Blood of the Prodigal

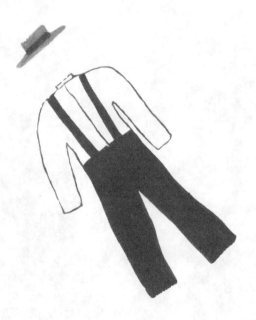

Blood of the Prodigal

AN OHIO AMISH MYSTERY

P. L. Gaus

Ohio University Press
Athens

Ohio University Press, Athens, Ohio 45701
© 1999 by P. L. Gaus
Printed in the United States of America
All rights reserved

ISBN 0-8214-1276-0 (cloth)

Preface

All of the characters in this novel are purely fictional, and any apparent resemblance to people living or dead is coincidental.

Many of the places in this novel are real, and the author has strived in those cases to make them as true to life as possible. For Holmes County, in particular, most of the descriptions and locations are authentic. The same is true of the Bass Islands area of Lake Erie, near the towns of Port Clinton, Lakeside, and Marblehead. For those interested, the best Holmes County map can be obtained at the office of the County Engineer, across the street from the Holmes County Court House and the old Red Brick Jail. Millersburg College is entirely fictional. Leeper School is still in use, but it is not located in the Doughty Valley.

I am grateful for the kind and valuable assistance of Seaman Anthony Muccino, U.S. Coast Guard, of Holmes County Sheriff Tim Zimmerly, and of Wooster, Ohio, Police Chief Steve Thornton. Thanks also to Pastor Dean Troyer, Eli Troyer, and Kathy Chapman, as well as to Tony Hillerman for encouragement and advice. The author also most gratefully acknowledges the kind and expert assistance of the late Professor William I. Schreiber, whose excellent book *Our Amish Neighbors,* © 1992 by William I. Schreiber, can still be obtained through the Florence O. Wilson Bookstore, The College of Wooster, Wooster, Ohio 44691.

I am especially grateful for the insightful work of my editors, David Sanders and Nancy Basmajian, of Ohio University Press.

to my wife, Madonna

Blood
of the
Prodigal

1

Friday, May 22
4:30 A.M.

LIKE all Amish children of ten, Jeremiah Miller had known his share of sunrises. Morning chores had long since taken care of that. Every day brought the same duties. His grandfather had made it clear. Children were for working. Life was supposed to be hard. Generally, for Jeremiah, it was.

But lately, Jeremiah had discovered something new and wonderful in his dawn chores. Something exhilarating. Also a bit frightening, because he suspected it was forbidden. It was so simple, he thought, who could object? If he arose before the others and slipped out quietly, he could be alone, drawn awake early by the allure of a solitary Ohio dawn.

It had begun last winter. None of the other children had understood. After all, who would choose to be alone? So he kept it to himself, now. Even Grossdaddy didn't know. It was Jeremiah Miller's little secret. At so young an age, he had already discovered that the dawn could give him a sense of identity separate from the others. And this was his first act of nonconformity. Among the *Gemie*, that was considered evidence of pridefulness. And pride was surely the worst of sins. He worried that it could eventually brand him a rebel. Like his father.

He'd dress quietly in the clothes his grandmother had made —clothes that were identical to those of other Amish children. Long underwear and denim trousers with a broadfall flap. A light-blue, long-sleeved shirt with no collar. A heavy denim jacket. Suspenders. And a dark blue knit skull cap. If he escaped the house before the others awakened, Jeremiah Miller was free.

In the barns before sunrise, only the Coleman lantern kept him company, hissing softly as he drifted among the animals, in and out of the stalls. In winter, there was the enchanting, billowing steam his breath made in the crisp air. The delightful crunching of his boots in the snow. There was, especially, the peace and the solitude, and at only ten, Jeremiah Miller had come to reckon that dawn would always be his favorite part of the day.

Today, late in May, it was nearing the end of a season still often raw and bleak, the usual for a northern Ohio spring. Some days were almost entirely awash in gray. Yesterday, there had been only the barest hint of a sunrise, delicate shades of pink as he had worked alone at morning chores. Then an afternoon drizzle had developed into a steady, all-night rain as a storm front moved in off the great lake, a hundred miles to the north.

Jeremiah slipped out from under the quilts and sat, wrapped in his down comforter, on the edge of the bed. He listened there a while for sounds of his family stirring. Hearing nothing, he drew the ornate quilt around his waist, eased lightly across the plain wooden floor to the window, pulled back the long purple curtains, and peered out. Yesterday's rain had slackened to a cold drizzle. He saw no hint of sunlight at his window, but as he was about to release the curtains, the headlights of a rare car flashed on the foggy lane in front of his house. He briefly thought it strange, and then, hitching up the comforter, he let the curtains go slack.

He sat on the edge of the bed and pulled on his shirt and denim trousers. He glided down the hall, the wooden floor cool beneath his stocking feet. He passed the other bedrooms carefully and crept down the stairs. He eased through the kitchen unerringly in the dark, lifted his jacket from its peg, pulled the heavy oak door open, and slipped through the storm door onto the back porch.

There would be no supervisions on the rounds of his morning chores. No instructions if he worked alone. No corrections. No reminders to conform. The hours before dawn were his alone. The one time of each day when he owned himself entirely. Jeremiah had discovered that solitude was personal. More personal than anything else he had ever known.

On the back porch, he stuffed his feet into his cold boots and laced them, hooked his suspenders to the buttons on his plain denim trousers, and closed the hooks on his short, denim waist jacket. Reaching down for the green Coleman lantern, he gave the pump several adept strokes and lit the silk mantle with a wooden match. Then he rolled his thin collar up and stepped off the porch into the rain.

School would close soon for summer, he thought. He set the lantern on the muddy ground outside the massive sliding doors to the red bank barn. School wasn't so bad. And summers could be long. So why did Grossdaddy speak so bitterly of school?

He set his weight against the sliding door and forced it heavily sideways on its rollers. Grandfather would like the teachers, if only he'd come to visit the school. It was just down the gravel lane, less than a mile. Teacher stayed late every day, and they could talk. If only Grandfather would. The other men thought well of teachers, so why didn't Grandfather? Jeremiah only knew that something had happened long ago. Something that would never be discussed. He suspected it had something to do with his father.

A nervous black kitten launched itself through the crack between the sliding doors at his feet, and he sidestepped it superstitiously.

"Kommen Sie," he called gently after the cat, momentarily curious. He whistled for it softly, shrugged, picked up the lantern, and squeezed through the narrow opening between the doors.

The three-story bank barn was set into the side of a hill behind the big house. At the bottom of the hill, the sliding doors opened to the lowest level of the barn. The top of the hill gave access, on the other side of the barn, to the second level. There were nine stalls down the right side of the lower level, and eight down the left. The avenue down the middle was strewn with fresh straw. Five massive oak uprights stood in a line down the middle of the avenue, taking the weight of the roof. The crossbeams were made of walnut twelve-by-twelve's. The haylofts ran high above, on either side of the third level, planked out in rough-hewn maple and elm. Long runs of rope and chain looped through a large wooden block and tackle, which was hung from an iron wheel that ran high in the rafters on a rail the full length of the peak. Leather harnesses and collars hung in front of each of the stalls. At the far end, the rakes, mowers, and threshers stood silently in the wide avenue. Their iron wheels were easily a head taller than Jeremiah.

Inside, Jeremiah climbed onto a stepstool to hang the lantern against one of the upright beams, and hopped down in front of the first stall. He scaled the slats of the gate and made a clicking sound with the inside of his cheek against his teeth. He balanced on his toes near the top of the gate and reached up to stroke the nose of the Belgian draft horse, light chestnut brown with a creamy white mane. As it thumped ponderously in the straw, Jeremiah rubbed at its wet nose and bristling hairs, then jumped down with a laugh and took the tasseled whip from its hook beside the stall.

He snapped the black whip playfully overhead and grinned, mindful that his Grandfather's were the very finest of all the Belgians in Holmes County. That was good, not prideful, he thought. Not prideful to admire a good horse. After all, God had made them Himself. And hadn't Grandfather promised that his time would soon come to work a whip behind them? To learn to plow. To run a harrow. To handle a team of Belgians! A boy should not go to school forever, Grossdaddy had said. Why should a boy be smarter than a father?

As he played with the whip, the unexpected aroma of tobacco drifted Jeremiah's way. Startled, he remembered the skittish cat and the weird headlights earlier on the lane. He stood tip-toe on the stepstool, took down the glowing lantern, held it high overhead, hesitated a fateful moment, and moved apprehensively toward the far end of the barn.

IN THE milky light of dawn, a small girl in a black bonnet stood on the elevated lawn in front of the Millers' white frame house. Her bonnet was tied close against her cheeks, with thin cloth strands under her chin. Her narrow shoulders were draped properly with a black shawl that was knotted loosely in front and covered her hands. In the delicate morning light, her long pleated skirt showed the barest hint of rich peacock blue. She was motionless except for her large, tranquil brown eyes as they followed the headlights of a car approaching on the lane.

The hollow sound of slow tires crushing loose gravel ground to a halt as the car rolled up to a mailbox mounted on the white picket fence. The driver's window rolled down, revealing police insignias on the sleeve of a blue jacket. The driver reached out and flipped an envelope into the mailbox. As the girl watched silently, the car sped off, throwing gravel, its taillights disappearing into the lingering fog.

2

ON A clear summer morning, Bishop Eli Miller drove his top buggy into town along little-used township roads. The buggy was a one-seater, a boxy, covered affair of the typical Ohio Amish style. The large wooden wheels carried iron rims, not rubber, as was proper among the bishop's sect of the Old Order. The roll curtains on the side windows were tied up, as was the curtained windshield over the wide dash. The hooves of the horse swung left and right in front of the rig, and struck a steady gait of hollow clicks in the gravel. The horse was well-lathered and had started to tire, but the bishop, in a somber mood, kept after him with an unrelenting whip.

Bishop Miller was dressed in dark blue denim trousers with cloth suspenders, a long-sleeved white shirt, and a collarless black vest with hooks and eyes instead of buttons. He wore precisely the one type of white straw summer hat that was currently approved in his district. To the English who saw him that day, he seemed plain, Amish, nothing more. Certainly no different in dress and demeanor than any Amish man, on any particular day. In Bishop Miller's district, as for all Old Order Amish, that was the whole point. Look the same, live the same, stay the same. To live every day in tranquillity.

Today, only a few would be any the wiser. Those who, studying his face closely, could have discerned the weeks of anguish in his reddened eyes. Little else betrayed him. Neither his dress nor the buggy. Perhaps only the horse's unusually brisk pace and heavy lather.

The buggy was entirely flat black. It sported no frills. Nothing in the way of vain decorations, horns, mirrors, paint, shiny metal, or any other of the various ostentations of the more liberal Wayne County Amish congregations to the north. These, he thought, had compromised with the world. Surely in the north, the bishop mused, the *Gemei* had lost its way.

The narrow wheels of the buggy cut wispy lines into the berm. Miller worked the horse with the reins, staying carefully to the right. A car roared by, shaking the rig in its backdraft. The horse skittered, and he whistled softly and worked the reins to steady him. Another auto blared its horn and sped around. The impatience surprised Miller. Rather, it puzzled him. "English," he whispered disapprovingly, as a pickup blared behind and passed abruptly. A day spent among them was a trial. "Remember," his wife had said, "you have not chosen this." Wise, he thought. And righteous. "Thank you, Lord, for the counsel of a Godly woman," he prayed.

The deacons, too, had urged him. Use the pastor to approach the professor. If the professor wouldn't help, maybe the pastor would. Pastor Caleb "Cal" Troyer was known among the plain people. They would trust him, and Professor Branden, too, but no one else. Certainly not the law.

His grip on the reins went limp as he shook his head, lost in thought and prayer. Little Jeremiah had been taken nearly four weeks ago. The burden of his chores had fallen to the other children. And lately the bishop had begun to doubt. The deacons had sensed these doubts in his prayers. He hadn't spoken of it outright, but still they knew. Doubts about his outcast son bedeviled him endlessly, now, almost as much as the loss of his grandson.

It was the same for his wife, although she never spoke of it.

He knew that she never would. That was their way. So it had always been. *Es steht geschrieben*—it stands written. So it shall always be. From this, he assured himself, they drew strength for the life of separation. For the one true path to salvation.

Bishop Miller found himself staring down blankly at the reins. He forced himself upright and snapped the whip grimly. His son had been lost more than ten years ago. "Lord," he prayed today, "not my grandson too."

He had started out before dawn, carefully traveling the remote gravel roads and township lanes in southern Holmes County, heading up out of his Old Order Amish district, toward the city, where greater prosperity had enticed the brethren into easier lives. Into compromises with the world. It was the city that had drawn too many of the brethren away from the paths of righteousness.

Today was Thursday, a day for labor. He'd not normally have forsaken the chores of the farm for a journey into town. But the deacons had agreed. In point of fact, they had urged him to go.

After days of prayer, he had relented. The child had shown promise with the Word. Jeremiah's gift was to speak of the Book. He'd surely be called, in his day, to be a *Diener zum Buch*—a preacher. An interpreter of God's character in the scriptures. And he must not be sacrificed to the world. Not for so much as a single summer.

On the south edge of town, Bishop Miller watered his horse at the buckets set out in front of the Wal-Mart store and pulled the buggy into the parking lot of the Pizza Hut on the other side of the street. He stepped down and around to the back, lifted a faded green canvas feed bag out of the buggy, and walked to the front to hang the bag over the horse's ears. He tied the reins around a light pole next to a telephone booth, and then he ran his hand along the rump of the horse, reached up into the seat of the buggy, and lifted out his black metal lunch pail.

As he lunched with the horse, a teenage girl came out of the Pizza Hut and sauntered over to the phone booth. She looked him over disdainfully, made a quick call, and then stood impatiently beside the phone until a rusty truck arrived, driven by an older man in a ragged tee-shirt. As she got in, he gunned the engine, popped the clutch, sprayed gravel toward the bishop's buggy, and drove away shouting vulgarly out the window.

The bishop shook his head, took down the feed bag and carried it wearily around to the back. Then he tightened the lathered hip straps at the breeching, dried his calloused hands on his trousers, climbed back into the buggy, dropped the plain black curtains on the buggy's windows, and teased the horse into awkward back steps. Once clear of the phone booth, he snapped his whip, brought the horse to a determined pace, drove further north into town, and turned onto a side street in a working-class neighborhood. He traveled several steep blocks through the hills of Millersburg and pulled into the gravel parking lot of a white frame church. Out front there was a plain white sign that read: "Church of Christ, Christian. Pastor Caleb Troyer." It gave the times of the Sunday morning, Sunday evening, and Wednesday night services. A color poster planted on the lawn announced the details of this year's Vacation Bible School.

The bishop entered a side door of the small church and remained inside for nearly an hour. When he emerged, he turned around on the steps of the church to study the pastor's face. Cal Troyer was a short man with a round, leathered face that marked him in those parts of Ohio as likely descended from the Amish. He had flowing white hair and a heavy, tangled white beard with no hint whatsoever of its original color. He was dressed in workman's blue jeans and a denim shirt. He had a carpenter's belt strapped to his waist. A ladder stood against the gutters of the church house, where he had been working earlier that morning.

The bishop took his hand and shook it firmly, gratitude showing openly on his face. He gazed an extra moment into Pastor Troyer's eyes. With proper grooming, once shaved around the mouth, Cal Troyer would easily pass anywhere for Amish. Perhaps his hair was too long, but that was easily remedied. The deep tan on his face and the powerful muscles in his short arms had always brought him respect with the *Gemei*. Troyer was a preacher, but he earned his way in life as a carpenter. And the way the bishop figured things in these perverse times, that was not far at all from the true calling.

In truth, it was Troyer the bishop had wanted, but he was resigned now to the fact that, with the preacher leaving in a few days for a missions conference, that wouldn't be possible. But Troyer had vouched solidly for the professor, and the bishop had taken him at his word. The deacons had agreed. They would place their trust in Professor Branden if Troyer would assure them that they could do so. If not for that, the Bishop would have driven home and closed his doors, resolved to ride it out alone, without the aid of any English at all.

But, as he walked to his buggy, the bishop's hopefulness began to fade. Whatever else, wasn't Cal Troyer still one of *de Hochen*, the high ones, the "English"? Wasn't he of the proud people, not the plain? Not of our people, *unser Leut*. And if not plain, then perhaps not entirely trustworthy. He turned at his buggy and glanced back at Troyer on the steps of the small meeting house. A line from the *Liedersammlung* song book came to the bishop's mind. "*Demut ist de schönste Tugend*"; humility is the most beautiful virtue. He gazed a moment longer at Troyer and was reassured by what he saw. Cal Troyer was not *schtolz*, not proud. Rather, he was possessed of deep humility. Staring at Troyer from the seat of his buggy, Bishop Miller resolved finally to rest his hopes in the hands of Professor Michael Branden, on the word of this humble country preacher, the least prideful of all *de Hochen* the bishop had known—a fitting resolution of their dilemma, considering that all of their trials had begun, nine years ago, with the death of little Jeremiah's mother, the most profane of all *de Hochen* the bishop had ever known.

3

Thursday, June 18
11:30 A.M.

A MILE or so south of Millersburg, in the wooded hill country
sheltering the largest Amish settlements of Ohio, Cal Troyer
eased his truck over the berm onto an isolated lane and
dropped into a hidden glade near a long forgotten farm pond.
Tranquil glens tucked away in nearly every corner of Holmes
County hold spectacular bass ponds, made available to only a
select few, and those few almost exclusively Amish. This particular pond, stocked years ago with fingerlings, had been fished
by only Pastor Caleb Troyer and Professor Michael Branden.

They had acquired the privilege while working for a farmer
who could not otherwise have paid them. "Working a case," as
the professor's wife Caroline liked to tease. It had concerned a
chemical problem with fertilizers used on a nearby English farm,
plus runoff disputes, and the EPA. Children had taken sick.
Farmers in the valley had been blamed. The EPA, it developed,
had been wrong, at the cost of several livelihoods.

The bass pond had been Branden's idea. He and Cal Troyer
would accept no fees. But, in return for their help, they would
fish the pond for life. The land would never be sold without
provision for this.

Cal dropped the truck into low and chuckled, thinking it no
surprise to find Mike Branden fishing here, today, working the

far edges of the pond with a spinner bait. Troyer parked in tall weeds at the tree line, eased himself out of his rusty truck, and leaned back against the hood, watching, his short arms folded across his chest. His thoughts drifted to the first summer they had spent here, and his eyes turned up to the dilapidated farm house on the hill.

Branden cast into the shallows at the opposite edge of the pond and retrieved the spinner quickly, churning its blade just beneath the surface. At a point where the color suggested deeper water, a surge erupted under the spinner, and the bait jerked sideways under the impact of a strike. He played the bass on his arching rod, brought it steadily to him, lipped it with his thumb and forefinger, and held it up for Troyer, who acknowledged it with a wave, as Branden extracted the hook with a quick twist and tossed the fish back into the pond.

As Cal watched, Branden worked around the pond toward him, casting into each irregularity at the bank. He cast over weeds, tree roots, and stumps, the sport completely absorbing him. Here, nothing of Branden's academic life could reach into his mind. Neither the petty politics of academia nor the inflated egos of his colleagues. No pressure from the administration for speeches to rich alumni groups. No endowment headaches. No urgent phone calls from the dean. No manuscripts to review. No campus mail. No committees.

Today, he had nearly managed to forget the Federal Express envelope that lay unopened on his desk. A phone call yesterday from a southern university had prepared him. He was to be offered an endowed chair in the history department. Prestige and money he'd never known. Reduced classroom duties. "An escape from the small college arena" was how they had worded it. Now Branden wondered if he was obliged even to open the envelope.

To open it would, perhaps, prove altogether too complicated.

Caroline was strong again. They had buried two children, now, each miscarried without warning, and he and Caroline had sunk their roots deep into Millersburg during their grieving. People like Cal Troyer and Sheriff Bruce Robertson, both childhood friends of Branden, had helped them carry their burden of sorrow and loss, and slowly the void in their lives had filled somewhat, and healed over. So the question for him wasn't about prestige and money, anymore. At one time it might have been. Not now. Still the offer lay on his desk, and sooner or later Caroline would hear of it. Then the question would be, would it matter to her?

Branden glanced with a smile across the small pond at Cal Troyer. Branden knew that Cal would have his gear out soon. But not too soon. First Cal'd simply watch. See how they were hitting. Then, when he was ready, he'd have a go. They had fished summers together since they were boys, and, over the years, they had developed an abiding competition. Biggest bass. Most bass. First bass. Last bass. In this, at middle age, they were still precious little more than boys.

How long till Cal noticed that the strikes were falling short today, Branden wondered. Short strikes that hit only the trailing skirts of his lures. The first hour had brought him no luck. Then he had solved the puzzle. The bass were on an early spawn and striking territorially, not feeding. So he had trimmed the skirts back, added a stinger hook, and scored half a dozen in as many minutes. As he worked toward Cal, he bagged two more and released them.

At the pastor's truck, Branden leaned against the hood next to Cal. "I thought maybe you weren't coming," Branden said.

"Just held up, is all," Cal replied. He studied Branden's lure with unconvincing disinterest, saw the trimmed skirt, tapped the hemostat clamped to Branden's vest, and asked, "Short strikes?" as if it'd be obvious to anyone.

"Not at all," Branden said. Then he shrugged a smile and ambled over to the water.

Troyer followed.

"You're not fishing, yet," Branden offered. "I know you too well, Cal. Something's on your mind."

Troyer picked up a stone from among the tall weeds that had overgrown the lane next to the pond. He tossed it absently into the water and answered, "It's a missing child."

"How old?"

"Ten."

"How long?"

"About a month."

Branden wound slack line onto his reel. He thought for a moment and then said, "Police aren't involved?"

"It's Old Order Amish," Cal said. "Bishop Eli Miller. One of the strictest in Holmes County, though his sect isn't the most backward in the county. His grandson has turned up missing. He knows who has the boy, just doesn't know where. He wants to meet you."

"How would he know anything about me?"

"I reckon word gets around."

"I reckon you'll have told him something."

"Told him you're a mostly harmless, absent-minded professor who has little better to do in summers than wet an occasional line."

"He'll think me a shirker," Branden complained with a laugh.

"He did say something about idle hands doing the devil's work. So I told him of the various people you've helped over the years."

"*We've* helped."

"All right, we've helped. I could have told him more, but he seemed satisfied."

"I'm supposed to have used my summers to think deep

thoughts, write papers, attend conferences, that sort of thing," Branden offered. Then he grinned, held up his pole, and said, "Tenure does have its benefits."

"I leave Tuesday for the missions conference. I can help you get started locally, but that's about it." Cal shrugged and smiled apologetically.

"A missing Amish boy?" Branden asked.

"Kidnapped, essentially."

"Old Order?"

"Moderate Old Order. Weaver branch. One of the strictest bishops."

Branden's gaze drifted to the long-deserted farmhouse on the hill. Gutters sagging, paint chipped, shutters fallen down. "Remember the summer we worked here, Cal?"

Cal nodded silently.

"That case was also tangled up with the Old Order."

Cal held his silence, waited.

Branden mulled it over. After a few minutes, he asked, "And I'm to talk with the bishop?"

Cal nodded. "He'll be at Becks Mills. At the general store in the Doughty Valley, about an hour from now. I'm to bring you there, and then he'll want you to ride with him a spell. He said something cryptic like 'in a month, none of this will matter,' so we've only got that much time to find the boy. But, still, the bishop will want to take some time to get to know you, sound you out. It may take a day or two, I don't know. He explained the whole thing to me as if time was short, but I gather he's already sat on his hands a good while, as it is."

Branden thought about that while toying absently with the line on his pole.

Cal explained a little further. "Look, Mike. We've known it was like this with the Old Order since we were kids. It's just the Amish, that's all. He came to me, but he'll accept you. And you know it's flat-out amazing that he's come into town to ask for anyone's help. So I imagine there's more to this case than he's told me. It'll take time before he trusts us enough to bring us all the way in. For now, we're going to have to handle this the Amish way. Say little. Listen a lot."

"And what'll you do while I clatter around in his buggy?"

Cal reached down to Branden's lure, lifted it on the tips of two short fingers, noted where the skirt had been cut, and then grinned and helped himself to the hemostat clipped to Branden's fishing vest.

4

Thursday, June 18
1:00 P.M.

BRANDEN rode with the bishop on the plain buckboard seat
of the buggy, through the remotest Amish valleys of Holmes
County. From Becks Mills, they took a circuitous route out
onto 83, north to Township Road 122, dropped through Pan-
ther Valley, and traveled south on Route 58. Where 58 broke
into the Doughty Valley, they crossed Mullet Run and followed
Route 19 over the Doughty Creek itself. From there, they continued south and west and eventually wandered into the farms
of the bishop's district. They rolled slowly past luxuriant farms
and ramshackle affairs, what the bishop called *kutslich*, sloppy,
ill-tended. There were tall, splendid farmhouses, with no electric service. Immense bank barns and long runs of wooden
fence. Pastures and fields of barley, oats, and corn. Small bridges
over rain-swollen streams. Manure spreaders with their dis-
tinctive aromas. Children at play under clotheslines, with their
fluttering splashes of rich Amish blues, greens, and rose. And
everywhere tall windmills, Belgians hitched to slow and ponderous wagons, and light buggies pulled by spirited horses.

As they drove the narrow lanes of his district, the bishop
questioned Branden about his family. About his friends, and
about his profession. So Branden told how he and Cal Troyer
had grown up together, fishing on summer ponds. And how
Branden and Sheriff Bruce Robertson had spent winters hunt-

ing deer in the glens of the hardwood lowlands and pheasant along the hilltop pasture fence lines. And he explained how Cal Troyer had been changed—called to the ministry—the day Branden's parents had died in a highway crash, as an impatient tourist had swung out around a buggy in a no-passing zone and hit their car head on.

When Branden began to speak of his job at the college, the bishop questioned him sternly on his studies of war and the weapons of war. So Branden explained that his fascination with the Civil War arose from a scholarly desire to understand the origins of conflict and the impetus to arms. And how his fifth-grade teacher had sparked his interest in the Civil War by assigning a paper on the battle of Gettysburg. How his grandfather had taken him to a rifle range with a muzzleloader when he was ten and started Branden on his quest to understand the firearms of the period.

The bishop drove and listened as Branden rode on the buckboard seat beside him and told of his cannon, fired each Fourth of July as much to commemorate Lincoln's Gettysburg Address as to celebrate Independence Day. He spoke passionately of the eloquence of Lincoln. Of the valor of soldiers, and of bravery among common men. Of the memories his grandfather had cherished of summer afternoons spent on a country porch, listening to the ancient, grizzled veterans of that war. Stories told in turn to a young Michael Branden. Memories that now spurred his research into the letters and journals of Civil War soldiers.

As time passed, the bishop's attention seemed to stray, and Branden fell silent. On a long, uphill stretch of a gravel lane, the bishop let the reins go slack, content for the moment to have the horse trudge along at its own pace. He leaned back heavily against the buckboard and sighed like a man who had endured a surpassing loneliness.

"Professor," he said, and then faltered. Clearing his throat, he began again.

"The ban, Professor, is not cruel." He looked fervently into Branden's eyes. His expression was somber, and he seemed overwhelmed by the burdens he had shouldered. "The ban is a prayerful act. The last, joyless thing that a bishop can do to turn a soul around. Often, it brings repentance."

Branden leaned forward from the buckboard seat, rested his elbows on his knees, laced his fingers together, and studied the backs of his hands, listening, and indicating that he would listen as long as the bishop should need. The horse had brought them to the crest of the hill, and the bishop pulled carefully right and brought it to a halt in the shade at the side of the lane.

"It is a bishop's duty," he continued, "to know when to impose a ban. And it is his obligation to have the strength of will to do it.

"Sadly, there are those whose rebellion is so complete, or whose character is so disreputable, that a ban only drives them away. They become nearly irretrievable, Professor. They refuse to be restored to the community of faith. When this happens, the burden a bishop carries is terrible. Still, it is a necessary burden.

"In my years as bishop, I have imposed only three bans. Two were members of the church, and today, they are members again."

Miller lapsed into silence. Branden looked over and noticed a sheen of tears in the bishop's eyes. He allowed the bishop to remain with his thoughts, and then asked, "And the third?"

Miller groped for words. He seemed overwhelmed, vulnerable. He remained quiet for some time, enmeshed in a private, enduring sorrow. In time, and with effort, he bolstered himself and sat a little straighter. He took up the reins again and guided the horse back onto the lane, down a small hill, and around a sharp turn that carried them over a ford at a little creek. Turning onto a larger road, he headed the buggy out of the valley, toward the pond where Cal Troyer waited.

"The third one," Bishop Miller said, "was a lad of eighteen, who was not yet even a member of the church. Had not yet taken his vows."

"You put the ban on an outsider?" Branden asked.

"He was not an outsider, Professor. He was my son."

The bishop bowed his head, unable to continue. Branden hid his surprise and waited silently for the bishop to explain.

"The ban has other purposes, Doktor Branden. The community of believers have vowed to be submissive to one another, and the ban protects them from the destructive influences of proud and vain individuals. From those who insist on asserting themselves. Of holding themselves above the welfare of the others. Above the whole community.

"Such disbelievers, Professor, work their greatest evil on the young ones. Especially those in the years of running wild, before they take the vows. It is the *Rumschpringe*. We allow it for every youth, because our vows, baptism, are meaningful only for those who have seen enough of the world to know that they have chosen the plain life because it is a better life.

"So we have the *Rumschpringe*. They seem to get the wildness out of their systems. Mostly, they run in small groups, called gangs, and one gang will be a little more crazy than another. They are people, Professor, with all the flaws of any people, anywhere. And without the strong influence of the church, they make mistakes. I know you've lived among us long enough to understand that we are not saints, and that our young people can cause a lot of problems in their years of running around wild.

"Of all these people, my son was the worst. There was drugs, whiskey, sex. More self-assertive pride than we have ever seen in one person. His rebellion was so intolerable that he was starting to draw the wilder gangs away. Young people who were wild in their own right, but would have come home, in time, to their places in the faith. He also had a bad influence on young people from other districts. Those who made it to the town bars. I started to get visits from other bishops.

"So, for the good of the district and for the sake of the young people, I put the ban on my own son, so that those who knew they would eventually be coming home would not be drawn too much away by his example. My son would have nothing to do with his family, and I cast him out for the sake of the others. From that generation, we have lost only two. My son and a girl from another district, who ran with him.

"After that, he got worse. I believe he was what you call 'hooked' on whiskey. He lived with an English girl who poisoned any remaining hope he ever had of coming home. Some say I sacrificed my son only to save the others. But I thought the ban would bring him to his senses. Draw him back to us.

"Some have said it was cruel. In truth it was harder on my wife and me than anyone can know. She never speaks of it now, but I find her weeping sometimes when she prays. And I have prayed for him too, without failing, in all these years. We pray that to have cast him out will one day bring him home to us. Every day, Professor, we pray for his return. We always will. We never lose hope. I have even been praying for him now, as we have traveled together."

Branden looked over at the bishop and watched him snap his whip to bring the horse to a brisk pace. The look on his face made it plain that he did not intend to linger in the memories of bygone years. Having said what needed to be said so that Branden would understand, he now evidently considered the matter closed.

"My son will not be lost forever," he declared. "Only God can understand the reasons for the ban. And only God can restore my son to us. His sinfulness endangered us all. Now it endangers my grandson, too.

"It is our son, Professor, who has the boy. Jonah, who has been lost to us all these years, has our grandson."

Reaching beneath his vest, he drew out a carefully folded

note and handed it over without comment. Branden opened it, read it, refolded it, and handed it back to the bishop. The bishop gestured for him to keep it.

"My son intends to keep Jeremiah for the summer, but he does not know the danger," Miller said. "He never really did. The danger of the world. Less than a month remains now, and my son does not know as much as he thinks he does."

"Why would your son take one of your grandsons?" Branden asked.

"Because he is the boy's father."

Branden's eyebrows lifted with surprise.

"After the ban, my son lived in town with a wretched woman he had met in the bars. At least he lived with her when he wasn't in jail.

"Then, apparently, he left town altogether. At least we have heard nothing of him since then, up until he left this note. After he had been gone several months, Jeremiah's mother gave birth, and we have pretty much raised the boy since he was a few months old."

"And the boy's mother?"

"Dead," the bishop said curtly.

Branden waited for an explanation. When it became clear that no further details would be forthcoming, he tried another tack.

"You put the ban on Jonah when he was eighteen?" Branden asked.

"Thereabouts," Miller said.

"And he ran with a wild crowd living in town?"

"And in jail."

"Then, for all you know, he just moved out and went away. Nothing from him in those years?"

"Nothing until about a month ago, when he put that note in our mailbox and took Jeremiah away."

"Then you want us to help you find Jonah?"

"Not so much my son. It is Jeremiah we seek. But with restrictions, Professor."

Urgently, then, as they finished their drive back to the pond, the bishop explained his restrictions. The terms under which they could accept his help. The extraordinary fact that they had decided to ask any Englisher for help at all.

When they returned to the pond, the bishop nodded approval to Cal Troyer, shook Branden's hand warmly, whipped his horse back up the lane, and headed the buggy home.

HIS TRIP had been successful, the bishop mused. The professor and the pastor would help. And the professor had given his word. He would abide by the deacons' restrictions.

There would surely be great risk for the district, not to mention for the boy. But the deacons had agreed. The bishop consoled himself again with an urgent prayer. This was the only way. Sad, he thought, what assurances a bishop needs in these perverse times. In this perverse world.

Once, life had seemed flawlessly simple. As it was written, so it had always been. Their lives need never change. But now, there was the ever-clamoring pressure from the outsiders. First it had been the land. Always scarcer, and repeatedly divided among the boys. Few parcels worth farming still remained. Those that came up for auction these days were priced well beyond his means. He had seen that pressure coming for years. What he had not seen coming was the pressure from the tourists. Gawking city English, with their billfolds full of money.

But the land had been the start of it. The pressing need for money to buy new land. And the boys who worked in the sawmills and the wheel shops had become, inexorably, ever more accustomed to the world. No less the girls who worked in the restaurants. And in the quilt shops. Worldly enticements at every turn. That was where the liberals had gone astray. Today had confirmed it for him as nothing else could have. What greater proof might a bishop need than a single trip into town?

The bishop could see, with perfect clarity, what threatened his people. Rumbling over the back roads, he prayed for insight and for strength. There would surely be many tests to come. He asked for resolve, steadfastness, and simplicity. His fingers tightened on the reins. He prayed for protection from the world. As his thoughts turned to the families of his district, an answer was given to his prayers, and a sense of peaceful belonging returned to him.

There had been no serious infractions, lately. At least none that had been brought to his attention. One girl was suspected to have worn a dress with fewer than the proper number of pleats. When warned, she had submitted. A good sign. On the northern edge of the district, a lad had been found letting his hair grow past the earlobes. Again, easily corrected. Radios with batteries were a challenge, but they could get through that, he figured. In truth, there had been no serious challenges of authority or custom since his son's. And his ban had assuredly taken care of that.

His authority as bishop was rarely challenged, now. Why couldn't the other bishops understand? Of course he had a reputation for severity. But didn't they know that the real issues were never the color of clothes or the number of pleats in a skirt? Not the length of hair, or the style of a summer hat. The real issue was, and always had been, authority. The willing, dutiful submission of a serene people. Righteousness thereby preserved. The profane world held at bay.

The strength of the people was not available merely to individuals. It rested only upon the whole, the *Gemei*, through hard work, plain living, and obedience. Submission to one another by denial of the individual self. Through sacrifice and, above all, lack of pride. And hadn't he kept the *Gemei* pure through a tireless vigil of leadership? His people understood, better than any, that to be different was to be proud. To be profane.

There, precisely, was the root of evil, he thought. It was pride that caused nonconformers to assert themselves. Pride, the greatest of all sins. Such, he recalled heavily, had been the downfall of Jonah. He thought again of little Jeremiah, gone a month now.

He knew Pastor Caleb Troyer. A good man. If he would only forsake the world and become a farmer, then surely a righteous man. And the professor, Michael Branden. Serious. Not worldly. Not profane. Certainly not *kutslich*. And yet, still one of the vain ones. One of the proud. One of the English *de Hoche*.

Miller wondered again how much these two English should be trusted. Certainly more than the police, that was clear. But not yet entrusted with everything. Not yet trusted to the uttermost. Perhaps only trusted completely if the next month came to naught. May God forbid that so grim a need should ever arise.

5

"I TOLD Cal you'd take the case, Michael," Caroline said as she gathered up the scattered pages of her manuscript, smiling outwardly at her husband and inwardly at her gentle mischief.

Branden carried two more mugs onto the spacious back porch and poured coffee for himself and Cal. "It's wiser to be a historian than a prophet, Caroline," he scolded.

Caroline turned to Cal, taunting. "The Professor doesn't like to be thought so predictable."

Cal held out his palms in mock surrender, laughed, and side-stepped the jab by pointing to Caroline's loose stack of papers. "Another book?"

"It's a revision of a collection of children's stories I edited a few years ago," Caroline said. She stacked the pages on edge, laid the manuscript on the glass-topped patio table where she had been working, and joined them in white wicker chairs by the porch windows. The day had begun brightly, but now a front was coming in from the north. A cool afternoon breeze blew through the tall screens of the porch.

The porch was more than spacious, running the entire length of the two-story brick colonial, extravagantly wide and screened on three sides, with windows stretching from floor to ceiling. Because of a gentle slope to the Brandens' long back yard, the porch seemed to hover over the lawn, so that the Brandens and their guests enjoyed a spectacular view of the eastern hills and Amish valleys. In summers, the porch had come to be Caroline's favorite place to work, and often, Branden would find her standing there, watching the hawks ride thermals, or gazing at the patchwork of Amish farms and fields in the distance.

Caroline sat in an old-fashioned, low and wide wicker chair, her legs crossed casually. She peered at Branden and Troyer over a fresh mug of coffee. "You did take the case," she said.

"Wasn't up to me," Branden said. "The bishop made the decision. I just showed up for the interview."

"How'd that go?" Cal asked.

"Slowly, as you predicted," Branden said. "We toured Holmes County for over an hour before he asked anything about me."

"Typical," Cal said.

"Mostly we talked about the people and the farms we passed. In remote regions of the Doughty Valley. He showed me each of the family farms under his leadership. Named all of the children, parents, grandparents, land holdings, livestock, relatives, and relationships. Even courtships. Essentially, he introduced himself to me by detailing all of the district over which he serves as bishop. Eventually, he wanted to know about me. And Caroline. And whether we had any children."

Cal glanced at Caroline and saw the memory of her losses pass heavily across her eyes. Troyer and Branden exchanged glances, wondering how she would handle a case involving a child.

Eventually Caroline asked, "Does he have a lot of children?"

"Fourteen. Thirteen living," Branden answered gently, grateful to see her strength. He wondered again, briefly, how he'd mention the Federal Express envelope to her. Wondered how she would handle the prospect of moving to the new university professorship he had been offered.

He took a moment, turning his coffee mug in his fingers, sipping from it thoughtfully, and then said, "Actually that's the whole point of this case. His children, that is. One of his sons, Jonah Miller, is dead to them, but still alive."

He glanced from Cal to Caroline, giving them a chance to think it through.

"He left home?" Cal asked.

"Shunned," Branden answered, pointedly.

"His own son?" Caroline said. "That's hard to believe."

"He's the bishop," Branden answered. "If anyone in that district were to have been mited, the bishop would have done it himself."

"I would have hoped the mite was a thing of the past," Caroline said.

"He wouldn't have had any choice," Branden said. "He's the bishop."

"Many of them would not so much as have spoken his name," Cal added.

"Then there's more to this case than the custody of a boy," Branden said. Cal and Caroline waited for an explanation. "Bishop Miller did actually speak his son's name, once. At the end of our interview, Cal. He said something like, 'It's my son, Professor, who has the boy. Jonah E. Miller. He's been lost to us for nearly ten years.' Then he handed me this note."

Branden gave the note first to Cal. When Cal had read it, he passed it, disquieted, to Caroline. She read it out loud.

Dear Father.
I want my boy to see some of the world.
You'll have him back in time for harvest.
Do not try to find us.

                                                Jonah.

"Extraordinary," Cal said after a pause. He ran the fingers of both hands back through his long white hair.

"Because of the note?" Caroline asked.

"Yes, but more," Cal said. He slouched in his white wicker chair, his stocky legs out straight and crossed at the ankles, coffee mug balanced on his belly, eventually saying only, "There must be more."

"Agreed," Branden said. "Let's think it through." He leaned forward, rested his elbows on his knees, and counted out each assertion on the fingers of his left hand. "First, the bishop put the ban on his own son, ten years ago." The first finger went up.

"Must have been good cause," Cal said.

"Indeed," Branden said, and another finger went up. "Also, the bishop evidently thinks there's good cause, now, to involve outsiders in this case." A third finger popped up.

Cal stood up, walked over to the large windows of the screened porch, ran his eyes out toward the far hills in the east, and said, "He'd not have mentioned his son, or have involved us in this case, if it were simply a matter of a father taking his boy for the summer."

"Precisely," Branden said, and held up a fourth finger.

"Whatever the reason, his Dieners would have concurred," Cal said.

"Right again," Branden said, and lifted his thumb.

"You'd think that if the bishop were really worried about his grandson, he would have gone to the police," Caroline said.

"They don't trust them," Branden said.

"Partly," Cal said. "More likely, they think it's not yet necessary. They simply haven't gotten to the point where they think that the police need to be involved."

"So," Caroline said, "you've been asked to help the Old Order Amish find Bishop Miller's grandson, who has evidently been taken for the summer by his father. The father was earlier shunned by his people. The note says that the boy will be returned at the end of the summer."

"By harvest," Cal interjected.

"Where's the boy's mother?" Caroline asked.

"Dead, according to the bishop."

"Do we know who she was?" Caroline asked.

"No," Branden said. "The bishop wouldn't speak of her at all. Just that Jonah met her in a bar and left town before the child was born. The bishop and his wife took in the boy as an infant and have raised him since then. That's all he would say."

"Should be easy enough to find out who she was," Caroline volunteered. "Doesn't sound likely she was Amish."

"No, and that could mean her folks would be more willing to talk about Jonah," Cal observed.

After a moment in thought, Branden said, "It's unusual for the bishop to have approached Englishers for help. And I agree with Caroline. Why come to us instead of the police?"

"That's not out of line at all. They'd be unlikely, whatever the circumstances, to involve the police," Cal said, and eased himself back down into one of the white wicker loungers.

"If you push this concept through to its logical extreme, this is a kidnapping case," Caroline said. "It's not just a 'grand summer away with father.'"

"Their distrust of secular authority runs deep," Cal said. "It's part of their suspicion of outsiders. And governmental authorities are the most suspect of them all."

Branden stood, paced to the far end of the porch, stuffed his hands into his pockets, and said, "I still don't see a compelling reason for them to have come to us."

"Perhaps one summer out in the world is more than they think the boy can handle," Caroline offered.

"Yes, but there's got to be more to this case than Miller's let on," Branden said.

"We'll get little more out of him at this point," Cal said. "We've already been told more than I would have expected."

Branden said, "Then we'll have to find out more from other sources, obviously."

"That'll take some time," Cal said.

"There really isn't much time left at all, when you consider what a cold start we'll have finding Jonah," Branden said. "The bishop gave it a month. Said something like 'a month from now and it won't matter anymore.'"

"He said the same thing to me," Cal told Caroline.

"Before what?" Caroline asked. "If you believe the note, at the very worst, the boy'll be gone for the summer and then brought home for harvest."

They each fell silent and thought, Cal and Caroline seated, Branden pacing in front of the windows. Dense, billowing clouds had gathered over the valley. The afternoon breeze had grown chill.

Eventually, Branden said, "I keep coming back to the fact that the Amish, who insist on independence and self-reliance, have engaged the assistance of outsiders to solve what is essentially a family dispute over a boy."

After a few quiet moments, Cal said, "We need to know more about the boy's father, Jonah Miller."

"How?" Branden said. "No one will talk to us about him."

"No Amish will," Caroline said. "But how about the authorities? Police, social services, schools, neighbors who are not Amish. Anywhere someone might have known Jonah E. Miller."

"Or those who know Eli Miller," Cal said.

"Good point," Branden said. "Also the preachers and deacons in neighboring districts."

"How about relatives of the boy's mother?" Cal said.

"Maybe her folks have been in touch with Jonah," Branden said.

"Good luck," Cal said with obvious pessimism.

Branden stood at the windows for a while longer with his gaze focused on the distant hills, pale green under cover of gathering clouds.

Caroline asked, "Didn't his teachers ask about Jeremiah?"

"The bishop told them he was needed on the farm," Branden said.

Cal scoffed and then said, "I've got a few days yet. Maybe I can work on Amish folk who know the bishop. I might find one who's willing to talk."

"A few days before what, Cal?" Caroline asked, concern evident in her tone.

"Sorry, Caroline. Next week's when I leave for the missions conference."

"How long will you be gone?" Branden asked.

"A week. Too long for me to be of much help to the bishop. I'm hoping you'll have it wrapped up before I'm back."

"We'll need your help, Cal," Branden said. "Especially for talking with Miller's neighbors."

Troyer shrugged apologetically and said, "I've got half a week before I leave. I'll get you started, Mike, but mostly you're going to have to work this one yourself."

"Then I'll help," Caroline said. "Teachers, newspapers, neighbors, that sort of thing."

"Don't you have a deadline on your book?" Branden asked.

Caroline shrugged and said, "I'll do what I can, Michael."

As they cleared the dishes, Branden added, "Just one more thing. I don't know why, but the bishop has insisted on special conditions. He's accepted our help only because he trusts that we'll abide by those restrictions."

He paused to let his words have effect and then said, "We can't let on to anyone that the boy is being held against his will. Or that he might be harmed. We are especially not to tell the law that Jonah has Jeremiah. He only wants us to investigate whether or not the boy and his father can be found. If they can be found, we are supposed to decide, without approaching the father, whether or not we think the boy can be returned to the family. I have also given the bishop my word that we will not attempt to take the boy from his father. We're simply to locate the two of them, find out the boy's condition, and advise the bishop. Nothing more."

Caroline and Cal glanced curiously at each other and then at Branden, waiting for an explanation.

"For some reason," Branden said, "the bishop is afraid to force the return of his grandson. If we can't turn something up in the next few weeks, he'll wait out the summer until harvest, rather than cause a ruckus now."

"I don't get it," Caroline said. "Does he want the boy back or not?"

"His restrictions, for now, are quite specific," Branden said. "We can look for the boy diligently, but we are not to make it appear that Miller is seeking to force the return of his grandson. He was very clear on this. Said something like, 'For now, Professor, we must be very cautious. Just see if you can find him, and then let me know.'"

"To what end?" Caroline asked.

"I don't know, exactly," Branden said. "Maybe he just wants to make sure that the boy will be safe until harvest. And that's all we can do. Maybe once he knows where the boy is, he'll bring him home, himself. Keep it in the family. You know how clannish they can be. Secretive, even. That's why I promised to abide by his restrictions. They'll not accept our help on any other terms, and they'll certainly never go to the police with the matter. So finding the boy is something we'll have to do on our own, and even that, as little as it is, is an amazing and unusual thing for a bishop to have asked an Englisher to do."

"Working through the sheriff's office would be the best way to find them quickly," Caroline said.

"We can't tell the law, any law, about Jeremiah's being gone."

Cal said, "You'd expect that sort of resistance from Old Order Amish."

"I think the bishop is being a little foolish," Caroline said.

Branden reiterated, "They won't take our help unless it's on their terms, Caroline."

Cal said, "But Caroline's right, of course. The sheriff could do this faster."

"Believe me, I agree," Branden said. "That's not the issue. It's the bishop. He's setting the rules, and I promised I'd do things his way, so that's the way it has to be. He was very specific about that. Said that if the law got tangled up in the matter, he'd deny ever having a problem in the first place."

6

BRANDEN stood looking down at the legs of Jeff Hostettler, jutting from under the front bumper of an old pickup. Hostettler wore black boots and a dirty pair of blue mechanic's coveralls. From under the engine, Hostettler said, "What makes you think I give a damn about Jonah Miller?"

Branden answered, "I've been looking for him precisely one day, Mr. Hostettler, and that's today. First place I went was social services, and the first thing I learned was that you fought the Millers in a custody battle over your nephew."

"So what?" Hostettler said and pushed out on his roller pad from under the truck. He stood, walked over to the workbench in his garage, took down a wrench, lay down again on the creeper, and slid back under the truck.

"So, you'd have good reason to know where I could find Jonah Miller."

"If I knew where Jonah Miller was, I'd do more than just open that custody hearing again," Hostettler said indignantly. "But I don't know where he's at, and I don't care anymore." He rolled out again, looked up at Branden, and added, "I've had all I can stand from that Miller bunch, as it is."

"We've reason to believe that Jonah has returned to the area," Branden said.

Hostettler lay still and thought for a moment, then rolled back under the truck. Branden heard the wrench clinking into place and saw Hostettler's legs lift at the knees as he grunted with the exertion. There was a slip, a thud, and the clanging of the wrench on the concrete floor. Hostettler pushed out from under the truck, holding bloody knuckles in his hand. He hauled himself upright, cursing, and stepped to the workbench. He took a clean towel from a drawer and began patting it on his black and greasy knuckles, where blood and pink skin showed through the grime.

Hostettler wrapped his hand in the towel and spoke in an angry tone. "The Millers have been nothing but trouble to me since my sister took up with Jonah. I hate them, and I don't mind telling you so. First, they as much as killed my sister, and then they took the boy. I've got nobody left now, Professor. Got any idea how that feels? Nobody except that little boy, and him I never get to see. They're raising him Amish, too, as if taking him from me wasn't enough. Amish! He's gonna grow up to be one of those dirty little buggy brats, and I can't do a thing about it."

Branden said, "There's worse things than growing up Amish."

Hostettler took an impulsive step toward Branden, fist raised. He fumed instantly to a bitter hatred and shouted, "Not the way I see it!"

Branden let Hostettler cool off a moment. "Look, Hostettler. I'm sorry. I didn't know about Jeremiah. I didn't even know about you until this morning."

Hostettler held his knuckles in the towel and grumbled, somewhat cooler now.

Branden added, "I'd just like to find Jonah, and I thought maybe you'd know something. That's all."

"Why should I help you?" Hostettler asked.

Branden stuffed his hands into his front pockets. "If we were to find Jonah, and that's all we want to do, but if we were to find him, what difference would that make for you?"

"None at all," Hostettler said. "The guy's a doped-up alcoholic, wherever he is, anyways."

"So what harm could he do you, if we were to bring him home?" Branden asked.

"He'll never come home," Hostettler said.

"Why not help us find him?"

"I don't know where he is."

Branden thought there was hesitation in Hostettler's answer. "But you do have some idea where we might look."

Hostettler stood for a long time with his fingers wrapped in the towel. His hands were blackened from his struggles with the engine of his truck. His coveralls showed more dirt than blue. His boots were old and worn. He wiped at his brow and smudged his forehead with black grease. He leaned back against the workbench and began to talk.

"It's only me now, Professor. When my sister died, Jeremiah's mother, I lost the last one there was. Then Jeremiah, too. Those were rough and wild times for me, and just like Jonah Miller, I did my share of drinking. We were good people, and I lost the family home snortin' cocaine. It's no wonder the courts put Jeremiah with the Millers. Now, all I've got is this little house, a couple of beat-up cars and trucks, and a job I've been able to hold onto for the last seven years. It pays the bills, nothing more.

"So when you came at me with Jonah Miller, it threw me. There isn't another name in all the world that could have thrown me like that. Now, you want to know where he's at, and there's nothing I'd like less than to see his sorry face back around here.

"I'm going to tell you one thing, though, and then I want you all to leave me alone. Somebody mentioned him to me last spring. I won't say who, and I won't tell you why. But, I got a call in early May saying that this certain someone had run onto Miller up in Cleveland.

"That's it. That's all I'll say, and now I'd just as soon you leave."

With that, Hostettler threw the bloody towel down on the floor and stomped into his house, letting the screened door to his garage bang shut behind him.

As he walked down the short gravel drive to his car, Branden wondered what Hostettler had meant when he had said, "First, they as much as killed my sister."

7

Friday, June 19
3:00 P.M.

DONNA Beachey stood awash in memories at a dirty window in Leeper School and watched a horse-drawn wagon roll along slowly in a distant field. She ran a finger along the dusty sill and then absently brushed cobwebs away from a corner of the glass.

She turned to Caroline and said, "I can tell you exactly why they sent you to me. It's the same reason I asked you to meet me here. The story of Jonah Miller starts here, with me, and they all know it."

Donna glanced around the single room, seeing a grade-school classroom, filled with happy Amish children of all ages. "This was my first teaching assignment. One of the last groups of children to have been taught in Leeper School." She wondered, somewhat amused with herself, why she had agreed so impulsively to this meeting.

Her hair was tied neatly in a bun under a white Mennonite prayer cap. She smoothed out the plain apron in front of her pleated aqua dress and walked slowly to the chalkboard at the front of the classroom. There was still an eraser in the tray, and she picked it up out of habit, lost again in memories.

Caroline stood quietly in the middle of the empty room and waited. She had interviewed three teachers today. Two had mentioned Leeper School. The third had also spoken, in hushed tones, of Miss Donna Beachey.

"Funny," Donna said, "how you forget." She dropped the

eraser back onto the tray and dusted off her hands with a some-what wilted expression. "That was almost twenty years ago."

"Why did you want to meet here?" Caroline asked, glad at last to be talking.

"This is where it started."

"That's what I've been told," Caroline said, delicately.

Donna Beachey noticed Caroline's restraint, and smiled appreciately. "I'm surprised you don't have the whole story," she said. "There used to be better gossips in these parts."

"I know very little, really, if anything." Caroline held back, wondering what she'd learn from the one person who evidently knew it all.

Donna Beachey returned to the window with an air of resignation. She was surprised by how much she had forgotten. Being here again, and using her old keys to open the school-house door, had brought it all back. She had cherished the feel of the curved sandstone as she had climbed the worn steps outside. The familiar noises the hinges had made as the front doors swung open. The aroma of chalk dust and the creaking wooden floor. She stood at the window for a long time, with her memories upwelling.

Caroline let the minutes pass quietly. In time, the teacher motioned for Caroline to join her at the window.

"It's pushing twenty years since they closed this little school, but the view here hasn't changed in the slightest."

Caroline stood behind her and looked out over the top of Miss Beachey's head covering. Rows of hay, recently turned, lay in the fields beyond. A few shocks of corn stood along a fence where they had been stacked last fall. A flatbed wagon with large black rubber truck tires eased along silently in the distance, drawn by two Belgian draft horses. The driver sat lazily on the plain wooden buckboard, dressed in a summer hat, white shirt, black suspenders, and denim trousers. He held a whip, tassels high overhead, but seldom employed it.

"I was a rookie teacher then, Mrs. Branden. They usually

had their own. It would be one of the young mothers from a nearby farm, or an unmarried daughter with time on her hands. In earlier days, the teachers might not have had much more education than their oldest pupils. I think it's better now, and sometimes there will be one with an actual teacher's degree. But for a spell, it was the Mennonite colleges that sent most of the teachers here, like me.

"Now as far as Jonah goes, by the time I started, he was in the fifth grade, and already reading at a high school level." She turned to look at Caroline, wondered briefly if she would understand, and then turned back to the window with a sigh. "The Amish choose a lifestyle that seems backward, but that doesn't mean they choose to be stupid. It just means that they have different rules.

"Take that wagon," she said. "See the rubber tires?"

Caroline nodded.

"See how they're inflated?"

"Umhmh."

"In some districts, that'd be disallowed. Some bishops might approve rubber tires, but not inflated rubber tires. Just rubber pads on the rims. Others rule out rubber altogether. They use iron or wooden rims only. An inquisitive child wouldn't understand why. But, when they take the vows, all Amish acknowledge that they have accepted the rules. That was the hard part for Jonah Miller. Accepting the rules.

"You see it in the kids. Especially the younger ones. Like in the fifth grade. They want to know 'why.' Fair enough, wouldn't you say? They just want to know 'why.'

"Most of them eventually accept such answers as they get, and the rules, too. They finish school, have their year or so for the *Rumschpringe* and then come home and take the vows. Some are ready earlier. They don't need a year. Don't have any doubts. No questions. No *Rumschpringe*.

"But once in a while you'll see one who needs to know more. Wants to know why. Really wants to understand why rubber tires are not to be inflated.

"That was Jonah's problem. He needed to know 'why.' Even by the fifth grade. I tried to give him something special in school, because he was so intelligent. At first, he responded well, but eventually, I lost him."

Donna paused and looked at Caroline again. She walked over to the desk in front of the chalkboard and stood facing out into the classroom, obviously struggling with regrets. Caroline leaned against the windowsill and gave her time. Calmly, at last, Donna Beachey began to tell what she knew of Jonah Miller.

"Jonah was a rebel," Donna said, "at a time in my teaching career when I was too young to appreciate what that would mean in Bishop Miller's district."

She pointed into the back of the room and remembered the little desks. "When Jonah took his seat, he'd scoot the desk two or three inches to the left. Always to the left. Just enough to be out of line with the other children."

"You think that was important?" Caroline asked.

"Yes, because he always watched me, to see if I had noticed."

"Some rebel," Caroline said.

"Don't underestimate that," Donna said. "He also began rolling his pants into a tight, high cuff. As a fashion statement. He always did it after he was on school property. Before he left, he'd roll the cuffs out again."

"It doesn't seem like a very big thing," Caroline said.

"Ah, but he was Old Order Amish, Mrs. Branden," Donna reminded her. "Soon after that, his father—"

"Bishop Miller?"

"Yes. Bishop Miller came to me after school and asked if it were true that Jonah was 'hitching his britches up' in school."

"And?"

"Jonah never did it again," Donna said. "The tragedy is, Jonah had intellect. He knew. Or suspected, anyway. You know —that the world holds marvels. It tormented him."

"He quit school like the rest do?" Caroline asked pointedly.

"He had no choice. That's the way of the Amish. His grand-parents, parents, uncles, aunts, brothers, sisters, cousins, and neighbors all quit school earlier. If the state did not now require them all to attend, most would quit sooner."

"It doesn't sound to me as if they get much of a chance," Caroline said.

"That's just their view of life," Miss Beachey explained. "There are two Amish proverbs. First: 'The Peasant Believes Only the Father.' Second: '*je gelehrter, desto verkehrter.*'"

Caroline waited for a translation.

"The more learned, the more confused."

"You said that was your first year teaching," Caroline re-marked, "almost as if you have learned better in the years since then."

"I have," Donna said and laughed almost inaudibly.

After a pause, Donna meekly said, "I had forgotten some of these things, Mrs. Branden. Our memories are carefully selected, it seems, but well preserved."

She looked disconsolately around the empty classroom and out through the open front door. Her hand slipped beneath her apron, and she drew a plain white handkerchief from a pocket in the side of her dress. She pulled herself up straight, and held the handkerchief briefly to her eyes.

"Jonah was different. I could tell it as early as his fifth grade, even if I was only a novice. And not just because he was my first bright student.

"He never could have lived truly Amish. I believe that, ab-solutely. Like with the cuffs.

"And I saw it in his schoolwork. He was a scholar. And a dreamer. He asked about the stars, about ships at sea, Indians, everything. Sometimes I'd find him on the steps of the school when I arrived in the morning. Always so full of questions.

"And I encouraged his studies, not realizing, then, what that would do to him."

She stopped and straightened the front of her apron, only a little bit self-conscious, now. She looked at Caroline and wondered anew what it was that had caused her to speak so freely. Perhaps it was being in Leeper School again. Funny that she had kept the keys. It was even stranger, she thought now, to have asked Caroline Branden to meet her here.

"With Jonah," Donna said, "well, I thought I was making a difference. But now I realize that I only accentuated traits that his father considered to be flaws. I encouraged attitudes in Jonah that ended up driving him from his family.

"At the end of his fifth grade, I gave Jonah a book of American poems. You know—Whitman, Sandburg, that sort of thing. And two novels, *Moby Dick* and *The Last of the Mohicans*. Then I transferred to Massillon, to be closer to my congregation, and soon after that they closed this little schoolhouse. Jonah went on to another parochial school.

"Years later, on the day after Jonah's sixteenth birthday, Bishop Miller drove his buggy into Massillon and waited for school to close. After the children had left for home, he walked into my classroom and laid those very same volumes on my desk.

"Then he said: 'You'll remember, I'm sure, Jonah Miller. You gave him these books when he was in the fifth grade. Jonah is beyond his school years, now, Miss Beachey. I intend no disrespect, but *Wir sind Bauern. Verstehen Sie Bauern?* Do you understand? We are *Bauern*, peasants. We have chosen this life freely. It is our hope that Jonah will choose it too. As peasants, we have a saying: 'The barn is not to sit in, and books are not helpful in plowing.'"

"He brought back the books that you had given Jonah?"

"More than that," Donna said. "He wanted me to know that he intended to put a stop to Jonah's 'overly inquisitive nature.'"

AFTER Miss Beachey had left, Caroline sat on the steps of the one-room schoolhouse and tried to imagine an Amish bishop making the forty-mile drive into Massillon simply to return three used books. In the end, she decided that she could not imagine the scene at all. As she left, Caroline came down the worn sandstone steps slowly, thinking about the schoolhouse. Thinking about a fifth-grade boy whose life as a rebel had started in the tiny, one-room Leeper School.

She walked around to the playground at the side of the schoolhouse and stood under a tall silver maple. There was an old rusty swing set with patches of mud underneath, and she walked absently over to it. There were small footprints in the fresh mud. Children still came here to play.

She sat on the swing and, side-stepping the mud, gave a gentle push with her toes. She closed her eyes and felt the slight, passing breeze on her face. She remembered her own cherished playgrounds and the long-forgotten, joyful sounds of children at play. The faces of childhood friends, the pleasant aroma of newly sharpened pencils, and the soft texture of wide-lined paper under her fingertips.

She opened her eyes and swung peacefully for a while gazing at the small schoolhouse, red brick walls patched in earlier days with white concrete. Lately, it hadn't been patched at all. The square belfry needed white paint. One of the gutters had swung loose and now hung from the roof at an angle.

A small figure wearing suspenders appeared around the corner of the schoolhouse, and Caroline waved. The child retreated bashfully behind the building, and Caroline thought again of Jonah Miller in the fifth grade. Of Donna Beachey and the things she had said.

There was more to what she had said than the mere words

she had spoken. For one thing, she had said that she remembered a single student from her first year of teaching. Evidently, she remembered Jonah Miller well. She had also plainly said that she had unwittingly given young Jonah Miller something that would eventually drive him from home.

But Caroline also found herself thinking about the things that Donna Beachey had not said. Had she forgotten them, or simply avoided them? Probably the latter. At any rate, others this morning had seemed to have little trouble remembering. They had whispered it all to her eagerly. They had remembered and so, surely, did Donna.

For one thing, Donna Beachey hadn't mentioned that Jonah Miller had fallen openly in love with his fifth-grade teacher and that the boyish crush had not ended when she left the district. She hadn't mentioned that he had ridden to see her several times the next year at her new school in the city. Or that ever since the fifth grade Jonah had taken to questioning his father about all matters Amish and not Amish. That his year of the *Rumschpringe* had come when he had finally quit school, and that Jonah Miller's year of decision had exploded into a decade of rebellion.

Finally and most significantly, Donna Beachey had not mentioned that she alone had visited him in jail.

8

Friday, June 19
9:30 P.M.

JEFF Hostettler's news that Jonah had been seen that spring in Cleveland was Branden's first hard fact in a case that offered no sensible beginnings. Notwithstanding Caroline's information about Donna Beachey's somewhat nostalgic recollections, and beyond the details of Jonah's troubles that she had been able to provide, Branden thought, he still had only Hostettler's slim lead on Miller, and everything else pointed to trouble.

Bishop Miller's account of his son had been bleak enough, and yet he hadn't said a thing about Jeff Hostettler's sister, Jeremiah's mother. Nor had he mentioned how she had died, despite Hostettler's assertion that "they," whoever they were, had pretty much killed her themselves.

The custody battle over Jeremiah, no doubt heated, was another thing the bishop had neglected to mention. That, together with what the teacher had told Caroline, had put a nervous kink into Branden's spine, and the mysterious reasons for the bishop's one-month deadline heightened his concern.

From the second-floor bedroom Branden used as his study, he called out to his wife through the walls. "Caroline. Did Donna Beachey say she had any idea where we might find Jonah Miller?"

Caroline came into the study dressed in a summer nightgown and said, "No. She did say on the phone that she got a call from him, once, from Texas. That's all."

"Too far away," Branden said. "He was in Cleveland last May."

"I really didn't make a point of asking her," Caroline said, and pulled up a desk chair beside him at his computer.

He logged onto the internet, called up a search engine, selected a people finder, and typed in a search for Jonah Miller. He chose "find it," and they watched as the search was run. Zero hits in Ohio for a Jonah Miller.

Branden modified the search to cover the whole nation and got only seven hits for Jonah Millers, altogether. He scanned the addresses, but found only distant states: North Carolina, Vermont, Kansas. No Ohio addresses, and nothing close to Ohio. He saved the data anyway.

"Maybe a derivative name, like John," Caroline said, and pulled up a little closer to the screen.

Branden modified the search parameters to read John Miller and got sixty-two hits for Ohio. Only two were in northern Ohio, and neither of those was from Cleveland. Again, Branden saved the results. There were nine names, now, in total, and any one of them could be their Jonah Miller, he thought. More likely, none of them was.

Casting further, he ran four more searches. Jon Millers in Ohio, 45. Jon Millers nationwide, 337. J Millers in Ohio, 819. J Millers nationwide, one thousand, plus.

He sat there for a while with Caroline, gazing at the screen, and then printed out the seven hits for Jonah Millers in the nation, plus the two for John Millers in northern Ohio, one from Lorain and one from Sandusky.

In their bedroom, Caroline propped up some pillows and sat back on the bed, her legs crossed at the ankles. Branden sank into a soft chair and tapped a finger on the printout.

"This is a start, but it's likely not going to be enough," he said.

Caroline said, "At least two are northern Ohio."

"I know, but he was only 'seen' in Cleveland."

"You think he's living somewhere else," Caroline said.

"Could be anywhere."

"Then how'd Miller expect you to be able to find him at all?" Caroline asked.

Branden responded with, "And why the one-month deadline?" Then, apparently offhand, he added, "I need to talk to the sheriff."

Caroline nodded. "I'll start calling Jonah Millers tomorrow."

"Right," Branden said and fell silent.

After several minutes had passed, Caroline said, "Maybe we shouldn't be looking for Jonah Miller. Maybe we should look for Jeremiah."

Branden mumbled, "How?" and shifted uneasily in his bedroom chair.

9

"FANCY pants!" Enos Coblentz shouted over the scream of the ripping blade. Branden stood well back from the saw and cupped his hand to his ear to signal that he hadn't heard.

"Jonah Miller got fancy pants," Enos shouted again, watching Branden's face for signs of comprehension.

Branden shook his head and then Coblentz held up all the fingers of each hand, pointed to the clock, and shouted, "Ten minutes!"

Branden nodded and walked outside where lumber was stacked, sorted by size and variety—maple, walnut, oak, hickory, and cherry. There was the pleasant aroma of freshly cut wood and a mound of sawdust outside. After several minutes, his ears began to recover from the intolerable noise inside.

The sawmill consisted of two rough pole buildings of corrugated aluminum and a shed for horses in winter. There was a summer corral of whitewashed boards in the back and a picnic table on a patch of grass under some trees. Two customers' buggies stood hitched in front, one horse nervously pawing at the gravel. Even at a distance, the noise of the saw astonished Branden.

He had begun his rounds with Cal Troyer before dawn in the districts south and east of Millersburg. There had been a slow walk through a plowed field with one of Troyer's distant cousins, an hour spent as the sun came up, retracing their kin-ship back to the day when Cal's grandfather had quit the Amish life. Since then, Cal's line had lived entirely English.

Then there were gentle questions for the cousin's neighbor, a brother-in-law. Branden had held back while Cal had probed delicately through a maze of family relationships, clanships, splinter groups, and the inevitable offshoots of several districts. At each step they had learned incrementally more about Eli Miller and his son Jonah. Sometimes they had found a willing-ness to talk forthrightly about both. More often they had not. Sometimes Cal had exploited the tendency for clannish rivalry between differing bishops. Other times he had sensed that they'd get little more than the bashful nod of a head or a silence that confirmed without comment.

Branden also marveled that most of the folk with whom they had talked had known something of Pastor Caleb Troyer before-hand. They knew him by reputation, and they trusted him.

When he had sensed from a wry smile or a cocked eyebrow that it would be productive, Cal had pushed with his questions into the fringe, seeking details about a man most had managed to forget. In the course of the morning they had spoken with a short man whose neck was puffed on one side by a goiter. There had been an elder Dutchman with a favorite pipe, sitting on an overturned barrel behind a hardware store in Kidron. A younger fellow with a denim apron in the tack shop at Charm. Someone had revealed that Jonah Miller had run with several friends—accomplices, he called them—from Sugarcreek. A vis-iting neighbor had confirmed it with a hesitant nod.

And so Troyer and Branden had made their way through the morning. The wheel shop in Moreland. A harness shop south of Fredericksburg. Troyer's bakery in Charm. A cheese factory in Sugarcreek. Well-shaded businesses with low ceilings and oil lamps, or white-glowing silk mantles hanging from ceiling fixtures. Off the tourist routes. Too far back in for tour buses. Each time learning better what to ask. What not to ask.

But eventually, sometime toward noon, the two began to notice that the people they approached seemed somehow to have known they were coming. Word had gotten around. The bishops had passed a ruling, and the people had become less forthcoming, more suspicious. But not before Cal had uncovered the name of one man—Enos Coblentz—who would surely know, if anyone did, whether Jonah Miller had come home. Then the pastor had been called to his other duties, and now Branden stood outside the sawmill where Enos Coblentz worked.

In ten minutes, Enos Coblentz strolled out through the large overhead door, slapping sawdust from his apron. He eased off his plastic safety goggles and put on small, round spectacles, hooking them carefully behind each ear. He pulled the ear plugs from both ears. His black hair hung precisely to his earlobes, in straight Dutch style, and his beard was full, unkempt, and laced heavily with sawdust. His face was shaved clean around both his upper and lower lips, forming an oval accent around a delicate mouth.

"Jonah Miller got fancy pants," Enos said again and brushed sawdust off his arms. "Near as I can remember, it started with pants. Cuffs or something like that. Can't recall exactly. But he was told. Proper and private. Everybody knew it."

Branden was dressed in blue jeans, a plain blue tee-shirt, and hiking boots. As usual, the soft waves of his brown hair were slightly tousled, and his brown beard was trimmed close, showing gray at the temples. He opened a can of pop and offered it to Coblentz. Coblentz declined, and Branden said, "Are you sure? I've got more in the truck."

"Thank you," Enos said, "but I have lunch in the buggy."

Branden followed Coblentz to a black one-seater parked beside the corral. It was of the classic Ohio style, the sides slanting in at the bottom to meet oval springs. Branden noticed the rubber-padded rims on the wheels and tapped at them, not thinking anything in particular, but aware nonetheless of their significance. Coblentz was not Old Order. At least not conservative Old Order. Surely not from Eli Miller's district.

Coblentz eyed the professor and then said, almost grinning, "Can you think of a reason why a buggy shouldn't be comfortable?" Then he lifted a black metal lunch pail from the buggy and ambled to the picnic table under the shade of a willow. A push mower leaned against the trunk of the tree. A quiet stream lapped past the exposed roots of the willow. Branches mingled lazily into the water and gave the small glade a peaceful, easy quietness, the saw having been stopped for lunch.

"I've been at it all morning," Branden said, "and you're the first person who's been willing to talk much about Jonah Miller."

"I'm not surprised," Coblentz said while unwrapping the wax paper on his first sandwich.

"Can you tell me about the ban?" Branden asked.

"What's to tell?" Coblentz remarked. "Jonah asked for it."

"Then can you tell me what actually precipitated the ban?" Branden said.

"Pride."

"How so?"

"Like I said. Jonah took to fancy dress. He was admonished. Everyone knew it."

"Yes, but what else?" Branden instantly regretted his impatient tone.

Coblentz ate slowly. The tranquillity in his eyes gradually gave way to an expression of rising inner turmoil. "It was a long time ago," he said eventually. "I can't recall everything that happened, but the way I see it, the ban actually started most of Jonah's problems."

He glanced into the corral and said, "See the bay? How she trembles there, standing? She don't like people much. Mostly just likes to run. Too spirited for her own good. That's the way Jonah was."

Coblentz fell silent again, and Branden waited, standing at ease beside the rough-cut picnic table, watching as Coblentz ran the puzzle of Jonah Miller through his mind. A breeze pushed delicate branches of the willow into Branden's hair, and he absently brushed the slender leaves aside.

Coblentz laid his sandwich down on the smoothed-out square of wax paper and stared unseeing at the cluster of standardbred horses and a single Morgan in the corral.

"I do not think Jonah was really so bad," Coblentz said. "First it was only simple matters, but in Miller's district, any indiscretion was invariably handled decisively. Chastised for small mischief, there. Do you realize, Professor, that I am not Old Order?"

Branden nodded and slid onto the bench on the opposite side of the picnic table.

"Our rules are not quite the same," Enos explained. "It's a revelation for me to think of him this long after our year of mischief. The grand *Rumschpringe* of Jonah Miller and Enos Coblentz." He shook his head and smiled.

"I've got a brother, Professor. Jonas. He started in the mills, just as I am doing now. So, should Jonas be blamed that the only farm that came up for auction had electric already in it? Of course the rules can be changed. Who would insist that Jonas disconnect the power? Thing is, Eli Miller would have insisted."

With that, Enos Coblentz seemed to have lost his appetite. He rubbed at his temples in slow circles and said, "It's a marvel how the mention of an old friend's name can affect us so much after all the years gone by. It has been a long time, Doktor Branden, since Jonah Miller's name has come to my ears. Is there a reason his name comes to them now?"

"Yes," Branden said straightforwardly, but offered nothing more.

A pause, then, "Can you tell me what it is?"

"Partly, I can," Branden said.

Coblentz considered that and then asked, "Would I be doing a bit of dreaming if I were to think that Jonah has come home?"

"Not entirely," Branden said and then explained the reason for his questions. He told of young Jeremiah, now spending the summer with his father. He told of their search for the boy. And of Bishop Eli Miller's request for help.

"The bishop came to you for help?" Enos asked, clearly surprised.

"Yes," Branden said, fully aware of what that would signify to Coblentz.

"Doughty Valley's gonna be sure abuzz this summer," Enos said with a mischievous smile.

"The bishop hopes that we'll be able to locate the boy," Branden said.

"I would not be calling that an exaggeration, by any means," Enos said and laughed. He picked up his sandwich, chuckled a bit, took two eager bites, and spoke with his mouth full. "What you are saying, Professor Branden, is that Bishop Miller wants the boy back."

"Is it that obvious?"

"Well, you sure won't need to explain that to anyone in these parts," Coblentz said with his eyebrows raised.

Branden tapped his fingers on the picnic table, thinking while Coblentz finished his lunch. He rested his chin in a palm and rubbed thoughtfully at his short brown whiskers.

Why had the bishop said they could search for Jonah but not make an effort to recover Jeremiah?

"Can you tell me," Branden said at last, "what provoked the falling out between Jonah and his father?"

"As I said before. Fancy pants," Coblentz said, loosened now to talk. "Jonah wore wide leather belts and store-bought fashion jeans. And he secretly carried a pocket watch on a gold chain."

"Even after warnings to conform?"

"Especially then," Coblentz observed. "Jonah was a rebel. He gave the bishop no choice. Everyone agreed. Jonah asked for it.

"But that wasn't the end of the matter," Enos said as he packed the remains of his lunch into the black metal pail. "We ran together in our year of the *Rumschpringe*. Eventually it had come to smoking dope, drinking, and women. I quickly got my fill of it. Went home and took my vows.

"Jonah moved to Millersburg after the ban. He moved in with a girl he had met in a bar. She was one of those '*Amish Lieben*.' English who fancy the Amish. Seems I remember she came from a good family, but by the time she met Jonah, she was pretty well gone on dope. And she was a regular at all of the bars. Six months after Jonah left town for good, she delivered a baby boy."

Enos stood and frowned, his memories evidently difficult. Branden sat gazing up at Coblentz from his seat at the picnic table and studied his face as Coblentz thought the puzzle through. He realized, by the set in Coblentz's jaw, that he would learn little more here today. Coblentz acquired a distant look for a brief spell and then focused his eyes again on the professor.

"Everyone saw it coming," Enos Coblentz said morosely. "After all, a leather belt betrays a prideful heart."

With that Coblentz went back to his mill, leaving Branden to return to his truck, frustrated over how little he had really learned about the Jonah Miller of today.

10

"LET HIM on through, Ellie," the sheriff hollered from the back of the jail. "That's Doc Branden."

"You're Professor Branden?" Ellie Troyer asked, flustered. "I'm sorry. I'm new."

Branden nodded and smiled sympathetically.

"I'm Ellie Troyer. You can go on back," Ellie said.

Branden asked, "Any relation to Cal Troyer?"

"No," Ellie said. "He's the preacher, right?"

"Right," Branden said and then held up a finger mischievously. He leaned forward with both elbows on the counter and said, "Let's listen a bit."

Sheriff Robertson's deep voice carried easily along the halls and through the thin walls inside the jailhouse. It had been paneled in the fifties with light-brown pine, and it had looked rustic then, and fashionably western, just the way the sheriff at the time liked it. Now the panels were faded, and the nails showed through as little rusty dots. The thin wooden walls carried the current sheriff's voice like an amplifier.

"I don't want to see your young butt back here EVER again, Crist Detweiler," Robertson roared. "Someday you'll want to grow a beard and take the vows. How you think I'm gonna feel meeting your wife on the street then, knowin' your drinking habits as I do?"

In the moment that followed, Branden and Ellie Troyer heard muffled, penitent assertions in Low German.

"All right then," the sheriff bellowed unsympathetically. "You want your Amish or your English clothes?"

Again, there came a soft, contrite answer in German. Branden whispered to Ellie, "Looks like I've caught the sheriff in one of his moods."

"Do tell," Ellie laughed. "He's been pumped for two straight days, now."

"So it'd be fair to guess that all of the deputies will be conveniently out of the jail on any missions they can dream up," Branden said.

"Wouldn't you hightail it?" Ellie asked. "You know how he gets."

Branden nodded and smiled, knowing as well as anyone how his old friend could "swing a mood." Robertson could be up, and then nothing could touch him. He also could be down, sometimes frighteningly so. To compound matters, Robertson characteristically refused to take the medication prescribed to moderate his mood swings, saying, "I'm way too good at this when I'm up and on a run. Can't risk losing that, now, can I, Mike?"

"I'm going to keep your English clothes, then," the sheriff said, still much louder than necessary. "I'll give them to someone who can use 'em. Consider it a fine, and don't let me see your butt in here EVER again. Verstehen Sie?" and then almost explosively, "DOST DU VERSTEHE?"

Seconds later, a wilted Amish teenager stepped backwards from the sheriff's office and glanced ruefully down the hall. When he saw Branden leaning against the counter, his delicate skin flushed crimson under black Dutch hair, and he slipped out through the back door, into the alley, utterly mortified to have been seen.

Sheriff Bruce Robertson followed shortly, carrying a brown

grocery bag stuffed with English clothing. He dropped the sack onto the counter and shook his head. An anxious deputy sheriff came out of Robertson's office and joined them at Ellie's front counter.

Branden peered into the sack and turned up his nose at its odor of cigarettes and beer. Then he grinned at Ellie behind the front counter and said to the sheriff, "You're going to get fired someday, Bruce, barking at youngsters like that."

"Don't make me laugh, Mike," Robertson said with exaggerated confidence. "People in this county love me, and you know it."

He turned to Ellie and introduced Branden. "Ellie Troyer," he said, beaming, "this is Professor Michael Branden. Civil War history and suchlike. Boyhood friend. He's the grand pooh-bah of Gettysburg. The one with the cannon out on the east cliffs."

"I know that, Sheriff," Ellie said. "We've just met."

"Well, good. Then look, Ellie. The professor always gets through. Understand? Day or night. Always put his calls through. Always send him straight back. Verstehen sie?"

"No problem," Ellie assented. She pretended to busy herself with papers at her desk and smiled brightly. "The professor always gets through."

Robertson spun Branden around heartily and ushered him down the hall with an arm clamped around Branden's shoulder. He motioned for Deputy Ricky Niell to follow. Jovially, he said, "How many cases have we worked on, Mike?"

"Ten? Twelve. Not sure, anymore," Branden said, enjoying the familiar company of the ponderous lawman. They had grown up together in Millersburg. Gone through the grades together with Cal Troyer. Branden glanced sideways at his sizable friend as they marched down the hall. In or out of uniform, Sheriff Bruce Robertson would always look to Mike Branden like a chubby, boisterous, irrepressible, and mischievous boy of ten on a grade-school playground.

"And when did we ever have more than one or two cases a year with the Amish on the wrong side of the law?" Robertson continued in stride, turning the corner into his office.

"One or two a year, if that many," Branden said.

In the office, Robertson introduced Branden and Ricky Niell, his newest deputy, with the department only a week. That done, he said, "You two want to tell me what these Amish kids are doing showing up in town bars in English dress?"

"Such as that fellow just now?" Branden said.

"Exactly. Seems I get one or two a week, now."

Robertson sat on the front corner of his antique cherry desk and Branden dropped into a low leather chair beside it, legs out straight, ankles crossed, relaxed. Niell stood awkwardly near the door.

The sheriff's office was large, occupying fully a quarter of the first floor of the house-like, red brick jail. Two of the tall windows looked out onto Clay Street, which runs north and south through Millersburg past Courthouse Square. The north windows of the sheriff's corner office gave a view of the courthouse lawn, with its Civil War monument. The sheriff's desk stood with its back to the south wall. Several straight wooden chairs and a few leather easy chairs were scattered about the office. Behind the sheriff's desk stood a full-length, floor-to-ceiling bookcase, holding an assortment of photos, plaques, books, and trophies. One section of the bookcase was devoted to Robertson's collection of vintage Zane Grey western novels, all valuable collectibles, each thoroughly read. On the paneled wall to the sheriff's right, Robertson had stapled his collection of some seventy to eighty police department arm patches. They were tacked to the wall haphazardly, in whatever location had happened to suit the big sheriff at the moment. The jumbled, spontaneous array worked pleasantly on the eyes only because of the sheer number of patches, not because of any care he had given to their arrangement.

Robertson snapped a cigarette out of a pack of Winstons on his desk, lit up, and blew out the match, his thoughts shifting impulsively. He pointed the lit end of his cigarette at Branden and mocked a grave tone. "City Council's got a problem with your cannon again, Professor. Some old ladies want me to shut you down. They know the chief can't do anything because you're outside the city limits." He gave his words a serious inflection, and glanced sideways, hoping to find Niell watching. Niell was, intently.

Branden noted the conspiratorial glance. "We've been over this before," Branden said, calmly for Niell's benefit. "And you know I always wait until noon."

Robertson seemed disappointed. "Doesn't matter, they still want it stopped."

"In that case, I'll cannonade at precisely midnight."

"Certain old ladies on the council don't think you can do it at any time, day or night."

"Then let 'em read their own statutes. I've been outside the city limits for ten years. Special dispensation. You know it and so do they."

Robertson drew slowly on the remains of his cigarette and chuckled. Then he studied the smirk on Branden's face, shook his head, laughed and said, "Same time?"

Branden eased smugly into his chair, and said, "Twelve, noon. I presume you'll attend?"

"Wouldn't miss it for anything," Robertson said and slapped Niell on the arm as he walked to a sideboard and poured a cup of coffee. He offered to Niell, who declined with a self-conscious wave of his hand. Robertson poured a second cup, added cream, gave it to Branden, and sat again on the front edge of his massive desk. After a sip, Robertson asked, "Is this a fishing trip, Mike, or are you here on a case?"

"It's a case," Branden said and blew across the creamy coffee. "I'd hoped you could provide us with a mug shot out of county records. We're looking for Jonah E. Miller."

"Whew-eee," Robertson whistled loudly and shot Niell a glance. "Jonah Miller's back in town?"

"I don't know where he is. I'm simply trying to find him," Branden explained and set his coffee cup on a coaster on the sheriff's desk.

"Why?" Robertson asked, suspicious, but scarcely pausing before clicking on the intercom and asking Ellie to have the jail photos of Jonah Miller sent over from the courthouse.

"We go back a long way, Bruce," Branden said and propped himself a bit straighter. "You'll have to believe me that I can't actually tell you why I'm looking for him."

"Good grief, Mike. You have any idea what that name means around here?"

"Not really," Branden said. "I can only say that Bishop Eli Miller has asked me to find him."

"And then what?" Robertson asked.

"Simply tell the bishop where Jonah Miller is, so far as I understand the matter," Branden said discreetly.

The sheriff walked around his desk, sat in his swivel chair, and leaned heavily back with his toes balanced against the floor, elbows up, hands clasped behind his head, cigarette between his teeth.

"If you do find him, Mike, I'd advise you to tell no one other than the bishop," the sheriff said, the remains of his cigarette bobbing between his lips, eyes squinting against the smoke.

"You seem pretty certain of that, Bruce. Mind telling me why?"

Robertson drew again on the cigarette, rocked forward, and thumbed it out in a scarlet ashtray. Then he leaned back again, folded his hands across his substantial belly and said, "For his own good, that's why."

"Whose?" Branden said. "The bishop or his son?"

"Both!" the sheriff exclaimed. "Look, Mike. You're obviously out of the loop on this one. Think about it. Aside from a few youngsters in trouble, like that kid that just snuck out of here, the Amish have rarely been a problem for the law. In all the years you and I have logged in this town, we'll still not be able to come up with more than two or three serious cases between us. Maybe a couple of conscientious objectors and social security tax resisters in the old days. But never any real criminal trouble. Jonah Miller is the exception. Follow me?"

Branden nodded and asked, "What's so special about Jonah Miller?"

The mug shot photos were delivered to Robertson, and he looked them over and then held them up for Branden. "Cripes, Mike," Robertson complained, "most Amish don't even know what court is. Never seen a judge. Wouldn't know how to go about filing a police report."

"You don't have to tell me, Bruce," and then, "That's Jonah Miller?"

The sheriff nodded and then said to Niell, "You grew up around here, too, Ricky. You know of any real trouble with the Amish?

Niell shrugged and said, "Not really, sir."

Robertson handed the photos to Branden and kept at it. "Take those four boys last year that got caught busting up mailboxes at Halloween. Court date came up, no lawyers, no legal moves, nothing. Judge lined 'em up in front of his bench, read the charges, and asked how they pleaded."

"And?" Branden asked.

"Didn't know what it meant 'to plead.' So the judge explains, 'Guilty or Not Guilty?' Not one of those boys said a word. Probably too confused. Or embarrassed. Anyways, the bishop who brought 'em to court stood up in the back and said 'They pleads guilty.' End of case."

"What's the point, Bruce?" Branden asked.

"Point is, Mike, Jonah Miller is no longer Amish. He's way past that, now, buddy, let me tell ya. Closest thing to wanton lawlessness I've ever seen from a Dutchman."

"And?" Branden asked. He studied the front and side-view

photos of Miller. Short black hair in a crewcut, long black mustache, a sullen expression on his face, with a hint of wild defiance in his eyes. He passed the photos to Niell, who studied them briefly and gave them back to Branden.

"And, if Jonah E. Miller were to show his face in these parts, there'd be no end of trouble, all around. Amish included." Robertson leaned forward on his elbows and raised an eyebrow, saying, "Do you remember the Brenda Hostettler thing ten years back?"

"Brenda Hostettler—Jeff Hostettler's sister, right? I was on sabbatical then. What happened to her?" Branden asked.

"Suicide."

Niell looked startled and took a step forward. The sheriff waited for Branden to make the connection.

"Brenda Hostettler and Jonah Miller?" Branden asked.

"You're starting to get the picture," Robertson said indelicately. "Jonah Miller got Brenda Hostettler pregnant before he split."

Ricky Niell said, "I knew Brenda in high school," and sat down heavily in a chair in front of the sheriff's desk.

Robertson continued. "Some say he didn't know about the child, but plenty think he did. Something like ten years ago, now. You were still in the service, Ricky. You, my fine professor, must have been locked away in your ivory tower."

Branden rolled his eyes and said again, "I was on sabbatical, Bruce, all year at Duke."

"OK, whatever," Robertson said. "Anyway, the kid was born. Brenda took care of it for a spell. Then she walked out to Bishop Miller's house, left the kid on the back porch, stepped over the hill, and blew her brains out with a .357 magnum."

Branden groaned, shifted uncomfortably in his seat, and ran his fingers back through his hair.

Ricky Niell, shaken, muttered again, "I knew Brenda Hostettler."

Branden thought for several minutes, staring at the floor.

When he looked back to the sheriff, Branden said, "The child was Jeremiah Miller?"

"Right. So you do remember the case," Robertson said.

"Not really. I just know the bishop," Branden said, his mind racing. "Also, I'm looking for his son."

"Brenda Hostettler killed herself?" Niell asked.

"I think you two are catching on," Robertson said and smiled. Then he asked, "Why are you looking for Jonah Miller?"

"The bishop has asked me to find him," Branden said, and offered no more of the puzzle.

"Then don't you think it's a bit strange that the bishop didn't mention her to you?" Robertson asked.

Niell nodded once in agreement and turned his eyes on the professor.

"She wasn't Amish?" Branden asked, fishing.

"No." Robertson explained. "She was a bar-hopping tramp, but she came from a prominent family. Her father was dead at the time. Her mother has passed on, since. She has only a brother who survives her."

"And?" Branden asked.

"And he has vowed to kill Jonah E. Miller on sight."

As he left the jailhouse, Branden pocketed the photos of Jonah Miller and wrestled with the nature of the problem he had been handed. Clearly Miller would not be able to come home to stay. Evidently, he'd not likely try. And clearly it was obvious to everyone that Bishop Miller would stop at little, if anything, to retrieve his grandson. Also, clearly, the bishop did not want the disappearance of Jeremiah, a kidnapping really, placed into the hands of the law.

Branden drove the narrow, steep streets of Millersburg, thought about that, and realized he agreed with the bishop, at least for the moment. Even aside from the bishop's inherent distrust of the law, Branden knew instinctively that Bruce Robertson's bluff approach would be wrong for the delicate task of locating the bishop's grandson. And yet, without more to go on, there was little he could do, beyond what they had already planned, to find Jonah Miller and his son Jeremiah.

As he drove slowly up the hill to the college heights, Branden wondered what the bishop expected them to do. He had ruled out access to the resources of the Sheriff's Department, and, on their own, they had learned precious little. Jeremiah was with Jonah Miller, who would not likely appear in Holmes County any time soon. And Bishop Miller had decided to sit on the farm for a month, waiting for whatever leads a couple of English folk might turn up.

"There's nothing there," Branden mumbled as he turned onto the short street where they lived near the college. Nothing to lead them to Jeremiah. He also realized as he parked at the curb that, apart from the fact that he wanted his grandson back, the bishop had given him practically nothing to work with. There was just Jonah Miller's note, and that was cryptic enough. "Back by harvest" was how it had read. He wondered how he could ask Bruce Robertson to run some criminal records checks, without violating his promise to the bishop.

Then, as he walked into the brick colonial, set close to the curb, he asked himself the pivotal question in the puzzle they were working. Why, given the facts, or lack of them, in the case, was the bishop not content simply to wait it out, for Jeremiah to come home for the harvest?

11

CAROLINE rose from the small wooden breakfast table, carried dishes to the sink, came back to the round table, took Cal's cup and saucer, added hot water at the stove, set it in front of Cal and said, to him and to her husband, "I can't explain all the reasons why, Cal. I just know Donna Beachey thinks she's the cause of most of Jonah Miller's early troubles."

She sat back down at the table, wondering privately when her husband intended to speak of the FedEx envelope that lay unopened on his desk at the college. When he's ready, she told herself, sorry now that his secretary had ever mentioned it to her.

Cal said, "Jonah Miller had more troubles than can have been started by any fifth-grade teacher."

"It doesn't matter," Caroline asserted, "She still carries remorse over Jonah. A great deal of remorse."

"So what have we got here?" Branden asked. "A young dreamer of a student put too tight a roll on his trouser cuffs and ended up a smoking, drinking, fast-living scoundrel who deserted his pregnant girlfriend, drove her to suicide, kidnapped his own son ten years later, and is being hunted by his father who shunned him, and by the girl's brother, who has vowed to kill him. That about cover it?"

"Isn't that enough?" Caroline complained.

Cal rolled his eyes and shook his head. He sipped his tea and remarked, "There seems to be something missing. Something important."

"Something rather subtle," Branden said. "Did either of you get the impression that people were surprised to hear mention of Jonah Miller?"

"Very much so," Caroline said. "It took me all morning, and the better part of the afternoon, to find Donna Beachey. Until then, people were surprised even to hear mention of Jonah's name."

Cal said, "Same here. Most were uncomfortable to speak of him at all."

"I got something like that same reaction from Bruce Robertson," Branden added.

"So what's that tell us?" Cal asked.

"First, it tells us what the internet suggested right off," Branden said. "He hasn't moved back into the county. Also that he has not allowed himself to be seen, and that we might just as well start looking for him elsewhere."

"Elsewhere could be anywhere," Caroline said.

The phone rang, and Branden rose to answer it.

"Something else's been bothering me," Cal said to Caroline. "Why would the bishop ask Mike not to try to get the boy back if he found him? To leave him with his father? Everyone I spoke to acted as if it'd be obvious that he'd search for Jeremiah and demand his return. Relentless was a word someone used."

After a pause, Caroline said, "Maybe 'why' isn't the question. Maybe we should be asking 'who' the bishop doesn't want to learn he's searching for Jeremiah."

Cal glanced at Branden, still on the phone, and looking troubled.

To Caroline Cal said, "Among all of the people we've interviewed, it seems that Jonah has only one former teacher, Beachey, and one former friend, Coblentz, who might be inclined to think well of him. Eli Miller must be worried that Jonah will harm the boy." He thought a moment longer and then added, "Or that someone will make a run at Jonah, and Jeremiah will be caught in the middle."

Caroline grimaced. It was a good point. Almost anyone could be waiting for a chance at Jonah Miller.

Cal looked at his watch. "I've got to catch a plane tomorrow, and I haven't packed."

"Your conference?" Caroline asked.

"Yes," Cal said, "but Mike's going to need help finding this boy. Wish I weren't going now."

"He'll be fine," Caroline said. "Besides, he has Bruce Robertson if he really needs help."

"He said Bruce Robertson thought Jonah would be in danger for his life if he were to come home," Cal said, arguing the point.

Caroline said, "I'll help. Don't worry about going to the conference."

Branden returned from the phone and overheard. "It doesn't matter now, Cal," he said. "You can take all the time you want, and it won't matter to Jonah Miller." He sat down heavily, laid his palms flat on the table top, and studied the backs of his hands for several seconds. "That was Bruce Robertson on the phone. Jonah Miller is dead. Shot in the head less than half a mile from Bishop Miller's house."

12

"FOR Cripessakes, Andy," Robertson bellowed, glowering into the ditch from the berm above, "you've got enough pictures!"

Andy Shetler snapped off another six frames, clearly annoyed, wanting more. Impatient, aren't you, Robertson, he thought, irritated. Always in such a hurry. Wound too tight for police work, aren't you, Robertson, Shetler thought. It takes time to do things right, in case you didn't know. The shots were difficult. Body two-thirds buried in muck. Weeds obscuring all of the best camera angles.

Shetler squeezed off three more frames and then, with an audible groan, eased his foot into putrid goo at the bottom of the ditch. Bubbles of sulfurous gas gurgled up around his ankles, and cold muck seeped into his shoe. He pushed forward through the cat tails and shot several more frames of a body in Amish attire, lying on its side, arms tangled strangely, the back of the head destroyed by an apparent gun shot.

"How about it, Shetler? You going to let us get a look at that body or not?" Robertson had been pacing somberly along the berm, but now stood with his feet apart, hands planted decisively on his hips. Everyone had turned at the bark of his voice.

"All done," Andy said, gloomily pulling his shoe out of the mud. As he scaled the bank, he held the Nikon high over his head and said, "All yours, Sheriff. No need to hurry. He's a mess."

Robertson pulled two pairs of latex gloves out of his back pocket and shouted in the direction of a deputy standing guard at the yellow police ribbon, "Let the professor through."

Branden eased past a cluster of Amish folk gathered silently on the roadside. He ducked under the yellow tape and walked, hands stuffed into his pockets, to the side of the road where Sheriff Robertson stood amid a tangle of orange day lilies, glaring down into the muddy ditch. Only a light drizzle remained of the morning's storm. The skies were bleak, winds gusting, sun laboring ineffectively behind a drab cover of gray. If not for the green of the luxuriant crops that lay under the clouds in every direction, it could easily have been mistaken for a day late in fall.

Robertson handed Branden a pair of the rubber gloves and said, "Notice how the arms and legs sprawl?"

"You think he was dead before he landed?" Branden asked.

"Went limp before he touched down."

Branden grimaced, snapped his hands into the rubber gloves, and followed Robertson down into the ditch. Robertson pushed the cat tails aside and studied the face, washed clean by the rain. "Lousy job of shaving, wouldn't you say, Mike?"

"You mean the nicks?" Branden asked. The skin was ashen, mousy gray, and the open eyes were vacant. Tiny nicks in the skin showed around the mouth, shaved recently smooth above and below the lips. A small hole showed under the chin, ringed by a patch of black powder and burnt skin.

"I'll warrant he was not well practiced with a straight razor."

"Clothes are new," Branden said as they turned the body slightly.

The black vest hung loose, unhooked, and the plain white shirt was buttoned to the neck.

"They found a new straw hat nearby," Robertson remarked as he used a pencil to lift a revolver out of the mud beside the body.

"You figure that's the murder weapon?" Branden asked.

"Or suicide," Robertson said.

"Out here? Surely this has got to be a murder, Bruce. Especially considering all the trouble Jonah Miller has caused over the years."

"Can't rule out suicide at this point," Robertson replied.

"Check the hands," Branden said.

Robertson straddled the body and pulled one hand from the muck in the ditch. "Coroner's going to have to rule on powder residue," Robertson said, showing Branden the thick mud that encased the right hand. Then he pointed to the left arm, pinned at a strange angle under the torso and said, "The left hand, too."

Branden straightened beside the body and studied the crowd of curious Amish gathered on the road above. "Who found the body, Bruce?"

"Kids driving by in a surrey, as far as I understand it," Robertson said, his attention still on the body.

"And how do we know this is Jonah Miller?" Branden asked, as he tried to superimpose the booking photos from ten years ago onto the face that lay in the ditch.

"Oh, it's Miller all right," the sheriff said, and then, "Hey, look at this, Mike. No wallet, no comb, no nothin'." He had deftly pulled both of the pockets inside out.

Branden nodded bleakly. Robertson said, "Let's get out of here," and scrambled awkwardly up the bank to the road.

Once on top, Robertson hitched his pants up in back, gathered his shirttail under his sizable belly, and then waved for the deputy. "Coroner on her way?"

"Yes sir," the deputy replied.

"We're finished, here. She can have the body."

Branden studied the faces in the crowd that had gathered behind the yellow ribbons and asked Robertson, as he peeled off his gloves, "You figure that's a bullet hole under the chin?"

"No doubt, but I'll want to hear what Taggert has to say, too." The sheriff tilted his glance towards the back of the station wagon, where the deputies were sliding out a stretcher.

"You been over the road?" Branden asked.

"Yep. No skid marks here, if that's what you mean."

"Any idea what Jonah Miller was doing on this particular road?" Branden asked.

"No," the sheriff said.

"Do we know why he's dressed Amish?"

"No," the sheriff said, with increasing impatience.

"Any eyewitnesses?"

"None," the sheriff said, scowling.

Branden stood on the wet pavement, thinking. There were no witnesses and few details. And Professor Michael Branden was a man accustomed to details. Most of his cases had finally come down to them, one way or another. So, too, his research on the Civil War. The larger questions always fell into place only in context of the details. Here there were few. Instead of details, there was only a single, overarching implausibility: Although it was not uncommon for the Amish to become the victim of a careless driver on a country lane, it was decidedly uncommon for one to be shot, perhaps murdered—and that after a bishop had retained a private investigator to find him.

Branden studied the crowd that had gathered, glanced down despondently at the body, and struggled to frame the larger questions. Most of all, Branden distrusted the coincidences. "Bishop Miller," he said to himself, "must have held something back."

At the cruiser, Robertson leaned over, reached in for the microphone to his radio and made a call as he stood next to the black-and-white. "Ellie, I want Jeff Hostettler picked up for questioning."

"Jeff Hostettler, right away," Ellie answered.

"That's the brother I told you about," Robertson explained to Branden. "The brother of Jeremiah Miller's mother."

The mention of the boy's name sent a shock through Branden. Where was Jeremiah? His thoughts whirled momentarily out of control. Branden seized on the hope that Jeremiah must now be home, and felt the urgency lessen. Jeremiah must surely be at his grandfather's house, just up the road. First work the scene, then go to the bishop's, he told himself, calmer. Take the time here to do things right, and then go to the Millers'. That's where Jeremiah Miller will be. Back with his family.

"I'm gonna walk a ways," Branden said nervously, and started off in the direction of the nearest crest in the road. Robertson watched him intently and then waded into the crowd of onlookers, asking questions.

Branden walked slowly along the road, eyes down as he marched off a zigzag path from one side to the other, inspecting the shoulders. Puddles from the night's storms dotted the pavement. A remnant flash of lightning appeared in the eastern distance. The steamy haze over the pavement carried the scent of tar and earthworms. The thickets of trees overhanging the road were silent except for the occasional slight splashing of drops on the pavement as the wind dislodged water from the branches overhead.

It was the type of back-country Holmes County road that saw little car traffic. Doughty Creek, brown and swollen from the overnight rains, surged at turns as it ran alongside. The road, sometimes black-topped and sometimes gravel, ran over hills, around sharp corners, and through stands of timber beside the stream, along the north side of the valley. Small gravel lanes intersected the larger road at intervals, and today their surfaces showed numerous thin, overlacing buggy tracks, made after the rains.

In some of the remotest regions, the road narrowed and passed directly beside an Amish house, sometimes separating house from barn by a mere ten paces. It was a road meant exclusively for buggies. It meandered through a sequestered community nurturing a slower, more deliberate culture than can be found in larger America. Like dozens of others in the Doughty Valley, it was never a road meant for autos, nor for any of the other intrusions of modern life.

At the crest of the nearest hill on the lane, Branden stooped over, gently touched a rain-softened tire mark in the loose gravel, stood pensively upright, and then walked purposefully over the crest of the hill.

On the other side, not quite out of view from Robertson, Branden leaned over and picked up one of several wet cigarette butts from a scattered pile beside the road. His gaze worked along the road, away from the body, beyond the crest where he stood. When he had spotted what he was looking for, he whistled for the sheriff with his fingers stuck against his teeth, and stood by the pile of burned cigarettes.

Robertson arrived, breathing heavily from the exertion of the climb and carrying his yellow rain slicker loosely over one arm. "This better be good, Mike. Body's back down there, in case you hadn't noticed."

Branden pointed to the road at his feet.

"Cigarette butts in the dirt?" Robertson asked.

"Not just that. Look, it makes sense. Suppose Jonah Miller was walking this way, toward his home. Rather, toward his father's home."

"And?" Robertson asked.

"And, someone stood here, watching. Waiting. See how you can just look over the crest of the hill, down along the road?"

"So far, I'm with you, but what makes that interesting to us?" Robertson said, glancing back over the crest of the hill to the place where the deputies still talked to the crowd around the coroner's wagon.

"That," Branden said, pointing in the opposite direction, at a long skid mark that arose in the berm and played out onto the pavement, leaving a sizable patch of mud and burnt rubber.

"So you figure someone stood here," Robertson said.

"And smoked cigarettes waiting for Jonah Miller."

"And when Miller came along, he . . . ?"

"Or she."

"Right," Robertson said. "He or she got in the car, popped the clutch, and came over the hill. It just doesn't seem likely. For all we know, those are Miller's cigarette butts. I figure he stood here thinking something through. Then he walked down there and shot himself under the chin."

"Why suicide?" Branden asked.

"Why not?" Robertson said. "These skid marks could have been made a week ago."

"The mud wouldn't have been there a week ago," Branden retorted. "Besides, why would he kill himself?"

"Jeff Hostettler might have had a good reason to kill him," the sheriff offered.

Branden thought it over. "So you think Jeff Hostettler could have lured Miller back home, somehow? It's worth a shot. I notice you didn't waste any time having him picked up."

Robertson swivelled to face the cruiser where it stood by the body in the ditch. He signalled to a deputy and indicated the pile of cigarette butts. As the deputy climbed the slight rise, Robertson said thoughtfully, "Still, if it's murder, then there's one thing I can't figure. How would Hostettler know that Jonah Miller would be walking along this road, at this time? For that matter, how would anyone have known?"

"His father's house is just down the way," Branden offered, not entirely certain himself what that might signify.

As they walked back toward the cluster of onlookers, neither spoke. The deputies had the body tucked into the coroner's wagon.

"I'll grant you that we can't rule out murder," Robertson said. "But killing himself out here in Amish dress is the kind of wacked-out thing Jonah Miller was always capable of doing."

Branden said, "The gun could have been dropped there after the murder, to make it look like a suicide."

"The gun wouldn't be in his hand, anyway," Robertson said. "Most guns fly out of the hand in a suicide."

"Will Missy Taggert be able to tell us anything down at the coroner's labs?" Branden asked.

"You bet," Robertson said, and lowered himself awkwardly into his cruiser, intending to follow the coroner into town. Branden stood beside the cruiser, shut the car door, and then leaned down to speak quietly through the window.

"I'll see you later, Bruce. In town. First, I thought I'd stop by Eli Miller's house."

"You know where it is? It's hard to find," Robertson said.

"Been there once before. In a buggy," Branden said, and then walked away, slowly working through the crowd of curious onlookers, who still maintained a vigil behind the yellow police-line ribbons.

At the Miller house, Branden parked at the end of the driveway, pulling off to the side to allow a buggy to enter the yard where several other rigs were already parked on the grass. A plain white picket fence surrounded the yard. A large black mailbox was mounted on the fence near the gate. Canning jars were set to dry upside down on several of the fence posts. Behind the fence, large shade trees dominated the front yard. A new concrete walkway led from the driveway to the porch. A large round trampoline was set on the lawn, but no children were in sight.

The windows of the white, two-story, frame house were covered inside by heavy, full-length, dark purple curtains. As he approached on the sidewalk, the curtains of one downstairs window were pulled back to reveal a child's face, that of a small girl in a bonnet. After an unhurried, curious look at Branden, she disappeared from view.

As Branden stepped onto the porch, a short, round woman

came out through the front door. She was dressed, as was the girl beside her, in a bonnet, long gray dress, and black shawl.

"Mr. Miller is not home, at present," she said formally.

Branden introduced himself. He explained where he had been, mentioned that the bishop had sought his help, and inquired apologetically when the bishop might be expected.

"I'll tell him you were here," she said politely. She held her hands gingerly in front of her waist. Her fingers were bent with arthritis. On one finger, she nervously twisted at one of the magnetic iron bands favored among the Amish for its effects on rheumatic heart disease.

A young boy slipped bashfully through the screened door and stood beside Mrs. Miller. Jeremiah? Branden wondered. About the right age, he thought. The lad wore plain denim jeans, a plum-colored shirt with no collar, and a straw hat. A young man appeared, dressed to match the boy, and stood before Branden, somewhat in front of Mrs. Miller, who stepped back and fell silent.

The young man spoke with a tone of extreme formality bordering on animosity. "I am Isaac Miller. My father is with the Dieners," he said, cocking his head toward the large red bank barn on a slope beside the house. "He'll not need to be talking to you anymore, I reckon."

"And Jeremiah?" Branden asked.

"You need not concern yourself," the young Miller said firmly, and drew the younger boy closer to himself. "The bishop feels that he does not need your services any further, but he'll be happy to speak with you about it sometime next week. But Professor, as you can see, even now the family is gathering."

Branden turned and saw a procession of three more buggies wheeling down the drive. He excused himself, walked past the line of parked buggies to his truck, and drove into Millersburg.

BRANDEN found the sheriff at the coroner's office. In the

examination room, the coroner worked at her task. She had cut the shirt away from the torso of Jonah Miller, and she had set a pan under the large exit wound at the back of the skull.

Robertson, squeamish, was standing in Melissa Taggert's office, making a show of studying the diplomas from Ohio State that hung on her walls.

Taggert was average in height. She had soft brown hair tied in a ponytail and tucked up under a pale green scrub hat. She was dressed in green scrubs to match, and she wore amber latex gloves and a clear plastic bibbed apron. She had a pleasant face and a nearly constant happy disposition, which sometimes irritated the changeable sheriff to the point of distraction. "Missy," he would say, "you can't always be happy." "Bruce," she would answer, "why in the world not?"

The coroner knew that Robertson liked her for it, and she wasn't above using the advantage when she needed something unusual for the labs. She also knew that Robertson was not altogether comfortable in her examination room, and she took more than a few opportunities to needle him about it.

"Bring me those forceps, Bruce," she was saying as Branden arrived. "Second drawer down. The little ones."

Robertson stepped into the lab, walked over to the drawer and took out small forceps. "Melissa, even I can see that you won't find anything in that wound except blood, brains, and bone."

Robertson liked Melissa Taggert. He liked her because she was competent, professional, and strong-minded. Also because she was smart. He even liked the way that she teased him in the morgue. He liked the fact that, on forensic problems, if she did not have an answer, she said so honestly. And then, in nearly every case, she set about the business of coming up with answers, no matter what it took. Most of all, he liked the fact that he could push her hard on any case whatsoever, and she had never faltered.

She took the small forceps, scolded him by waving them wordlessly in front of his face, then bent over at the back of Miller's head and began searching for debris. After several minutes of washing the wound into the pan, she smiled with grim satisfaction and pulled out a small sliver of copper metal. "I expect this'll match the copper casings on the hollow points that are left in that revolver you found," she said.

Robertson nodded briefly, and, relieved to have the interruption, turned to Branden and asked, "What'd you learn at the Millers?"

"Nothing. Absolutely nothing," Branden answered. "There's a house full of relatives and neighbors out there, but no one's talking. Does that seem strange to you, Bruce? A house full of mourners for a man who was shunned?"

"No stranger than this," Robertson said. He stepped closer to the body. "Look at the clothes. Old Order Amish, head to toe." Then Robertson asked, "You about done there, Doc?"

"Only with the preliminaries," Melissa said. "It'll take some time before we have the rest."

"We'll need to know if there's gunpowder burns on his hands," Robertson asserted. "He probably shot himself."

"As usual, you sound blissfully sure of yourself, Bruce," Melissa said playfully. "I, on the other hand, being actually responsible for a professional opinion, will need to run some tests." She winked at Branden.

"Go right ahead, Doc. But look," Robertson said, "let us have a little peek at the body first."

Melissa shrugged, pulled off her surgical gloves, and stepped into her adjoining office. The sheriff and Branden moved closer to the table.

Jonah E. Miller was laid out straight on his back. His hair had once been cut in a flat-top style. Now it was unkempt, grown somewhat long, and lay down limp and straight, where there was still any left. His face had about half an inch in growth of beard, shaved clean around the mouth, top and bottom, in Amish style.

He was dressed in a plain white shirt, a black vest, blue denim trousers without a cuff, and brown work boots. All but the boots were new. The boots were stained with smudges of black tar.

There was no jewelry, nothing in the pockets, no watch. The plain straw hat that had been found at the scene lay muddied at his side. The sheriff inspected the hat and studied the hands.

"Still a carpenter," he said, pointing to callouses.

"Why the clothes?" Branden asked.

"You mean 'why the brand-new Amish' clothes," Robertson said.

"Why the brand-new clothes, and why was he walking along that road?" Branden asked.

"And where's his car?" Robertson added.

"Do you think he had one?" Branden asked.

"Jonah Miller?" Robertson scoffed. "Oh yeah, he had a car all right."

The phone rang next door. Melissa Taggert came out of her office and said, "Bruce, they need you over at the jail."

When the sheriff had left, Branden stood beside the stainless steel table where Jonah Miller lay. The Jonah Miller he saw was fitted out Amish, proper in almost every detail. The hair was not long enough, and neither was the beard. But that was it. The upper lip was shaved smooth, and the costume was regulation "Bishop Miller Old Order" all the way.

Simple questions began to wander into Branden's mind. Was Jonah walking toward home? Had he been alone? Had he been taking Jeremiah home? Was Jeremiah at home now? The young Isaac Miller had seemed to imply that, but he had never really said it outright. All he had said was that Branden should consider himself out of a job.

Branden walked outside to the parking lot beside Joel

Pomerene Hospital. The skies had darkened again, and a steady rain came down. He pulled the hood up on his thin green raincoat, walked to his truck, and thought about the biggest question of them all. As Jonah Miller was walking along that road, had he killed himself, or had someone smoked a dozen or so cigarettes, and waited for Jonah Miller to wander into a trap?

13

Monday, June 22
3:45 P.M.

AS MUCH as he liked Melissa Taggert, and as well as he tolerated her teasing, Bruce Robertson still hated visiting the morgue. In truth, he hated hospitals in general. In particular, today, he had hated the sight of Jonah Miller's body on the slab. He had barely been able to keep up pretenses for the sake of his reputation. Once again, Taggert had almost joked her way past his rough facade.

As he left the coroner's office for the jail, his thoughts turned morose, dwelling on a mental list of his more depressing memories. In the parking lot of Joel Pomerene Hospital, his outlook darkened rapidly, poised to give way to the depression that sometimes gripped him. From this state he could fall into a world of limitless bitterness and stay there for days. For most of his life, he had thought everyone was this way. There were ups, and then there were downs. When he was down, his depressions could become almost debilitating. Debilitating, that is, unless he saw them early for what they were, and fought back with the medicine. He was supposed to take it all the time, but he used it only sporadically. Today he took the medicine bottle from the glove compartment of the cruiser and swallowed two of the pills dry.

In the rain, Robertson drove down off the little hill where the hospital sat along the Wooster Road. Pounding his fist on the steering wheel in frustration, he drove south past the old Victorian homes, along the winding streets of Millersburg, stacked on a tumble of hills like a river town. On the square, he sat in his cruiser for a while and studied the old jail. It was two and a half stories of weathered red brick, with faded yellow trim, and gray bars over the windows of the two-story cell block attached to the rear. The rain pinged steadily against the hand-hammered tin gutters and window moldings. In the blocks he had driven from the hospital, Robertson's mind had refocused from a somber and diffused state of ineffectiveness to a purposeful, elevated state of action. He lumbered out of his black-and-white cruiser in a steady downpour and marched purposefully across the blacktopped parking lot strewn with earthworms, his head down under his uniform rain hat, hands stuffed in his pockets, his long yellow slicker pulled back and hanging carelessly open in front. He stomped to the back of the old jail with his sense of order and purpose restored. Ellie had put it out on the radio that the deputies had brought in Jeff Hostettler.

Robertson pushed through the door at the rear of the jail and slapped his rain hat several times against a cold steam radiator, knocking off a small shower of water. Ricky Niell, in uniform, stood in the long paneled hall outside one of the two interrogation rooms. Robertson's large office was situated to the left, across the hall from these two small rooms. Ellie Troyer was at her desk at the far end of the hall, where a right turn led, through the wooden counter's swinging door, to the front entrance of the jail and the first-floor gang cell behind a black iron door.

Robertson stepped out of his slicker, gave it a snap, and hung it, with others like it, on one of the Shaker wall hooks outside his office. He glanced questioningly at Niell, who nodded at the closed door to Interview B. Robertson ducked into his office across the hall, lit a cigarette from a pack on his desk, inhaled hugely, held the smoke, stepped out into the hall again, looked down the hall toward Ellie Troyer, and blew out the remains of the smoke gratefully. He paused there, watching Ellie work the dispatch radio, drew again heavily on the Winston, and rubbed at the back of his neck while rolling his head in a slow circle. Niell stood quietly at ease, letting the minutes pass, knowing instinctively to hold silence.

When he was ready, Robertson turned to Niell, jabbed his smoldering cigarette at the door to Interview B, and softly asked, "Hostettler?"

"Yes, sir."

"Been there long?"

"About an hour."

"Does he know about Jonah Miller?"

"Knows he's dead. I can't say whether he knows more than that."

"Has anyone talked to him? Questioned him?"

"We're saving that for you."

"OK, Ricky," Robertson said. "We're going to play this for Hostettler like it's a murder. Could be a suicide, but I want to sweat him anyway. We've got nothing to lose, and we might learn something that'll tell us why Jonah Miller was there and whether or not he actually did have a reason to kill himself. So, play it like we think we've got a murder on our hands."

Niell nodded.

"What's he done while he's waited?" Robertson asked.

"He sits mostly. Sometimes stands to stretch. He seems almost sleepy, if you can believe that."

"Perhaps he's been up all night watching the road to Jonah Miller's house?" Robertson offered. "What's he wearing?"

"A forest green cammo shirt, khaki slacks, hiking boots. When we picked him up, he was packing a van. He says he's going camping."

Robertson scoffed, "Right," and then asked, "Have you looked his van over?"

"No blood, if that's what you mean."

"Mud on the wheels, under the frame, anything like that?"

"It's just been washed. Besides, you gotta figure the rain," Niell said.

"How perfectly convenient. Any other vehicles out at his place?"

"There's an old Chevy pickup under a car port, and it's been washed too."

"Did you look it over carefully?"

"Not really. Mostly we just brought him in, saying that you wanted to talk with him about Miller."

"If I remember right, he's not too big. Not too smart, either. About five-five. That about right?"

Niell nodded yes.

"So, if he comes at you, you could take him?"

"I believe so."

Robertson frowned, thought, and then said, "OK. Now, has he asked for anything?"

"Coffee and cigarettes."

"What kind does he smoke?"

Niell shrugged.

Impulsively, Robertson popped the door open to Interview B and stuck his head in at a startled Jeff Hostettler, who was sitting alone at the end of a rectangular gray metal conference table. Hostettler was a boyishly small man, looking to Robertson a decade older than his actual thirty-seven years. His brown hair was not graying, but it had thinned to baldness on top. He wore the rest of it combed back above his ears in long, thin strands. His blue-gray eyes were bloodshot in the whites and in the watery lids. Their hollow look confirmed the story of how he had squandered his father's money on drugs.

Robertson held his head in through the crack in the door and asked, expansively, "What brand do you smoke, Mr. Hostettler?"

Hostettler looked skeptical, but Robertson held his gaze. Hostettler eventually replied, "Camel Lights." He was obviously exasperated.

Robertson closed the door with a dutiful smile, stepped down the hall, pulled a deputy who was just coming on duty out of the locker room, and whispered instructions for him to go out to Hostettler's to have another look around outside. "I want a report before we finish with Hostettler here."

Then Robertson returned to Niell and said, "You get two packs of Camel Lights. Two packs, Ricky. Bring 'em in and drop 'em as arrogantly as you can on the table in front of Hostettler. No matches. I want you to glare at him like you think he's worse than pond scum and then take up a position behind his chair so he can't see you unless he turns around." And then, because Niell was new, Robertson explained his plan in detail.

When Niell had ducked out of the back door carrying an umbrella, Robertson slipped down the hall to Ellie Troyer's desk, poured two cups of coffee, creamed and sugared one, carried both down the hall, balanced the two Styrofoam cups in the upturned palm of his left hand, turned the doorknob with his right hand, strolled imperiously into the room, and blurted out, "Lord, I hate these rainy days."

The sheriff set the two cups of coffee in front of Hostettler, on the right end of the gray metal table. He drew a chair up to the corner beside Hostettler, sat down to Hostettler's left with a sigh, leaned back casually, and said, in a bantering tone, "You sure picked a fine day to go camping."

Hostettler looked puzzled momentarily. Snapping back, he blustered, "I don't see that's any of your business."

Robertson ignored the tone, leaned forward, pushed the two

cups of coffee toward Hostettler and asked, "Black, or cream and sugar?"

Hostettler took the black one and sipped at it with a brooding antagonism, eyeing Robertson over the rim of the cup.

Robertson took the creamed one, stirred idly at it with a little red and white plastic stick, smiled broadly and lied, saying, "Good. I like it sweet." He watched Hostettler for a spell and then added, "Jeff, I'm glad you agreed to come in."

Hostettler griped, "Like I had a choice."

Robertson noticed the condescension in Hostettler's voice and looked the man over carefully. He seemed no bigger than a thoroughbred jockey. Next to Robertson's bulk, Hostettler was a distinctly small man.

"I know, Jeff, and I'm sorry about that," Robertson said, pleased by how easy he found it to sound genuinely apologetic. He intended to pratter inconsequentially over a cup of coffee and a pack of smokes, all afternoon if necessary, and learn everything Hostettler could be tricked into telling. He focused on the light brown coffee, and after a moment added, "Jeff, I figure it's been eight or nine years since you and I last tangled, and I have to say you've showed me I was wrong about you. Seems like you turned out OK."

Robertson peered at Hostettler intently and was satisfied to note an uneasy constriction around his eyes. Hostettler sipped compulsively at his coffee, turned his head left to face the sheriff, and rubbed at the right side of his neck, one eye squinted shut, the other eye watching Robertson suspiciously, evidently deciding against saying anything.

The truth was, the sheriff ruminated, both Brenda and Jeff Hostettler had been raised in a fine, prominent, Millersburg family. Their father had owned a feed-stock business, and the Hostettler kids had enjoyed every privilege and advantage that could be given children in an upper-middle-class family. But, for some reason, Brenda Hostettler had gone completely wrong, and Jeff Hostettler had wasted a college education and the family fortunes on cocaine.

Robertson waited until he thought Hostettler'd be suitably unprepared to hear it, and then said, with affected tenderness, in a manner that wasn't altogether unconvincing, "Jeff, you know how sad I was about your sister."

Hostettler sat back straight in his chair, and Robertson saw antagonism flood into his eyes. Hostettler turned again to face the sheriff and said pointedly, "I did not kill Jonah Miller."

"I believe you, Jeff," Robertson answered passively, dominating an urge to berate. "Believe me I do. But you've got to understand that my deputies, who don't know you quite so well, think you're good for this one, and there's nothing I've been able to do about that. I agreed that they could bring you down here only because I thought that'd be the best way for you to clear things up."

Hostettler shifted sullenly in his metal chair, turned away from Robertson, and reached, out of habit, for a pack of cigarettes in his shirt pocket. There were none there.

Robertson noticed the instinctive reach of a smoker, considered an impulse to offer him one of his Winstons, decided coldly against it, lit one up for himself, and let the minutes pass in silence.

Hostettler thought matters through from several angles and then seemed to relent. Gaze focused on the far end of the table, he started to talk about the time Brenda and Jonah Miller had spent together. The bar hopping, the booze, and the dope. He spoke with mounting bitterness about the terrible days before Brenda had killed herself. How she had kept her baby, hoping against reason that Jonah Miller would one day come home to her. How she had beseeched Eli Miller to send for his son, bring him back, cancel the Mite. How the bishop had insisted that Jonah would have to come home on his own accord. How

Miller had explained that Brenda did not belong with The Low Ones, either, and that she should forget the Amish altogether. Mostly she should forget Jonah and think of her son.

Hostettler's account took only a few minutes. He finished matter-of-factly, as if rehearsing the lines of a grade-school poem. As if he had pushed the play button on an old recording and had settled onto a hard bar stool to listen to a favorite song from a bygone day. Then he straightened in his chair and faced Robertson with a scornful coldness. "Sheriff, if Jonah Miller had shown himself around here in those days, I'd have ripped him open in a heartbeat."

Robertson held his gaze unwaveringly for nearly a full minute, until Hostettler looked away, disquieted.

Robertson stubbed his cigarette out in a glass ashtray on the table and said, "And now you'd have me believe that you didn't kill Jonah yesterday, when he did come home."

Hostettler gave a disaffected wave of his hand, and, as Niell came in through the door and dropped two packs of Camel Lights abruptly onto the metal table, Hostettler said, wearily, "I told you. I didn't kill him."

Niell muttered, as previously instructed, "Right," disrespect-fully, and then stood in the corner behind Hostettler's chair.

Robertson shot an exaggerated, angry scowl at Niell, held it long enough for Hostettler to notice, and said, "Knock it off, Ricky." Then he reached into his shirt pocket to extract a pack of matches. He tossed them to Hostettler and said, with a slight chuckle, "The deputy doesn't like to be sent on my little ciga-rette errands, Jeff. Don't take it personal."

Hostettler muttered something, opened one of the packs, and lit up.

Robertson glanced briefly at Niell, who stood with a satis-fied smirk, dripping water in the corner behind Hostettler. Niell knew instinctively to watch Robertson's eyes. He knew from the stories that nothing would show in Robertson's chubby face. No tell-tale pulsing of the veins in his bulging neck. Nothing in Robertson's expression. No changeable lines or wrinkles around his eyes. Nothing from his lips. Niell watched only the dance of the sheriff's eyes.

Robertson sat perfectly still, legs crossed in a casual pose that belied a taught inner focus. His massive hands lay delicately in his lap, motionless, almost floating. His head was cocked at a curious angle, the short gray hairs on his head standing somehow straighter than usual. His breaths came regularly, easily, relaxed. Everything about him seemed nonchalant, disinterested. Everything except his eyes. Ricky Niell stood behind Hostettler and watched Sheriff Robertson's eyes as they danced over his subject, taking in everything: Hostettler's lips, his pulse, his posture, attitude, and gaze. Robertson scanning, probing, thinking. His mind racing headlong, anticipating what Hostettler might say or do, evaluating every possibility, shifting adroitly with each thing Hostettler did or said. As the interrogation continued, each sentence opened new avenues, closed off others. Robertson's mind raced easily ahead with the chase, master of the conversation, his entire personality having swung "hard a-lee," keeled over dangerously in a gale like a close-hauled sloop on a manic tack.

When he had finished, Robertson had learned everything Hostettler would have to say about Jonah Miller. How he had hated him for deserting his sister. How Hostettler had looked for Miller in those early days, certain that he would come home, sooner or later. The ordeal of the custody hearings. In college, Hostettler had pretty well forgotten Jonah Miller. After college, Hostettler had found trouble of his own. There had been numerous drug arrests. Probation. More arrests, and finally a charge of burglary with criminal trespass, which landed him in the county jail for seven months. Finally, he had smashed up several cars in a D.U.I. and drew three years in the state penitentiary. Released on shock probation, he had found the courage to straighten himself out enough to hold a job in a grocery store for the past several years. Last, Hostettler added sarcastically, with all that in his life, where would Robertson figure he had time to worry at all about a jerk from ten years ago, much less plan to murder him?

Under the circumstances, most people were intimidated by Robertson, whatever his mood. They walked a circumspect path around him, not knowing whether they'd get Good Bruce or Bad Bruce, his moods almost impossible to judge, unless they had, like the deputies who stayed on, learned to read Robertson's eyes. Now, Ricky Niell looked into Robertson's eyes with a growing admiration, guessed correctly that he should push harder on Hostettler from behind, and quipped, with an insulting tone, "Jeff, here, says he's going camping."

Hostettler craned his head around to the deputy, thought about saying something, reconsidered, and turned back to the table. He knocked the first line of ash off his seventh Camel and said, "Like I was saying, I did not kill Jonah Miller."

"But you can understand how we might think you did," Robertson said directly, eyes still dancing.

Hostettler shrugged a noncommittal answer.

Niell came right back with, "Oh, he did it all right; he's no better than his sister was."

Hostettler bolted out of his seat, skittering the metal chair at the wall as he turned to lunge at Niell.

Niell ducked a solid right hook, and in a single, smooth action, pinned Hostettler's arm to his back, pushed him against the wall, spun him around, and slammed him back into the chair next to Robertson.

Robertson looked reproachfully at Niell, slowly and deliberately lit another Winston, and calmly remarked, "I don't see any reason for rough play here, Deputy." He motioned with a backwards jab of his thumb over his shoulder that Niell should leave them alone.

Hostettler, released, leaned over on his elbows, and picked nervously at his fingernails, waiting for Niell to disappear, angry with himself for the outburst.

Robertson waited until Niell had closed the door indignantly, said, "Relax, Jeff. I'll be back in a minute," and left Hostettler alone in the room.

Outside Interview B, Niell leaned sideways against the wall in the hallway, shaking his head with a smile. Robertson gave him a slap on the back and then marched down to Ellie's desk to ask her to phone the coroner for news.

While the sheriff stood behind the jail's front counter, Sergeant Wilsher came through the front door, and Robertson took a report from him about the condition of Hostettler's Chevy truck. Then he led Wilsher back down the hall. There, he instructed his deputies precisely where to stand, Niell leaning casually against the left wall of the narrow hall, Wilsher against the right. When he opened the door to Interview B, Robertson leaned in and softly said, "Jeff, you can go now. We've got what we need."

When Hostettler emerged with the two packs of cigarettes, Robertson stepped back from the door, blocked the way down the hall to the front entrance of the jail, clamped an enormous left arm over Hostettler's shoulders, said something expansive and jovial about keeping the cigarettes, and marched Hostettler down the hall, between the two deputies, who forced Hostettler and Robertson closer together as they passed.

When he returned from the back exit of the jail, Robertson told Niell and Wilsher, "Either he's a cooler head than I figured, or he's telling the truth. Anyway, find out where he's going camping. Follow him if you have to, anywhere in Ohio, and back. Then bring him in again. In the meantime, I'm going to get a warrant to search his place."

14

BRANDEN drove home slowly from the coroner's lab. When he came onto the hills where Millersburg College stood at the east edge of town, he drove past the college grounds to the south point where the cemetery held the highest ground. He parked beside the low chain fencing and walked to the little cupola that faced out over the valley. He took a seat on one of the rough wooden benches, laid his raincoat at his side, and sat quietly, thinking. The rain slackened to a drizzle and then to a mist. After nearly an hour, when he was satisfied that he could not think of a single good answer to the several remaining questions in the Jonah Miller case, he got back into his small truck, drove home, and found Caroline in the living room, talking with Donna Beachey.

Caroline introduced her husband to the teacher, adding that Miss Beachey had only just arrived. Branden crossed the room to shake her hand, and then he took a seat on a couch. He noticed that Donna Beachey had been crying.

"I understand that Caroline spoke with you at the old schoolhouse," he said.

"Yes," Miss Beachey said, "I can't believe that Jonah is dead. So close to home. It doesn't make sense." She dried her eyes with a small lace hankie and said to Caroline, "I've been upset with myself since we first talked. I'm afraid I left the wrong impression about the Millers. Well, at least about the bishop."

Branden asked, "Miss Beachey, do you think Jonah would kill himself?"

Beachey looked puzzled for a moment and said, "I don't know, I suppose. A lot of time has passed. But the way I heard it, he was shot."

Branden nodded silently.

Caroline said, "You were going to explain something about Jonah." She looked with interest, first at the teacher, and then at her husband.

"The sheriff and I go back quite a ways with Jonah Miller," Donna said. She paused, expecting one of the Brandens to have questions. Neither of them pressed her, but they seemed interested, so she began explaining herself.

"That summer when Jonah was locked up at the county jail, I used to drive down to see him there. Sheriff Robertson was a scoffer. He told me to quit wasting my time. I told him to pretty much mind his own business.

"Then, after about five or six visits, Jonah began to open up about his father and the ban. We talked mostly about why I thought he ought to try to go home, and about why Jonah felt he never could. Never did resolve anything, but I think he liked the company.

"Then, when I spoke with you, Mrs. Branden, at the school, I couldn't seem to shake the notion that the whole sorry mess was the bishop's fault.

"Well, now that I know Jonah is dead, I realize the troubles weren't all Jonah and they weren't all Eli Miller, either. It was their circumstances, I guess. If you look at it fairly, the ban was righteous, and Jonah deserved it as far as any folk in these parts will ever think. But Eli Miller was also at fault for being so stubborn about Jonah's behavior. The father pushing the son and the son pushing back, so to speak.

"At any rate, I want to clear it up, if I gave you the impression that Bishop Miller was out of line. Given his culture, he couldn't have done anything else. And given Jonah's temperament, he had few other choices."

Donna paused and studied the carpet, hoping they would see what it was that she was trying to tell them. Hoping that the death of Jonah Miller and his coming home were things that they could be made to understand. Eventually, she said, "What I didn't tell you is that, from everything I've heard about the bishop since the ban, he has hoped and prayed for his son's return. It wasn't done in anger, you see. The ban I mean. If anything, Eli waited longer than most, hoping that his son would change."

Caroline said, "I don't think you gave me the wrong impression, Donna. I only came away with a feeling that the whole thing was tragic. That the bishop had little choice. At least that's what I've come to think once I put your conversation alongside of other things we've learned." She looked to her husband, encouraging him to agree.

Branden said, "Most people have told us that the ban was proper."

Donna said, "There's something else, though, that I didn't tell you, Mrs. Branden. Do you remember that I said that the bishop drove his buggy to my school in Massillon?"

Caroline nodded.

"Well, Jonah's younger brother Isaac did the same thing. For a different reason, but he also drove all that way to talk to me about Jonah. It was in those days when I was visiting Jonah in the jail.

"It was strange, but I believe to this day that his father put him up to it. You see, Isaac asked me to convince Jonah to come home when he got out of jail. And I believe the bishop wanted the same thing. He was behind it, I think. He used Isaac to talk to me, to talk to Jonah in jail, to tell him he could come home if only he'd take his Amish vows."

After she had left, the Brandens sat in the darkened living

room and talked about the death of Jonah Miller. Branden mentioned that he still had not seen Jeremiah.

"What did Bruce say about that?" Caroline asked.

"Haven't said anything to him yet," Branden said. He saw Caroline react in disbelief.

"You can't be serious, Michael," she chastized.

"I've been close to telling him a number of times, but things keep popping up that don't make sense. There's something I don't understand. Maybe several things that I don't understand, and telling Bruce about Jeremiah just hasn't felt right. First, I believe Jonah was murdered and that someone dropped the gun to try to make it look like suicide. Or more likely, just to get rid of it. Second, we really don't know that Jeremiah isn't home with his family right now."

"Jeremiah Miller has been missing all this time, and may very well now be at peril from someone who has killed his father, and it hasn't felt right to you to report it?" Caroline scoffed. Heat rose in her cheeks. There was the promise of tears as she stood in the living room, thinking instinctively of the gravest possible dangers.

"Michael, you've got to take this case to Robertson. You probably should have done that in the beginning." Her voice was strained and starting to show her panic.

"Caroline," he said, trying to assuage her, "we had good reason to honor the bishop's distrust of the law when we first took the case. I'll admit that Jonah's murder changes a lot, but as far as Jeremiah is concerned, we'll probably find tomorrow that he is home, and that he is safe."

"You don't know that he's safe," Caroline berated.

"Neither do we know that he isn't at his grandfather's house, Caroline."

"Why didn't you ask about him when you were out there?"

"I did."

"And?"

"I didn't exactly get a straightforward answer."

"See?" Caroline challenged. "They don't know where he is either."

"We can't be sure of that."

"You've got to go to Robertson."

"I promised the bishop that I would not."

"Michael, everything has changed."

"Maybe. Maybe not. Their culture remains the same. Bishop Miller did not want the sheriff involved in finding Jeremiah. I doubt, now, that he'll even cooperate with the investigation into Jonah's murder."

"That ought to tell you something right there," Caroline said. "If he still feels that way about Jeremiah after Jonah has been murdered, then he's pegged himself a fool."

"I don't know how he feels, Caroline. Don't know what he thinks. I can't even tell you what he knows now or what he knew when he had me promise to keep the law out of this. But he did that, Caroline, and to break faith with that would betray not only his culture but also my promise to him when we took the case."

"Fine. You'll honor your promise. Remain true to the culture of those who have withdrawn from the world. But you're not Amish, Professor Branden, and the day is going to come when you'll have to explain this whole sorry mess to the sheriff."

Her eyes were moistened with tears, and Branden crossed the room to her and took her into his arms. He whispered, "Tomorrow, Caroline. Just until tomorrow. Then I'll have an answer from the bishop, and we'll know if Jeremiah is safe at home."

"He had better be, Michael," Caroline said, "or I'll go to Robertson myself."

15

THE TALL Miller house stood quietly in the morning light behind the silver maples that shaded the lawn in front. The gravel drive was muddy and rutted from the visitors of the day before. There were three standardbreds hitched at the fence, and their buggies were pushed off to the side, lined up neatly along the driveway as it led to the house. The trees and the lawn still held water from the all-night rains, but the sun was coming out strong, and birds and squirrels were foraging. Half a dozen robins worked the lawns for bugs and worms. A band of jays marauded through the yard and raided a corn feeder the Millers had put up on a white pole. The black rubber middle of the children's trampoline sagged more than usual with the soaking it had taken, but the yellow bumpers were beginning to dry and brighten as the sun slanted in from the east.

Branden walked down the drive past the south end of the house and found three women with two younger girls scrubbing and cleaning vegetables beside the house. Mrs. Miller sat barefoot on the slanting boards that served as a cover to the outside cellar stairs. She and the two girls, evidently her daughters, were cleaning small carrots, lettuce, onions, cucumbers, and snap beans. The girls' dresses were dirty, and so were their hands, but their faces were bright. They were barefoot like their mother, and their feet seemed leathered and tough. There were brown grocery bags from the market at Becks Mills, folded empty next to the women. They each had a plastic bucket and a pail of water beside them. The work seemed to be about half done as he approached them. The two older ladies who had been sitting with the bishop's wife got up directly and moved their work onto the more private back porch.

He stopped to exchange greetings and found Mrs. Miller unwilling to say much more than simple courtesy required of her. She worked awkwardly with a large knife to slice carrots. Her fingers were roughened by years of labor, and the skin was cracked and darkened at the knuckles and near her chipped fingernails. Her hands were twisted with arthritis.

Branden asked about her son Isaac, but all that she would say was that he was working behind the house.

"And how is the bishop?" he asked.

"He is all right, yet, I suppose," she said and reached down for the handle on her pail. She spoke curtly to her daughters and moved straightway with the girls onto the back screened porch.

Branden judged that they had paid him less attention than was warranted, considering that her husband had made an extraordinary effort only a week ago to enlist his help. He decided to push his inquiries beyond simple pleasantries, and stepped up to the screened door. The girls scurried behind the women and watched bashfully from behind their dresses.

With his palm cupped to shade his view through the screen, Branden said, "Then I am sure you must be glad to have Jeremiah home again."

Abruptly, she raised up, puzzlement showing on her face. One of the girls began to answer him, but Mrs. Miller hushed her, and sent both girls into the house. She dried her hands on her apron, said, "The bishop is around to back," and disappeared into the house with the other women.

Branden pulled back from the screen, rounded the far back

corner of the house, and stepped down a steep and awkward slope to the lower level toward a two-story, red bank barn. He heard a gasoline engine and then saw the tumbler of an old, white cement mixer beyond the corner of the barn. There he found Isaac Miller and his father on a little knoll about thirty yards beyond the barn, working with two older Amish men to shovel fresh concrete mix into wooden molds planted in the ground. A large rectangle was marked out with wooden stakes and yellow strings. The men had poured and worked about seven or eight of the footers. They would need fifty before the job would be done.

When he saw Branden approaching, Bishop Miller broke off working, called the other men with him, and anxiously motioned for Branden to come down the slope to the tall doors to the barn. The three Amish went in quickly, motioned for Branden to follow, and hurriedly closed the giant doors behind him.

On the lower level, with the doors rolled shut, there was scant light reaching down through the haylofts above. There was a propane lantern, and one of the men started to light it. The bishop quickly spoke against it.

Miller took his hat off, and scratched at the top of his head. He looked to both of the men and then introduced them. They were two of his five deacons. As Branden's eyes adjusted to the dim light, he saw a clear and deep anxiety on each of their faces.

Miller began to speak to the men in their low dialect and stopped. He then pulled them aside and whispered urgently with the deacons for a long time. When Miller did finally speak in English, Branden thought that the deacons seemed relieved of a mighty burden.

"It's Jeremiah," the bishop spoke in a low voice. "Are you still willing to help us find him?" The deacons drew closer to hear Branden's answer.

Branden did not answer right away, partly because he was

taken by surprise. He had suspected something still was badly wrong at the Millers' since the day before, when Isaac had dispatched him so abruptly. He had sensed there was trouble with the Jonah Miller case when he had driven home to Caroline. Even after their talk with Donna Beachey, his doubts remained. Not as strong as Caroline's, though now it seemed that she had been right.

Branden had not truly prepared himself for the notion that the bishop might have stood idly by, all the while knowing that the boy was still missing. It was the one thing Branden hadn't allowed himself to consider, in order to explain the way the family had responded to him and to Jonah's murder so close to home. But Caroline had said it for him. Maybe the case of finding Jonah Miller was closed, but what of finding Jeremiah? He groaned aloud, remembering Caroline's words last night.

"You don't have Jeremiah?" Branden asked.

"Can you help?" the bishop implored.

"You don't have the boy."

"No."

"Then it's out of my hands. You've got to go to the sheriff."

"We cannot do that. We cannot let you do it either."

"Your son is dead, Mr. Miller. You don't know where your grandson is. It's time to get the police involved."

"Just another day or so will not matter."

"It will matter a great deal. Every day that Jeremiah is gone increases the risk of something happening to him."

"We know that. But not the law. Not yet, Professor. Remember, you promised. You do not know everything about this matter, as it stands.

"Everything has changed now. Why can't you see that?"

"Nothing has changed for us, Professor."

"Why?"

"Because it was a policeman that my youngest daughter saw on the lane the day our Jeremiah was taken from us. A policeman, Professor Branden. We cannot trust the law. So we have put our trust in you."

"There's not much that I can do, now."

"Professor. We know what we are asking. We have three days. I cannot tell you why, now, but we have still got three days to find him."

"I'll go to the sheriff myself."

"We cannot have you doing that."

"What if I do?"

"We will deny that there is any trouble."

"This isn't the best way, Bishop Miller. Not the best way at all."

"We are not fools, Professor. Trust us. Give it three more days, and then we will go to the law ourselves."

As he walked back up the drive past the house, Branden muttered angrily to himself, rankled by their lack of trust and by the lost hours their mistrust had cost him. Had cost Jeremiah. Gradually he became aware that he was exasperated at least as much with himself, because, as the buggies had begun to fill the drive, when he had had the chance to ask pointedly and specifically about Jeremiah yesterday, he had somehow failed to get a clear answer. He stopped on the drive, looked back at the front porch, and shook his head, remembering how Isaac had turned him away.

On the lane where he had parked, Branden found Ricky Niell's black rig behind his own small truck, with the deputy standing casually, chewing on a blade of grass. Niell was dressed in civilian clothes. He wore trim cut blue jeans, creased meticulously down the front. The cuffs were pulled down over polished cowboy boots. He had on a sheriff's department field cap. Niell watched, arms folded over his chest, as Branden approached along the gravel lane.

"I'm surprised to see you here, Professor," Niell said as Branden came alongside. "You know, with Jonah Miller being dead."

Branden slipped in between the two trucks and leaned back against the tailgate of his truck, one heel propped up on the chrome bumper. "I see you have a taste for big rigs, Ricky," Branden said, and motioned at the full-sized truck, sport-rigged and jacked high on its wheels with after-market lifters. Then Branden said, "I'm still looking into the matter for the family."

"Robertson said you wouldn't let it go," Niell said, and smiled.

Branden shrugged and asked, "You here on business?"

"I was just delivering a message on my day off," Niell said. "The sheriff wanted the Millers to know that it'll be a while before the coroner releases the body."

"Does that mean Bruce suspects someone out here?"

"To tell you the truth, Professor, I'm not altogether certain what Robertson thinks. He talks as if it was possibly a suicide, but he's going about the investigation as if it were a murder."

Branden nodded sympathetically.

"Take yesterday," Niell said. "We interrogated Jeff Hostettler for nearly two hours, and then Robertson sent him on his way as if it were nothing. I thought he was locked in on Hostettler, and the next thing I knew, Robertson was escorting him out the door like an old friend. But he also put two of us on the job of following him, and he told us he didn't want us to go to any trouble to keep our tail at a distance."

"And you don't know what to make of that?" Branden asked.

"Not entirely."

"It's a game to him," Branden said. "Even if Hostettler doesn't seem right for this murder now, Robertson will keep pressure on, just to ratchet up the tension. If Hostettler is the murderer, he'll make a mistake sooner or later."

Niell thought about that and said, "It doesn't leave much room for subtlety."

"Bruce doesn't handle people with subtleties, Ricky. That doesn't mean he's a dimwit, either."

"You won't get an argument there," Ricky said.

"I'll bet you dollars to doughnuts he had some little skit rigged up for Hostettler's benefit before you even began with the questions."

Niell's eyes answered yes with his smile. "The sheriff had every detail worked out before we started on Hostettler."

"That's what you've always got to remember about Bruce Robertson," Branden said. "He looks like a simple man. Too big to be taken seriously. But he's smart. Smarter than most of the rest of us. And he's compulsive at times, which makes it hard to predict what he'll do next."

"You're telling me," Niell said. "Was he always like that?"

"Compulsive? Yes, even when we were kids. He'll get moody too. You've got to watch for that. Any of the older deputies mention that to you?" Branden asked.

"More than once."

"Then you know basically what you need to know about Bruce Robertson," Branden said. "If he's not happy, he'll let you know. If he thinks you don't get it, he'll explain it to you in very precise terms."

"I've been trying, but I can't figure out if he's angry with me or just grumpy."

"Might be both," Branden said. "But there isn't a disingenuous bone in his body, and if you listen, and work at doing things his way, I think you'll figure out how to handle him and why he's so good at what he does."

"Handle him," Ricky said. "That doesn't seem possible."

"Just watch Ellie Troyer. She's not too much longer on the job than you, and she already has Robertson figured out."

"Ellie Troyer?"

"Right. The only one before her who could handle Robertson was Irene Cotton, and she's dead."

"They say Cotton worked dispatch for Robertson," Niell said. "They also say Robertson wanted to marry her."

Branden nodded.

"Do you know about that?" Niell asked.

"It's a long story, Ricky," Branden answered. "I'll tell you all about it someday."

"Could you make it soon enough to do me some good?"

Branden chuckled. "How long have you been working for Robertson, Ricky?"

"A couple of weeks," Niell said, as if it had been a lifetime.

"And he's already using you in his little skits?"

"Yes."

"Then you're doing fine," Branden said, and changed the subject. "Let me ask you something about Hostettler. You said Robertson had him down at the jail yesterday?"

"Just as soon as we could bring him in," Niell said.

"And the interview? How'd that go?" Branden asked.

"I'm not sure," Niell said honestly. "I still can't tell what the sheriff intended or what he thought he'd learned. I know this much, though: We tailed Hostettler for half the night, and when I reported that he'd driven out to the Millers' house and parked down the lane, smoking in the car with the lights out, the sheriff radioed back twice to check in with me. But Hostettler just sat there a while and then drove home, and the sheriff called off the tail. No explanation. Just brought us in." Niell added, "With the sheriff, you think you've got one thing figured out, and then he pulls you in, and the whole game has changed."

"I know," Branden said. "But Bruce has always got a reason, and once you figure that out, you won't have a problem." Then Branden asked, "Ricky, does Robertson have only the Hostettler lead?"

"He does so far," Niell said. "I'm supposed to find out where Jonah Miller had lived or worked, and then we're going there, wherever that turns out to be."

"That seems sensible," Branden said. "Do you have anything yet?"

"No," Niell said, unhappily. "Any suggestions?"

"Not really," Branden said. "I ran a Net search on the name Jonah Miller and several derivatives, but it didn't turn up any obvious leads in the area. We tried calling the most likely names and nobody knew our Jonah."

"There's something going on at the coroner's," Niell offered.

"Ricky," Branden said. "If Bruce takes up any other serious leads, I'd be grateful if you'd let me know."

"Why's that?" Niell asked, immediately on his guard.

"Because I have a lead or two that I'd like to work myself, and I wouldn't want to duplicate efforts."

"Maybe you'd better let me tell the sheriff what you've got," Niell suggested.

"Believe me, he won't think much of it. For what it's worth, I got a call this morning from a girl who says she knows who killed Jonah Miller."

Niell gave him a skeptical look, and Branden said, "I don't think it's going to pan out, either, but I'm supposed to talk to her this afternoon."

"Then do me a favor, Professor," Niell said with a broad and mischievous smile. "Tell me what you learn a good half hour before you tell the sheriff."

Branden laughed and said, "No problem."

Niell climbed into his truck and rolled down the window. As he put the truck in gear, he eyed the professor hesitantly and asked, "Ellie Troyer?"

Branden said, "Right. You keep your eye on Ellie if you want to know how to handle Bruce Robertson."

16

Tuesday, June 23
5:00 P.M.

BRANDEN pulled off Route 62 into the lot beside an Amish restaurant near Wilmot. The old inn was set close to the road and was packed to overflowing almost every day since tourists had made its "discovery." Now a larger, more modern restaurant and inn was under construction on the hillside behind the original. In front of the restaurant, a Greyhound charter bus was loading passengers. Inside, there were the aromas of beef and chicken gravies, homemade breads, and fresh coffee.

Branden caught the eye of a matronly woman in Amish dress and nodded toward the kitchen, silently asking for her permission to slip on back. She recognized him, nodded in reply, and he disappeared through a swinging door. He checked briefly in the kitchen, and then walked out into the employees' parking lot behind the restaurant.

At ten after five, a substantial girl in a Dutch costume came out and stood next to Branden. She untied her apron, ducked out of her prayer cap, and wearily shook her hair out of its bun. After drawing a deep breath, she asked, "Mike Branden?"

"Right. You called this morning. You're Ester Yoder?"

The girl nodded and led the way to a black Camaro parked in a far corner of the lot. "I understand you're working on the Jonah Miller case."

Branden followed her to the Camaro with his hands in his pockets and answered simply, "Yes."

"I also hear that Jeremiah Miller is still missing."

He was startled to hear her say that, and his surprise showed in his expression.

"Of course I know about Jeremiah," she said. "Anyone close to the Millers knows Jonah has had him for a long time. I ran into Jonah in Cleveland in the spring and told him he had a son. He'd never known. Can you believe it? Figured then that he'd go for the boy."

She seemed eager to talk, and Branden drew closer and listened.

"So that makes your case a tad different, I would say," she said. "You're not looking for Jonah Miller any more. You're looking for Jeremiah. And now that Jonah's dead, you've got a problem knowing where to look."

"I had that problem from the very start," Branden said. He took his hands out of his pockets. "You knew Jonah had taken Jeremiah. Do you know where?"

"No. If I knew that I'd get the kid myself, take him back to old man Miller, and work out some reward. Who wouldn't? I don't know anyone who has a clue where Jeremiah Miller is now, because nobody knows where Jonah has been the last ten years or so. Except for Cleveland that one day."

Ester Yoder smiled with satisfaction, opened her car door and sat behind the wheel. Then she looked up confidently from her low seat, with the car door still ajar. Branden waited, eyeing the blacktop silently.

"I used to know Jonah," she said. "Before he went away. I also knew his brother, Isaac." She paused. "You ever hear of bundling, Professor?"

Branden nodded that he had.

"You've heard the saying 'five can be allowed to be an even number when it comes to lovers'?"

"Meaning the rules can be changed or overlooked for lovers?"

"Well, me and Isaac—you know," she said and paused again. She seemed embarrassed, now.

Branden waited, giving her time with her thoughts. He was astounded that she'd reveal the bundling so forthrightly to him.

She pulled the door of the Camaro closed, rolled her window down, punched at the cigarette lighter, lit one, blew smoke against the inside of the windshield, and tapped the steering wheel. "Isaac was approved by my parents. Jonah wasn't," she explained. "Going the other way," she added, "Bishop Miller never approved of me."

She stopped and considered her next words. There was regret in her voice when she continued. "I loved Jonah, but I would have settled for Isaac. So that pretty much turned the bishop against me."

Branden nodded again and fought an urge to question her.

"Here's something else you should know," the waitress said. "Bishop Eli Miller is almost out of land." She drew again heavily on the cigarette. "Started with something less than a hundred acres and a good barn his father left him, and got it up to nearly a quarter section when he was young. Since then, it's been divided to the boys, five of them so far. Jonah was next in line. Two years older than Isaac. Follow me? What you've got to ask yourself is, where'd young Isaac be now if Jonah were to be coming home?"

After starting the engine and putting the transmission into gear, Ester Yoder looked up at Branden and coldly added, "I wonder what that sanctimonious fool would say if he ever found out what his precious sons used to do with us girls in his barn." With a note of finality, she added, "I'll bet a week's tips that it's land that got Jonah Miller killed."

Then she sped off abruptly, flipping the cigarette out her window as she swerved onto Route 62.

Branden stood in place and watched the black Camaro disappear.

He strolled around to the front, sat in his truck, and watched absently as the Greyhound eased out onto the highway and headed east. Eventually it would turn north on 250, reach Wooster, and roll towards Cleveland, maybe Toledo. He idly inserted his key in the ignition, but did not turn it.

Motive, he thought. That was all about motive. She knows what she's saying. But why?

She's not practicing Amish anymore. Obviously.

So much more a reason to doubt her.

What had she really said?

For one thing, she had said that Isaac Miller, Jonah's younger brother, has motive. Or, at the very least, he stands to benefit from Jonah's death.

Is that possible? Murder among the Amish? Plainly, Ester Yoder wants me to think that.

Evidently it's the land. If Bishop Miller can't subdivide his original holdings to all of his sons, they'll have to move to another district. Perhaps even out of state. Land is everything. And a repentant Jonah Miller would obliterate Isaac Miller's chances for a farm of his own. And a wife. No land, no wife.

So why not take a job like Ester Yoder?

But there's no other acceptable occupation among Old Order Amish. Either you're a farmer or you're not living right.

Lifestyle's a matter of salvation. So it's not likely, he thought, under any circumstances, that Isaac Miller'd simply take a job.

Then he'd kill his own brother? Can't believe that. Not for a minute.

And the bundling. What was that all about? If he had understood her correctly, she had evidently bundled up with two of the sons of Eli Miller. Branden smiled slightly. Bundling used to be more common. Most Amish preachers in recent times had spoken against it. Heavy petting. Premarital intercourse.

They're peasants, really, not saints, he reminded himself. No big secret. Branden remembered the stories from his childhood. It used to be that the boys would drive home with girls in buggies, late at night on a Sunday, after a young people's social, and bundle up in a downstairs bedroom of the girl's house. Parents'd stay upstairs all night. Discreet. An old custom.

Not too surprising about the bundling, really. One girl and two boys. Brothers.

Clearly, she had loved Jonah. She had said it herself. Isaac was approved. Jonah wasn't. Pity.

That doesn't matter here, Branden told himself. Ester Yoder has plainly said that not everyone in the Miller district would have been pleased to see the return of Jonah Miller.

But Branden would not allow himself to consider Isaac Miller, any Amish for that matter, capable of premeditated murder. Not of murder of any kind. Maybe brief anger, or a long, unspoken resentment. But never murder. Donna Beachey had said as much, herself. The Millers wanted Jonah to come home to them.

Now, that all meant that his trip had been wasted. Frustration rose up within him. A day was gone, now, and he had seen only the Millers, Ricky Niell, and now the jealous, resentful, former Amish lover of both Jonah and Isaac Miller. The affairs had obviously driven her from her family. Or maybe she had left the sect on her own. Nevertheless, she had wasted his time tonight.

He thought it curious that she would consider him simple minded enough to have believed such a tale. He also knew he could not entirely dismiss what she had said. If nothing else, she had confirmed that Jonah had not been living in the county. But the day was gone nonetheless.

In truth, Caroline had admonished him strongly for not taking the whole thing to Bruce Robertson this morning. To her way of thinking, if Jeremiah were missing this long after the death of his father, then he was being held by someone, and it was kidnapping that they were up against. But it was kidnapping from the start, Branden had reminded her. And from the very start, when he had taken his first buggy ride, the bishop had steadfastly held him to the promise that he would not involve the law. Then there had been Donna Beachey's reassurances last night, and today's promise to the bishop that he'd give it three more days. Well, now the bishop had two days, Branden thought, sorry he had ever made that promise.

He hit the ignition and backed out, frustrated by the incongruity of it all. As he turned onto Route 62, he thought again of Ester Yoder, former Amish lass from Bishop Miller's district. So we have another suspect, Branden thought. Jeff Hostettler, and now Ester Yoder. Had she loved both brothers, or had she loved the bishop's land? Would the one brother's coming home change her plans? Or was it just revenge, like Robertson thought of Hostettler? Truthfully, it was Ester Yoder herself who stood the best chance of knowing that Jonah would be coming home the morning he was killed.

He drove for home, nervously tapping the steering wheel. He briefly tried the radio, then switched it off.

I don't like it, Branden thought. Why didn't Isaac Miller marry Ester Yoder?

He settled lower in the seat and drove slowly along the turns and hills of 62, southwest toward Winesburg.

OK, figure the bishop.

No, it's the two of them, both Isaac and his father Eli.

Headlights appeared suddenly in his rearview mirror. The car came around with its horn shrieking and mounted the next hill too fast for roads in Amish country. Branden saw the tail lights disappear over the crest and then shortly reappear on the following hill, swerving suddenly left into the oncoming lane. Branden shook his head, came over the hill and slowly up to the buggy he knew to expect, and eased gingerly around. He caught the driver's eye and waved. The buggy driver acknowledged him with silent reserve, nodding from under a black hat.

His thoughts turned to Robertson, "locked on Jeff Hostettler" as Niell had said. An apt description of the tenacious sheriff.

A vision crossed his mind of Robertson in a yellow slicker, intently working the murder scene in the Doughty Valley, and Branden smiled.

It began again to rain lightly, and a shuddering film of water gathered on the side window, collected into drops, and flowed back with the wind, along the glass at an angle.

He rolled slowly through Winesburg in the rain. Most of the shops were closed. At the antique store, the lights were out, but Annie Tedrow was at the front door, letting out one last customer. Annie'd stay open to sell a roll top desk, he thought. Probably nothing less. She'd been there twenty years. One of the first English to have recognized the coming market in Amish sales. Now the town, and others nearby, were filled with the shops of the non-Amish. Cheese Haven this, or Gingerbread that. Authentic Dutch. Real Amish. Millers and Troyers and Hershbergers. Only the locals knew the difference anymore. And *de Hoche* tourists seemed not to care. They gleefully bought everything that was offered for sale. It was Amish country. It had to be good.

What had Ester Yoder really said? That she was in love with Jonah Miller. Then later with Isaac Miller. She could well have loved them both. Now, one of them was dead.

A pedestrian in denim shot by in the rain outside his window, and the crime scene came to him again, with the image of Jonah Miller, sprawled face up in the mud, freshly dressed, and cleanly shaved. Washed by the rain amidst a crowd of onlookers.

A sudden, curious thought sprang into his mind. Why wasn't Eli Miller there?

Miller was the key. He had surely been nearby, if Donna

Beachey knew what she was talking about. At the house. Actually, Branden remembered, in the barn with the deacons. Isaac himself had said so. What were they doing?

And why all the people? Isaac had said on the porch, "As you can see, Professor, the family is gathering." What did that mean? Where was Jeremiah Miller?

He came up Bunker Hill into Berlin and stopped at the intersection with Route 39. The Berlin House Restaurant was open for a heavy evening trade, the large parking lot full of cars out back. He turned right to follow 62.

At the quilt shop, there was the dull orange glow of a lantern in a back room. Somebody's working late, he thought. Finishing quilts that couldn't be stitched properly with tourists in the store, boorishly probing with their constant and indelicate questions.

If Bishop Miller had known of the death of Jonah, then why . . . ? Why what?

It wasn't just a single question. That was it, wasn't it? More than one question came to mind. The answer to all of them probably hinged on one solitary fact not yet understood.

Surely Miller had known something. What was it?

The rain spattering the windshield reminded him of the face of Jonah Miller, washed clean of mud, and nicked by a straight razor.

If the bishop had ever thought either Jonah or Jeremiah was in danger for his life, then why not tell us that up front?

The rain came harder now, pelting the windshield.

When he knew his son Jonah was dead, why hadn't Miller told the sheriff, there and then, about young Jeremiah's being missing?

He remembered the body on the coroner's table, a new straw hat laid beside it.

Miller had to have known I was on his front porch yesterday, so why didn't I hear from him directly? Why did he wait until I came to him? But it was more than that, he thought. The truth was, Miller was laying a foundation in his backyard, when he should have been running a buggy into town.

Except for the boots, all of Jonah Miller's clothes had been new. None of them were improperly English. New, store-bought, and highly plain. Plain enough to be approved even by Bishop Eli Miller.

Eli's probably got a good idea who'd want to kill Jonah, so why hasn't he been to see Bruce about that?

People arriving in buggies at the Miller's house, while the body of Jonah Miller lay in a cold ditch.

He felt somehow, as if he were, mysteriously, very close.

If Jonah Miller was banned, why so many neighbors and relatives at his house the day he died? Was Donna Beachey right? Was Jonah still welcome at home, on their terms, after all those years in the World?

And finally, if Jeremiah Miller is still missing, what in the world has Miller thought was so important about the next three days?

The rain had stopped. The tires of Branden's truck hissed on the wet pavement as he climbed the hill to the eastern cliffs of town.

Branden felt as if a revelation hovered near at hand. It danced just out of range, flickering in and out of focus in the mist. He fought for a solid hold on it.

A singular, pivotal fact suddenly teased the edges of his mind. An image clamoring for recognition.

What was it? Something so obvious.

All of the images from the case washed through his mind again. Then, one image above all others rose into bright relief. An image of simple power and pure revelation. It had been there all along. It proffered only two sensible conclusions. One, on the day he was killed, a repentant Jonah Miller had been going home to take his vows. Or two, he had made it home, been rejected by his family, and then killed himself.

Slowly he checked over his thoughts, and then realized the truth. "It was murder," he said aloud. "I know that, and so do you, Eli Miller. So do you. Because if it were suicide, then Jeremiah would now be safe at home."

17

Tuesday, June 23
7:00 P.M.

ELLIE Troyer leaned sideways on her elbow against the back of the pinewood counter, grinning broadly, listening through the wall to Sheriff Robertson on the phone in his office, resting her eyes on the uniformed torso of Deputy Sheriff Richard "Ricky" Niell. He was slender and muscular, with jet black hair, fair skin, and intelligent brown eyes. His short black mustache was neatly trimmed. His uniform fit crisply, and she liked to watch the way he moved in it. All of this together had caused Ellie Troyer to take definite note of the new deputy.

A month ago, she had started on the secretary's desk, sometimes helping evenings on the dispatcher's console. Then, Ricky Niell had started, too, fresh from a tour in the Air Force. At first she had thought him cool, aloof. For so long he hadn't spoken. At least not more than duty required. Now she realized he was only reserved. Dreadfully shy. Perhaps careful. But certainly not arrogant or aloof.

She'd wait. Not push him. That'd be better. Let him ease toward it. He'd ask her out when he was ready. Better to leave it that way, she thought. She studied his uniform and listened to the sheriff's booming voice.

"Krimenentlies, Ben, you SURELY DON'T BELIEVE I laid a hand on him? No. Dog Gonnit! I DID NOT."

Niell set his coffee cup on the counter and leaned over it,

listening. That brought him closer to Ellie, who, he noticed, did not retreat. He glanced at her bashfully.

Was he right? he wondered. Had she been flirting with him? Not in what she had said, but how she had said it? Perhaps it was something with her eyes.

Ellie grinned, held her finger to her lips, and tilted her head to hear better through the wall.

"I'm telling you, Ben, for the LAST TIME I hope, that I have not been harassing Jeff Hostettler!"

Out in the front room, Niell whispered over the counter. "How long's he been like that, Ellie?"

"All his life, I guess."

"No. I mean on the phone," Niell said, chuckled, and straightened up to sip his coffee.

"All morning," Ellie said. "First with Jeff Hostettler's lawyers and now with the prosecutor."

Robertson's voice boomed again. "Ben, THAT'S NOT FAIR. You know Hostettler's our best suspect."

Niell eased around through the swinging counter door and poured another cup for himself from the coffee maker on a low table beside Ellie's gray metal desk. "What's the problem with the prosecutor?" he asked, nodding down the hall towards the sheriff's office.

"Ben thinks the sheriff's been heavy-handed with Jeff Hostetler on the Jonah Miller case. He has had Hostettler in twice for questioning," Ellie said. Then she added, sounding flippant, "Can you imagine? Our Sheriff Robertson? Heavy-handed?"

Again, she held up her finger and listened.

"You're tying my hands here, Ben," Robertson said, and then at intervals, "No. OK. No. Right. Right! I won't!" and slammed the receiver onto its cradle.

Niell gave Ellie a glance and then eased noiselessly back around to the front of the counter. Sheriff Robertson punched the intercom and shouted, "Ellie!"

Ellie winked at Niell, sat calmly down at her desk, and answered softly into the intercom. "I'm right here, Sheriff. No need to shout."

"For CRYING OUT LOUD, Ellie, I'm not shouting!"

She held Niell's eyes and answered, "Really, Bruce, when you get like this, we don't need an intercom. I can hear you just fine through the wall," and flicked off the intercom switch, smiling a triumph.

"Oh, is that right?" the sheriff hollered, switched off his unit, paced around to the front of his cherry desk, faced the wall separating him and his secretary/dispatcher, and shouted, "I suppose you can hear this just fine, young lady!"

"Yes," Ellie said coyly over the intercom. Niell shook his head, almost disbelieving.

"Then send young Niell in here as quick as he shows," the sheriff said loudly.

"Certainly, Sheriff Robertson," Ellie answered smoothly over the intercom. "Just as soon as he arrives."

Ellie Troyer looked up at Deputy Niell with a satisfied smile.

Niell said, "They say you're the only one's been able to handle him since Renie Cotton died," and finished his coffee.

Had Irene Cotton been so fearless? Niell thought to himself. How long ago had that been? Five years? Maybe six. About the time Ricky Niell had finished his first tour in the Air Force. Maybe a year later. Robertson had asked her many times to marry him, or so the stories went. And some said that she had finally agreed. Then Renie had died, and there had been rough times for the sheriff. Rough, too, for the deputies.

First Renie, Niell thought. And the sheriff had nearly lost reelection. Then a quick succession of four or five replacements for Renie, until finally Robertson had found one who looked like she would stay. Little Ellie Troyer, who could tie her hair in a bun, change her dress, and pass authentically for Mennonite anywhere. Niell stood across the counter and admired the one lady since Irene Cotton who had proved the equal of Big Sheriff Robertson. But there was more to it than that, he thought as he drained his cup. More than simply the way she handles her duties. Ellie Troyer had a handle on Sheriff Robertson himself. She managed him, just like Branden had said. And Robertson liked it. Irascible, smoldering, shoot-it-out Bruce Robertson, and she gave it back to him, tit for tat.

"You've been good for him, Ellie," Niell remarked offhand.

"Nonsense," she said, nodding toward the hallway. "You'd better go on back."

Ricky Niell found the sheriff standing behind his desk. His swivel chair was pushed back into the corner against the bookshelves. "You don't look tired to me," Robertson snapped. Niell instantly regretted stepping down the hall.

"Sir?" Niell said.

"Ellie says you've been working hard and I should be nice to you."

Niell stood up straighter and thought, Good grief, Ellie, thanks for nothing.

"You got anything for me on Jonah Miller?"

"Not exactly, sir," Niell said, uncomfortably.

"No address?"

"No, sir."

"No records?"

"None, sir," reluctantly.

"No employment history?"

"No, sir," embarrassed.

"Welfare records? Military service?"

"Not even a social security number," Niell said. "You know how they apply to get out of that, and he's probably got himself a job working 'off the books,' just like they all do. I've run every angle we discussed," Niell said and shifted his stance in front of the sheriff's large desk. "Even some we didn't. Outside of his family, Jonah Miller simply does not exist, sir."

"Then what's that lying in a drawer in the coroner's refrigerator?" the sheriff shot back, and stepped around the desk to eye the deputy directly.

Niell stiffened. He felt heat on his neck, and knew he was blushing, but didn't care. He didn't care if the sheriff saw him flushed, because he had tried. He had worked every angle. He hadn't found anything on Jonah Miller, because there was nothing to find. "There is no Jonah Miller anymore, sir," Niell asserted. "Hasn't been for ten years."

Robertson stood a scant six inches from the deputy, glowering at him from the side. Niell stood his ground in front of the desk, eyes focused on the bookshelves directly behind it.

"You said you checked on things we hadn't discussed," the sheriff said, this time less intensely, noticing the blush in the deputy's neck.

"Just trying to be thorough," Niell said.

"Tell me about that," Robertson said. He walked behind his desk, lit a cigarette, pulled his chair forward, and sat down.

"You know most of it," Niell said. "Like we discussed. Social security number, work, phone numbers, criminal records."

"You're satisfied there's no record of Jonah Miller?"

"Yes, sir, no record other than what you already have from ten years ago."

"You said you checked some other places?"

"Right," Niell said, slightly more relaxed, not entirely certain why.

"Tell me everything."

"It's not all that important," Niell hesitated.

"You might not think so," Robertson said and pushed away from his desk somewhat. He leaned the swivel chair back at a gentle angle. "Nevertheless, I want everything you've got."

Niell studied the sheriff's face, endeavoring to gauge the tone in his voice.

"It's OK now, Ricky. I'm over it. Sit down and relax."

Robertson waved his arm at the soft leather chair beside his desk. Niell took a straight-backed wooden chair in front.

"Here's the thing," Robertson continued, softly now, leaning forward to crush out the cigarette. He took another from the pack of Winstons on his desk, held it between his lips, struck a match, and then spoke as the flame developed.

The cigarette bobbed up and down with his words. "It's the details. You may not think they're important. But it's always the little things."

The flame had burned close to the tips of his fingers. He held the match a moment longer, brought it close to the Winston to emphasize his point, and then lit up at last and shook out the flame.

"So, Deputy Niell. Ellie thinks you look tired. I'm betting you're not. You're just coming to tell the Old Man you have nothing to report, and it made you nervous."

Niell shrugged, uncertain whether he should agree.

"Well, here's the thing, Ricky. If you say Jonah Miller doesn't exist, then I believe you. As far as you've looked. Point is, where have you looked?

"If it's county records and no luck, well, then, that's one thing. But if it's no Jonah Miller and you've looked everywhere —and I mean everywhere—all the places we mentioned and then some you cooked up on your own—then you can readily see that that's another matter altogether.

"So. I want to know the details. Not just what you found, or did not find. Also where you looked."

Niell shifted in his straight chair, ran his hand back across his short black hair, and pulled a spiral notebook from his uniform breast pocket. He looked at the sheriff, then at his notes, and began.

Out in the front room, Ellie Troyer smiled to herself with satisfaction, pulled her ear away from the wall and returned to her backlog of typing. After an hour or so, Sheriff Robertson came out behind Ricky Niell, with his immense hand laid confidently on the deputy's shoulder.

"Ellie, Niell here's got a theory. The stiff on the slab is not Jonah Miller. From what he tells me, I think he's right."

Ricky smiled weakly, embarrassed, and pushed through the swinging counter door. The sheriff poured a cup of coffee at the table beside Ellie, and glanced at Niell with an expression that might almost have shown outright approval.

"I'm going to the coroner's. You two can handle things here," the sheriff said, and strode back down the corridor to his office.

Ricky stood at the counter, thinking that he hadn't told Robertson everything. That he hadn't mentioned the stops he had made at law enforcement agencies in bordering counties. If any such agency happened to come across an abandoned car or truck, they were to let Niell know. Anything that looked suspicious.

Niell was glad he hadn't mentioned any of this to Robertson, because it seemed like such a lame move. But, if Jonah Miller had had a car, then someone was going to find it. And why shouldn't Niell be the one to bring that to Robertson? So, in the end, Niell was more than satisfied to have handled it the way he had learned in the Air Force motor pool. Never give them everything you've got. Always hold something back, against a rainy day, when you need a little something to pull out, just to look competent. Because, above all else, Ricky Niell hated looking incompetent.

The sheriff bellowed through the wall. "Can you still hear me well enough, Ellie Troyer?"

"Yes, Sheriff," Ellie said through the intercom, smiling demurely at Niell.

"Then tell young Deputy Niell there that, since we both

know he's smart enough to be chasing all the details on his own, he should be faster next time gettin' 'em to us."

"Right," Ellie said, watching the skin on Ricky Niell's neck flush red against his black hair and meticulous uniform.

Then the sheriff hollered, "Niell always gets through."

"Right, Sheriff. Deputy Niell always gets through."

18

CAROLINE let out a delighted laugh, standing behind her husband, both of them staring into the mirror at Professor Michael Branden in the simple glory of plain Amish attire. Millie Dravenstott, a particularly small Mennonite saleslady of about thirty years, had stepped down off the wooden crate where she normally stood to work her cash register, and had shown them into a rear washroom to use the only mirror in the store.

When he had arrived home in the rain the night before, the professor had explained his revelation about the Jonah Miller murder to Caroline. The realization that Jonah Miller had been going home as a changed man. And he had explained his promise to the bishop, that he'd give it only three more days. A chance, still, to find the boy, by tracing the last few days of Jonah's life. Then, in the morning, as soon as the stores had opened, they had started their search.

Finding this particular general store had consumed the majority of the Brandens' morning together. It was an old-style country store with groceries to the sides, hardware in the middle, and dry goods in the back, all stacked in careful piles on dented metal shelves. The worn and irregular wooden floor had taken a sag over the years.

They had started in the smallest towns. Walnut Creek, Sugar Creek, Berlin, Winesburg, and Charm, seeking out the hats, bypassing bolts of Amish cloth in approved colors—dull midnight black, deep peacock blue, chambray blue, ash gray, navy bean, surf turquoise, lilac, and spring jade. They had compared Branden's recollection of Jonah Miller's straw hat with those offered for sale. When it proved convenient, they had inquired into the styles of straw hats currently approved in the various districts of the area.

First, they had learned, there were the brims. All plain, round, and flat. But some brims were two inches wide, some three. Some were permitted stitching around the rims, others not. Some could be woven to leave holes in the brims at regular intervals, making patterns. Jonah Miller's was a flat-brimmed three-incher, with no stitching and no decorative pattern of holes.

Gradually, they had learned to inquire more knowledgeably into the matter of styles, and they had become expert at spotting the subtle differences. Not only the brims, but the crowns varied. Some crowns were creased, for sale mostly to the English tourists. Some crowns were flattened on top, others domed. Some crowns were tall, others squat. Eli Miller's people wore plain, round, five-inch domed crowns, without a crease.

In Berlin, they had found a near match. In Charm, the salesladies had recognized the style, but had sold out.

Then in Fredericksburg they had found what Branden had been looking for all along. Not only the proper style of straw hat, but the very person from whom Jonah had bought his own hat.

After confirming that the hat was precisely the style approved by Bishop Eli Miller, they had begun the task of suiting Branden in Amish dress. With Millie's help, they picked out each item, as Branden remembered it, to match the clothes on the corpse of Jonah Miller.

First the trousers. Plain dark-blue denim, no cuffs, no belt loops, and a square flap with the buttoned, broadfall style instead of a vertical zipper.

Then the shirt, a factory-made, long-sleeved white shirt with buttons and a plain collar. Millie Dravenstott assured them that Jonah had bought one like it. She also informed them that Jonah would have needed to replace it with a plain one, stitched up the front, with no collar.

Suspenders came next. Cloth, not rubberized. Never leather. They knew not to ask for a belt.

Last was the vest. He tried a dark denim jacket with snaps, but it worked against his memory of Jonah Miller in the ditch. Then a dark blue vest with buttons. Still not right. And Millie shrugged, stepped into an adjoining room marked "Employees Only," and brought out an exact duplicate of the one Jonah Miller had bought, saying it was the last. She had been saving it for him, but—well, now he wouldn't need it, would he?

It was made of black cloth. Midnight black, Millie said. It had no collar and no sleeves. There was no fancy stitching anywhere on the fabric. Instead of snaps or buttons, it closed with hooks and eyes. Branden put it on and left it hanging loosely open.

Last came the hat, and finally they stood together in front of the mirror, studying the perfect picture of Amish propriety in dress.

"Just shave around your mouth, Michael, and even Bishop Miller would have trouble recognizing you," Caroline said to her husband. She gave him a gentle nudge, moving him closer to the mirror.

Out in the sales area, Branden exchanged the straw hat for a broad-brimmed, black felt hat with a flat, three-inch brim and a plain, round, five-inch dome. Then he found Dravenstott behind the cash register, waited his turn bedecked in black, and asked how much for the entire outfit, including both the straw hat and the black one. A family of tourists gathered out front on the sidewalk and stared at him, chattering and pointing. A flashbulb popped white light through the window, but when he turned around to look, they were gone.

Millie rang it up from memory, looked at the paper slip and gave him the total. He picked out a straight razor, shaving cream, a little green bottle of Mennen Skin Bracer, and paid for it all.

"Could I use your washroom a bit longer?" Branden asked, gathering up his purchases. Millie checked the store for customers, nodded, and stepped down from her crate.

In the back room, after customers had cleared the store, Branden questioned Millie again about the clothes. "You're certain this is the outfit you sold to Jonah Miller?"

"Except for the black felt hat. I didn't sell him one of those at first," Millie said.

"At first?"

"Yes. As with the vest that you are now wearing, Professor, he asked me to set aside certain items. Said he'd ride back for them if everything worked out." She thought a few seconds, eyeing the vest, and then craned her neck to look up to Branden and added, "The little boy agreed. So I kept a few things aside for him."

Caroline gasped, "He had a child with him?"

"Yes," Millie said, puzzled. "He called him 'Little Jerry,' or something like that."

Branden turned to look in the mirror and asked, "The boy was dressed like this?"

Millie considered for a moment and looked up sideways at Caroline with an expression of growing curiosity. Then she said, "Yes, but somehow different."

"Please," Caroline said, "we're trying to find . . ."

Branden cut her off. "We're trying to find what became of Jonah Miller after they left your store," he explained.

"I'm not quite certain," Millie said, perplexed.

"Did they leave together?" Branden asked.

"Yes."

"Did they drive?"

"I don't think so."

"Buggy?"

"Not as I recall," Millie said. Then she looked anxiously back into the store, excused herself, and hurried with small, swinging steps to the front of the store, where she worked the cash register expertly from atop her overturned crate.

In the back room, Branden told Caroline, "We mustn't let her know anything about our looking for Jeremiah." She appeared eager to argue the point, so he explained. "There's still a day and a half before I have to explain any of this to Bruce Robertson. I gave Miller my word. Now, the only thing we can do, while the police do their work, is to trace Jonah Miller's path home. He bought clothes here, and as I said last night, that's very significant. Now we're going to stop for supper and then show up, out at the Miller's place, and let them know what we know. They all knew it too, on the day that Jonah was killed. If anyone in Miller's district is mixed up in this, perhaps we'll put enough pressure on to flush them out. The whole thing hinges on the fact that everybody out there knew what it meant that Jonah was dressed Amish."

"And if that doesn't work?" Caroline asked.

"Then whoever has Jeremiah has got to be a thousand miles away by now," Branden said grimly. "At least we will know that."

"And?"

"And then I'll have to go down to the jail and explain to the sheriff why I've withheld evidence in his murder case." He looked himself over in the mirror and added, "I'll be out in a minute."

At the cash register, while she waited for her husband, Caroline asked, "You said little Jerry looked somehow different to you. Different from the professor, that is. Was it his dress, attire?" Even on the crate, Millie came only to Caroline's shoulders.

"Been thinking about that," Millie said, and hopped down and around on tiptoes to straighten the gum and hard candies at the front of the register display. "It was his hair, I think."

"Can you be more specific?"

"You know. Not cut right," she said. "You get so used to seeing the kids come through the store. And they always look the same. It gets so as you're surprised when you see something different."

"Go on," Caroline said.

"Well, with the boy, his hair was cut too short. You know, not Amish style. And with his father, it seemed like he was trying to let his hair grow out. They both ended up looking strange. Everything Amish but the hair. Hats looked OK, but you wanted to see more hair under them."

Caroline thought about that and glanced to the back of the store, curious. "Can you think of anything else?"

"Just the complete change that the clothes made in him," she said. "They both looked so plain going out. Changed completely."

"What do you mean, completely changed?" Caroline asked.

"I'd have to show you. Mr. Miller came in here looking like he came from another world."

"You said you can show me?"

"Suppose it can't hurt any. I've still got his clothes. He asked me to save them for him too, just like with the vest. In case something or other didn't work out."

"Can I see them?" Caroline asked, stepping back from the counter to clear a way.

"Can't see any harm," Millie said.

In a corner behind the large, old-style white metal meat cooler, she bent over, lifted a cardboard box nearly as big as herself, and lugged it to the checkout counter. Then she stepped around the counter, mounted her crate, and watched Caroline open the box and lift out a Dallas Cowboys ball cap, a pair of

132   BLOOD OF THE PRODIGAL

slim-cut western jeans, an elaborately stitched leather belt with a silver Lone Star buckle, and a bright green western shirt with rose embroidery. There was also a gold-plated Zippo lighter and a silver wristwatch with an elaborate turquoise band. Caroline groaned, understanding instinctively that the search for Jeremiah Miller could take them anywhere, now. Anywhere at all.

As they stood at the counter, studying the fancy English clothes, the watchband, and the lighter, Branden emerged from the back room, grinning broadly.

"I knew it!" Caroline exclaimed and dropped the lighter onto the counter. "Michael Branden, I can't take you anywhere."

Millie leaned out over the counter, looked around the cash register toward the back of the store, and saw a plain-as-can-be Amish farmer. Flat-brimmed black felt hat. Plain black vest with no collar. White shirt with long sleeves. Dark denim trousers with cloth suspenders. Brown work boots. And a short, brown beard, trimmed Amish around his upper and lower lip where he had shaved himself clean, to resemble the corpse of Jonah Miller.

19

"I HAVEN'T been able to turn up anything under the name Jonah Miller," the sheriff was explaining to Melissa Taggert. They were in her small office next to the coroner's labs. Melissa sat in a swivel chair in front of her desk. Her arms were longer than the rests on the chair, and her wrists were bent over the ends. She wore a white lab coat unbuttoned at the front, with black slacks and a solid pastel green blouse. It looked to Robertson like silk.

Melissa studied the jumbled mess on her desk and laughed. "I don't see where you're going with this, Bruce, but I've got a positive identification of the body. From Bishop Miller, no less."

She pulled up in her swivel chair and began to straighten the papers on her desk. "Would Ellie Troyer let you keep such a mess down at the jail?"

Robertson reached a hand over, laid it on the papers she was shuffling, and said, "Missy, listen. I'm not actually saying it isn't Jonah Miller. I'm saying he has not lived as Jonah Miller in nearly ten years."

When Robertson had arrived, they had opened the files on top of the grey metal desk. Then they had sat together, pulled up to the desk, looking at Andy Shetler's photographs and Taggert's report on the autopsy. Now the file, the photos, the lab tests, documents, and a voice tape of the autopsy lay in a scrambled heap on top of her desk. And Melissa Taggert chuckled again at the spontaneous eruption of disorder that Robertson always managed to produce in her office. She thought to herself, "typical Class A personality—an overcompensated male."

Melissa Taggert was an organized and meticulous scientist. At the end of a day, there wouldn't be so much as an unwashed beaker or a flask out of its place. As she worked, she had formed the habit of organizing even the dirty glassware that accumulated. Her instruments, tools, equipment, and samples stayed clean and organized because she worked hard to keep them that way. It was the only way she knew to do science.

In the few years she had worked as Holmes County Coroner, she had learned to guard her labs jealously when Sheriff Robertson was around. He simply could not talk without fiddling with something. She had guessed correctly that it was because the morgue made him nervous.

Today, she had managed to confine him to her office, but there was no way to predict when the chaotic sheriff might spill over into her labs. She watched him take a tape cassette from the top of her desk and turn it idly in his fingers. She retrieved it with a smile and teased, "Bruce, I think I must make you nervous."

"Missy, sometimes I don't know what in the world you're talking about."

She sighed and said, "I know."

Robertson looked blankly at her, not knowing what to think. She was pretty. Not too slender. And she was easy to talk to. Robertson wondered why, and decided it was because she never took a tone with him. She never had gotten rattled when he had been in one of his moods. Truth was, he told himself, she was fun, happy, friendly, and he often came here because he liked being around her. Not her labs, though. It was her. He thought briefly that there was a revelation in that somewhere, but he dismissed it, thinking that everyone who knew her surely felt the same way.

Melissa Taggert was a keeper. He knew he couldn't say that out on the street, times being what they were, but it was true. Melissa Taggert and Ellie Troyer were both keepers. Still, Missy was different. She flustered him. Like now. He found himself blushing furiously when he realized, late, that she had been flirting.

He covered his embarrassment by forcing himself back on topic. "We need something to go on, Missy." He stared purposefully at the desktop, and then found himself looking up at her merry eyes. It unsettled him, and he said, "Maybe if you let me take that file, I could turn something up."

"There's nothing there, Sheriff," Melissa said. "You'd be wasting your time."

"Let's go over it again, anyways," Robertson said.

Melissa shrugged.

"There's got to be something, Melissa. One more time. Everything you've got." He had calmed himself.

Taggert sighed and recited, "Male Caucasian. Approximately thirty. In Amish dress. Killed instantly by a gunshot wound to the head. No other signs of trauma or foul play. Also, I'm sure you'll want to know that he smoked. Heavily, like somebody else I know. And drank. Evidently to excess. Calloused hands, probably a laborer, construction, most likely. All his clothes were new, except the boots.

"Next, there are the powder burns. He had them, but in unusual places. On the underside of his fingers. There was an intense line of burns that even the rain and the mud hadn't leached away. Well, at least not the burns. The powder residue is a trickier problem."

Robertson stopped her. "You said that he had powder and burns."

"He does," Taggert said. "They're just not displayed in the usual pattern for a suicide."

"You think someone killed him?"

"The burns are more consistent with his having a grip over the barrel and the cylinder gap," Taggert said.

Robertson pounded a heavy fist onto Taggert's desk. "As if he had a hold of the gun during a struggle."

"I think so," Taggert said. "Also, the bullets that were still left in the gun had fingerprints that do not match Jonah Miller's."

Robertson frowned and remained quiet while Missy stacked her papers into a neater pile on the desk and put away the folders and the other evidence she had gathered.

Eventually, Robertson said, "Tell me about the boots."

"There's nothing much to tell. The boots are old, worn, stained with tar, I think."

"Let's see 'em," Robertson said, interested.

Melissa retrieved them from an adjacent room, and sat back in the chair in front of her desk. Robertson held the boots together at the tops in his right hand, and turned them back and forth, the toes balanced on the fingertips of his left hand. The leather tops were heavily creased and, in places, had cracked open from wear. The shoestrings did not match; one was broken and had been retied. There were a variety of nicks and gouges in both the leather and the soles. "What do you make of these black smudges?" Robertson asked.

"It's roofing tar," Melissa said again. "Actually, roofing cement. It has tar in it, but it has binders, too."

"Did you get them analyzed?"

"Just the volatiles, on the G.C.," Melissa said. "It's ordinary roofing cement."

Robertson studied the boots another moment and then dropped them, soles down, onto the floor beside the coroner's chair.

"Can an analysis tell us who made it?"

Melissa was immediately intrigued. She thought rapidly as she turned her chair back and forth gently on its swivel, calculating how to make the sheriff's request work to her advantage.

Satisfied, she said, "I think so, but I'd have to analyze the solid additives, and I'd need more than a simple G.C. analysis on the volatiles."

"If that will tell us who manufactured the brand, let's do it," Robertson said.

Melissa replied, "We need a powder diffractometer to do that, Bruce. And a mass-sensitive detector for the G.C." She felt almost guilty because it had been so easy. A mass-sensitive detector had been on her "list" for months.

"Can you send it out?" Robertson asked.

"It would take a week or so at the B.C.I. labs," she said.

"I don't have a week. Isn't there another way?"

"Not for the binders. They're mostly inorganic solids. That'll take a powder diffractometer. They've got one at the college. They've got a mass-sensitive detector there, too."

"Can you use the college stuff?" he asked.

"They've got the right equipment. But do you want me doing this work up at the college? You'd owe them a favor, then."

"Do they have what you need?"

"Like I said, yes. But we need our own detector for the G.C. here."

"You want a mass detector?" Robertson asked.

"A mass-sensitive detector," Melissa said. "Yes."

"OK, I'll back you with the hospital board."

"It'll go to the commissioners," Melissa explained.

"OK, the commissioners, too, but you get up to the college today. Can you do that?"

To herself, Taggert shouted a quiet, triumphant YES! Then she said, "Right away," and began to stack the files on her desk.

"Look, Missy," Robertson said. "I doubt the commissioners will approve it. Even if they do, it could be months, even a year, before you get one."

"All I want you to do is try," Missy said.

"All right," Robertson said, smiling in defeat. "I'll try."

20

"HOW YOU gonna square that Amish beard with those cheese-balls out on the hill?" Robertson teased boisterously, as he worked a hole into his mashed potatoes and happily ladled in gravy.

Caroline encouraged the sheriff with more fried chicken.

"You mean up at the college?" Branden asked, running his fingers over the unfamiliar smooth skin around his now-Amish lips.

"You know exactly what I mean," Robertson said, gloating, and winked at Caroline.

Caroline smiled at Branden on the other side of the large, round family-style table in the Das Deutch Haus restaurant. A waitress in Dutch attire cleared the dishes in front of the Brandens and asked the sheriff if there'd be enough, or should she bring out more of anything?

"Just save me a piece of boysenberry pie," Robertson said and slid the last of the roast beef onto his plate. He had arrived only minutes ago, as Ricky Niell and the Brandens had been finishing an all-you-can-eat family-style dinner in a corner of the county not yet generally known to tourists.

Since early that morning, Robertson had had the deputies watching for the Brandens. It was Niell who had put Robertson onto that, by mentioning offhand that Branden had been at the Millers' the day before. Also Niell had reported, under questioning, that he thought the professor had been working on some angle of his own. Since then, Robertson had tried to reach the Brandens at home. He had even checked at Millersburg College with Lawrence Mallory, Branden's personal secretary. Then the sheriff had asked the deputies to watch for the Brandens' car, and at the end of his shift, Niell had called it in. He had found the Brandens at Das Deutch Haus.

"You don't think I can make this new look work for me on campus?" Branden asked, amused by how much his wife and Robertson seemed to be enjoying themselves at his expense. "I'll simply march into Arne Laughton's presidential offices one morning and tell his secretary that I've been researching Mennonite attitudes regarding combat in the Civil War. In two days, everyone on campus will know I've shaved. By opening convocation next fall, they'll all be surprised if I don't show up looking completely Amish."

The sheriff smiled and passed a bowl of creamed corn to Niell, who declined wordlessly and set it on the white tablecloth in front of him.

"Good thing Niell here found your car," Robertson said between mouthfuls. "He's got a theory I want you to hear."

Niell groaned privately and stared at his empty plate. His shift had gone off an hour ago, and now, seated next to Robertson, he had listened to the Brandens' explanation of their day of shopping, and had started feeling distinctly amateurish for having learned nothing himself about Jonah Miller.

They had told of the schoolteacher, Miss Beachey. Branden had recounted his conversations with various neighbors and friends of Cal Troyer, and with Enos Coblentz at the sawmill. There had also been discreet intimations about a bundling waitress, Ester Yoder. And then the clothes.

Niell sipped at his water while the sheriff worked away at

his dinner. Pretty impressive, Niell thought, for the professor to have deduced it from the clothes.

Niell hadn't uncovered a single fact about Jonah Miller, but he had done some deliberate checking on Branden, Robertson, and Troyer. Branden had grown up with Troyer and Robertson in the fifties and sixties in Millersburg. Troyer had taken conscientious objector status during the war in Vietnam and had carried a battlefield stretcher for a tour in country. Robertson had gone into the army after high school and had ended up an M.P., in Germany. And Branden had gone to college, where he drew a high draft lottery number, continued in graduate school, and came home to teach at Millersburg College rather than accept offers from several universities.

Niell heard the sheriff's voice, and pulled himself back to the conversation at the table.

Robertson said, "Go ahead, Ricky, tell 'em what you've come up with," and held up his empty coffee cup for the waitress to fill.

"Well, Professor," Niell said, tentatively, "it's just that we can't find a trace of Jonah Miller."

"Niell thinks he's been living under a different name," Robertson said and shoveled roast beef into his mouth.

Niell shrugged.

"That fits what we've been finding," Caroline encouraged.

"And it fits my idea about why he was killed," Branden said.

"On that score, you'll be happy to know that Missy Taggert has ruled it a homicide, too," Robertson said. He finished what was left on his plate, set his knife and fork delicately across the edge, crossed his arms over his barrel chest, and studied his three companions at the table. Caroline Branden was dressed in jeans, a sleeveless blouse, and a summer hat. Niell was still in uniform. And there was Branden in Amish attire. Sporting a brown Amish beard, grayed at the temples.

"So, Mike," Robertson said. "You got all that from the shaving cuts on Miller's face?"

Branden nodded.

"And from the new clothes," Caroline said. "Jonah Miller bought a suit of new clothes before going home. And he had shaved around his mouth."

"So?" Robertson asked.

"So he hadn't been living Amish," Branden said. "Just like your deputy has discovered. Jonah Miller the Amishman hasn't existed for ten years. And then, out of nowhere, he shows up on that lane down by the Millers' house in new Amish dress? And he had shaved with a straight razor, not a safety razor—or an electric one—as any sensible English man would have done. He used a straight razor, just as I did today, and with no more expertise. See the nicks?" Branden ran his fingers over the smooth skin above and below his lips. "No reason for him to have been so authentic about it, if he were just playing at being Amish for some reason. So I figured Jonah Miller was truly going home. I expect the bishop knows it, too."

Robertson finished his coffee and waited.

Branden continued. "Jonah switched to a straight razor and bought Amish clothes. He was walking, not driving. None of his old friends had heard of him in recent times. Then there's the little matter of the obituary."

Robertson said, "An obituary?" He was surprised.

"A big obit," Caroline said, "with a little verse, right along traditional lines. We found it in the *Sugar Creek Budget.* I'm guessing, but I'll bet it was written by the bishop himself."

"It's a traditional Amish obituary," Branden said, with emphasis.

"Now, who's gonna summarize what that all means?" Robertson asked, looking at no one in particular.

Niell stirred in his chair. "It means," he said, "that Jonah

Miller was going home on terms that would have canceled the Mite. That's why he was killed."

The sheriff acknowledged that with a nod and prompted, "And?"

"And it means that, if Eli Miller knows it, so does everyone else in the district," Niell asserted. "They all probably knew it the day Jonah was killed."

"Go on," Robertson encouraged.

Niell said, "Jonah Miller was headed back to Amish ways. He used a straight razor. New clothes. No car. Bishop Miller understands this and he also knows something else. Something he's been hiding. It probably has to do with why Jonah was killed." That said, Niell laid his hands flat on the table, waiting.

Robertson studied Niell for a moment and then commented to Branden, "You got all that from the shaving cuts?"

"First the shaving cuts," Branden said. "I wondered why he'd start growing a beard and use a straight razor to trim around his mouth. Obvious really. An electric razor would never do for a proper Amish shave. But I couldn't shake the weird look it gave him, nicks around his mouth, lying in the rain in that ditch.

"Then we shopped for an identical suit of clothes and found the lady who'd sold Miller his particular outfit in Fredericksburg. She'd even saved his old clothes. Fancy Texan. Pretty much the farthest thing from plain Amish a person could get.

"Also, we have the fact that old friends and neighbors have not seen Jonah lately. So that meant he hadn't been living nearby. Now, what Ricky has correctly deduced is also what every Amish man and woman surely knew the day Jonah's body was found. That's why they showed up in buggies at the Miller house the day I was out there. Remember? I couldn't understand why they'd show up if Jonah were still shunned, outcast.

"Well, he wasn't outcast by then. The word got out through

the entire district. Jonah Miller came home on the only terms his father could accept. And a traditional obituary has been printed by the Miller family in the *Sugar Creek Budget*. Jonah Miller came home to live on the farm. He had repented. He'd been forgiven. He's once again the son of Bishop Eli Miller."

The sheriff looked at Niell. "You agree?" he asked.

"Makes sense to me," Niell said.

"All right," Robertson said. "Jonah Miller was killed on the lane, less than a mile from his house. He was going home after ten years. Everybody knew it from the clothes. Now he's dead, and we still don't know who killed him."

Branden acknowledged the sheriff with a nod and said, "A waitress I talked to said that it was land that got Jonah killed."

Robertson looked blankly at Branden, waiting.

"That Eli Miller's son, Isaac, would have motive. And if not Isaac, then someone else in the extended Miller line would not want Jonah to come home. At least not come home Amish."

"Killed by one of his own family?" Robertson said, vastly skeptical.

"Or maybe one of his family knows, perhaps even the bishop. Why he was killed, that is. Knows who it was, but isn't telling."

"Isn't telling for what reason?" Robertson asked.

"I don't know," Branden said.

"Then how do you propose we move forward with the case?" Robertson challenged.

"That's what we've been talking about this evening, Bruce. I started out to buy the clothes just to satisfy my own curiosity. It helped me realize what the new clothes meant to Jonah. But now I'm going to confront Eli Miller tomorrow morning and let him know that *I* know that Jonah had decided to come home and live Amish. Then I'm going to take him aside and demand an explanation. Bishop Miller hasn't told us everything he knows, and I think it's time he started." To himself, Branden thought, "Besides, tomorrow is the last day of my three-day promise."

"The trouble is," Robertson said, "neither Eli nor Isaac is likely to have murdered Jonah."

"Probably someone they know, though," Niell offered.

"Or someone they're afraid of," Caroline said. "At any rate, Michael's plan stands the best chance of producing results, flushing someone out."

Robertson thought quietly for a moment, gazing into his empty coffee cup, and then said, "You're off tomorrow, Ricky. How you feel about a little overtime?"

Niell shrugged a yes, glad, now, not to have gone home after his shift. The Brandens had a better hold on a case that had been going nowhere.

After Niell and Robertson had left, Caroline said, "Michael, I still don't like this. Why didn't you tell Bruce about the boy? That was the perfect chance."

"Nothing's changed. We've been over this before, and you know how Robertson would handle it."

"I think you're selling him short," Caroline answered.

"If Bruce really thought he knew who had shot Jonah Miller, he'd have hauled 'em in by now, probably starting with Isaac and the bishop. Everyone in the bishop's district would know, and surely more would find out within the day. Especially whoever's got Jeremiah. You know how he can be. I can't risk it, yet. For now, we don't know who, if anyone, either in the Miller house or in the district, has got Jeremiah. To go out there as Bruce might handle it would destroy whatever chance we have of convincing the bishop to confide in us about the boy. Even then, we run a terrible risk of tipping our hand, especially if someone close to the Millers has killed Jonah and is hiding Jeremiah." Then he added, "Providing the boy is still alive."

Caroline shuddered. "Donna Beachey told us that the Miller household, or at least the bishop, has always wanted Jonah to come home and take his vows," Caroline said.

"I know," Branden answered. "The bishop told me the same

thing. In the end, it's the most rational argument I have for not telling Bruce about the whole thing right now. The Millers simply aren't involved."

"You're risking everything because you're not sure how Bruce might react."

Branden shrugged. "One more day, Caroline. For only another day."

"I don't like it, Michael, and that's not going to change. First Jonah Miller kidnapped his own son, and now you're covering it up."

"You're forgetting Jonah's Amish clothes," Branden said. "He can't have been part of anything like a kidnapping that's going on now with Jeremiah."

"And you are forgetting Jonah's fancy Texan clothes in Millie Dravenstott's little box. He was from Texas, Michael, and that means almost anyone could have Jeremiah, now."

Branden held his hands up, palms out. "Just another day, Caroline."

Caroline fell silent, and Branden drove toward town, first along County Line Road and then Route 83. In the fields at dusk, on the Amish farms, stolid Belgian draft horses pulled wagons, rakes, mowers. Clothes hung on backyard lines, giving serene splashes of Amish colors in the gloaming. Amish children played in yards bypassed by electric service. Caroline gazed out the side window, her head resting against the glass. An Amish lad of about fifteen stood at a fence beside the road and waved a greeting as they drove by. She glanced at her husband, still dressed in Amish clothes, newly shaved around his mouth, and thought of Jonah Miller. Then of Jeremiah. The dreary notion crossed her mind that Jeremiah could easily be dead like his father.

The road ran straight for a while and then turned, curved, rose and fell with the hills, followed a stream, and crossed the marshes of Killbuck swamp. On Route 83, Branden turned south into the hill country, away from the flatter, more fertile regions of Wayne County to the north, where the land begins to stretch out more distantly, almost like the plains in the northwest corner of the state, laid flat by glaciers. There, the private enclosures of the hills and valleys in Amish country do not exist. The farms become large, mechanized, prosperous enterprises where the horizon has been enlarged in every direction by the clearing of land, and where the farms are too valuable to be worked by mere teams of horses.

Jonah Miller had come up out of our secluded Amish valleys, ten years ago, she thought. And gone where? Where could he go? Anywhere. Everywhere. From peasant farms, into the twentieth century.

And little Jeremiah? What hope was there, now, for him? Still, in spite of that crumpled place in her heart, something convinced her that Jeremiah survived. What was it? Think. Jeremiah is still alive. She needed to believe in this. She choked back tears, and realized, slowly, what it was that could give her hope for the child.

With the sun long down, her head resting against the window pane, without looking at her husband, eyes nearly awash in tears, she said, "If you're right, then I'm guessing that the bishop knows who killed Jonah, or he knows who has the boy. He's being cautious about Jonah's murder because the boy's life is still at risk. Bishop Miller has been protecting the boy. He simply must have been."

21

Thursday, June 25
6:00 A.M.

"IT'S ELLIE Troyer," Jim Larson said gravely to Richard Niell Sr. He made his voice sound serious, but he grinned past a two-day stubble, showing several missing teeth, and elbowed Ricky Niell in the ribs.

They were seated in a booth at the McDonald's on the south side of Millersburg, Jim and Ricky on one side, Niell Sr. on the other. Younger Niell's eyes were haggard, and he had his nose parked over a large black coffee, pulling in aroma. He frowned, took a sip, rolled his eyes with a simmering animosity, and rubbed mirthlessly at his temples, exhausted.

He had been out all day yesterday, looking for the Brandens. Then the long dinner, which he didn't mind so much. Finally, up until three A.M. thinking it through. First from one angle and then from another. From all angles, even with coffee, it made no sense. There was no reason for Bishop Miller to have hidden anything. And yet, Niell had decided, that's precisely what Miller had done. Bishop Eli Miller had been hiding something important.

"I tell you it's little Ellie Troyer that's put a hitch in his shorts," Jim Larson gloated again, chewing the last of an Egg McMuffin. "She's the reason Big Deputy Niell, here, won't go huntin' anymore."

"For crying out loud, Jim," Niell complained, knowing it

148

was useless with Larson. The muscles at the base of his skull knotted painfully.

"You'll have to tell me again, boys, who Ellie Troyer is," Niell Sr. said.

Niell ignored Larson and said, gruffly, "She's the new dispatcher down at the jail, and I think it's about time you two told me why you drug me out of bed so early."

Niell Sr. explained, "We were out all night, raccoon hunt, down in the swamps and low forest lands, running the dogs, just like we used to. And Jim's right. Seems like you never go huntin' anymore, Ricky."

"Coon hunting's not legal this time of year unless you're a farmer and have a nuisance permit," Niell Jr. said.

"Then write us up," Larson challenged, half serious now, instantly more quarrelsome.

Ricky turned sideways in his seat and glared directly and disdainfully at his old friend Larson. Then, after a suitable interval, he turned purposefully to Niell Sr. and resumed, "And why are you telling me this?"

"Found a campfire, Ricky. Tracks all around," Niell Sr. said. "There was a gasoline smell, too, and Jim noticed a bumper sticking out of the water. He's still a little crazy, but we were both wearing waders, so it wasn't any trouble to ease out into the water, run the snakes off, and reach down to try for the door."

Ricky drank coffee and stared at this father with his head down, eyes high up in their sockets, reproachful.

"I'm getting there," Niell Sr. said. "Anyways, Jim waded to shore, took off his waders, swam back out to the truck, got the door open and the glove compartment, too. He wasn't under that long, but he managed to pull something out of the glove compartment."

With that, Ricky's father drew a sodden wallet from the top of his waders and laid it open on the table. He took out a plastic driver's license, dried it on his shirt sleeve, snapped it down onto the table in front of Ricky, and asked dramatically, "What do you think of that, young deputy?"

On the table beside Ricky Niell's coffee lay the driver's license with a picture of Jonah Miller, not much different from his appearance in the sheriff's photos.

Niell scrambled to comprehend all of what had happened. They had found the truck last night. Then by five A.M., they had shown up pounding on Ricky's door, their coon dogs still hot from the chase, waking up neighbors, bantering about getting Niell a promotion.

"You just got the wallet and brought the license to me?" Niell asked, trying to ignore the self-satisfied grin on Larson's face.

"Came straight to you," Jim said, "but I see you've been out all night," winking at Niell Sr.

"Jim, I'm only gonna tell you this once more, and then . . ."

Larson interrupted, "Then you're gonna what?" adding a challenge, "Everybody's seen her flirting with you."

"For crying out loud, Jim," Niell said, caught his father's smile, gave up, and muttered to himself, "For crying out loud."

Larson chortled a small triumph, pushed out of the booth, and sauntered up to the counter still wearing his filthy clothes, the stench of the swamp traveling with him.

Niell Sr. explained again about the truck. "Like I was saying, we really weren't looking for anything. First we found the campfire, out near Killbuck. It was used pretty light, maybe two nights at most. Then the truck. I remembered you said you needed to find one for Robertson. It looked to me like somebody pushed it in, hoping it would sink."

That'd be whoever had killed Jonah Miller, Ricky thought. His mind worked slowly at first. He rubbed at his hair, annoyed, and forced himself to think. Why would they sink the truck? Then again, maybe it was Jonah Miller himself who'd sunk the truck. Perhaps that'd fit. Before Jonah started walking home, either before he bought his Amish clothes or after, he drove to the swamp, camped, and . . . . what? Ricky Niell thought about that, came up with nothing, gulped the rest of his coffee, stood up from the table, and asked, "You said you found tracks?"

"Two sets for sure, maybe more," the senior Niell replied. "Trouble is, we stomped the place up pretty good ourselves, before we found the truck. But there were two sets of prints at least, one a man's, the other smaller."

"Small?" Ricky asked.

"Like a kid's," Niell Sr. said.

"Two tracks for sure?"

"Those two at least, plus ours. Gotta remember we didn't know it was your guy Miller that had been there. Then I recognized his picture. Got himself a different name on that license, though."

"Amish don't take pictures," young Niell said. "How'd you know it was him?"

"Oh, I'd know Jonah Miller's face pretty much anywhere," Niell Sr. asserted. "That kid was into more trouble than you'd believe for an Amish lad."

And now the picture of Jonah Miller lay flat on the table where Niell had been sitting. Thirty-one. Black on brown. Long black mustache, carefully groomed, and a flattop haircut. Killeen, Texas. Niell scraped mud from the corner where the renewal date was printed. The license had recently expired. The name on the license read Jon Fenimore Mills.

Niell lifted the license, wiped it clean, slipped into his back jeans pocket and said, "I've got to take it in right away. Then you'll need to take us out there."

In the parking lot beside his truck, Ricky added, "Let me tell the sheriff about the name on the license."

22

Thursday, June 25
9:00 A.M.

"SOME bozos will do anything," Ricky Niell barked for all ears to hear—the sheriff, Niell Sr., Branden, the deputies, Ed Lorentz on the tow truck's winch, and anyone else that morning who might have been near the southern reaches of the vast Killbuck watershed. As he spoke, Jim Larson came up spitting mud and wiped dirty water out of his eyes, exasperated to see them all standing there, encouraged to laughter by Niell, who wore an expression of utter disgust.

Larson swore profusely, waded with difficulty toward such shore as can be distinguished in a swamp, held up a hand, and was hauled out unceremoniously by Niell, who gave him a look that said "Listen, turkey—lay off."

Larson scraped muck out of his shirt collar and stomped over to the winch, dripping swampwater, mumbling to himself, fuming at the way the other men had seen Niell handle him. "This time, just give her a slow tug, Ed," Larson said, sounding bossy.

Ed Lorentz dismissed Larson's advice with a grunt, hitched his jeans up with a disrespectful scowl, and slammed the winch into gear. The cable tightened abruptly on the hook attached to the rear axle. This time the hook held, and the truck began to emerge tail first out of the swamp. It was a fairly new, full-sized, tricked-out Chevy, and it prompted whistles from a couple of the men.

Branden stepped well clear of the operation, waiting for water to surge out of the now-vertical truck. Ricky Niell came over to him and pointed at the license Branden held.

"Couldn't find Jonah Miller because he changed his name," Niell said matter-of-factly, and watched the truck spill water as it hung from the cable.

Branden studied the face on the license. Then he read the name again. Jon Fenimore Mills. He remembered the books Jonah's teacher had given him in the fifth grade and shook his head. Jon Mills, on its own, wasn't that different from Jonah Miller. The middle name Fenimore obviously came from Miss Beachey's gift of *The Last of the Mohicans*. Branden wondered about a man who had changed his first and last name so slightly, but also had given himself a name taken from a favorite author, as if he wanted to embrace the future, but couldn't escape his past.

"We'll be able to trace him, now," Niell remarked, eyes still on the truck. "But we've got another problem." Niell turned to face Branden. "The truck changes everything."

Indeed it does, Branden thought. There must have been a good Amish reason for Jonah Miller, aka Jon Fenimore Mills, to have abandoned the truck. A reason not to have sold it. Had he disdained the money? Maybe not. The Amish don't disdain money outright. And Jonah Miller could have used the money that the truck would bring. Or his family could have used it. But perhaps Jonah Miller had not simply been heading home. Perhaps there was more to his being on that lane than simply going home. "Got any ideas why he'd abandon the truck?" Branden asked Niell.

"You mean instead of selling it?" Ricky asked.

"For one thing, yes," Branden said. "But also, it's not just abandoned. Somebody also . . ." Branden stopped abruptly, thought a spell, and then asked, "You did say there were two sets of tracks?"

"Two at least. Several large prints, some small," Niell replied, interested.

"If it was only two sets, then who tried to hide the truck?" Branden asked.

"You figure it was more than Jonah's just not wanting the money from selling it," Niell commented, not needing an answer.

Branden nodded pensively, and remembered Millie Dravenstott, the saleslady in Fredericksburg who had kept back a box full of fancy western clothes for Jonah Miller, "in case things didn't work out." So Jonah Miller would have walked back to his truck, driven to Fredericksburg to collect his English clothes, and gone away, again, if his father had rejected him. But Jonah never got the chance to find out what his father would do, Branden thought morosely.

The sheriff had the truck doors open now, and Ed Lorentz had released the slack on the cable, letting the truck down on its tires.

Ricky Niell's posture had shifted perceptibly. He asked suspiciously, "You know who made the little tracks?"

"A boy," Branden said, and then added, "Deputy, I'm going to need your help."

Then Branden motioned for Sheriff Robertson, left Niell standing in place, met the sheriff halfway, and said, "Bruce, this license explains a lot."

"Sure does," Robertson said. He glanced approvingly at Niell and took the license from Branden.

"You'll be able to check it through? On the name Jon Mills, I mean?" Branden asked.

"No problem," the sheriff said, looking back at the truck. "But, we've got a lot of work here with the truck alone. It'll hold clues to his recent whereabouts, too."

"Then I'd like to go ahead with our plans out at the Millers'," Branden said and studied the sheriff's expression. "And I'd like to take the deputy with me," indicating Niell with a nod of his head.

The sheriff glanced over at Niell, still not in uniform. Up all night from his looks, the sheriff thought, either out on the town or hunting, maybe both. Then he had carried that license into the jail as cool as ice, laid it on the counter, and waited for Ellie to figure it out. They called back to me, and then waited without speaking for me to react. "Niell shows promise, don't you think?" Robertson commented in a low voice.

"That's why I need him out at the Millers'," Branden said.

"He's been piling up overtime," Robertson said. "Might not want to go."

"Oh, I think I can tell him a few things to entice him."

The sheriff looked back at the truck, saw Jim Larson leaning in over the front seat and hollered, "Not so fast, Larson," then to Branden, "OK," and made a hurried march to the truck, giving orders.

Explaining his intentions to Niell, Branden led the way back to his truck, tossing his hat in through the open window. With Niell on the passenger's side, he backed down the muddy path that leads into the town of Killbuck.

En route to the bishop's house, Branden told Ricky Niell the curious saga of Bishop Miller's request for help in finding his grandson Jeremiah. Of the note Jonah Miller had written saying the boy would be back by harvest. Of the bishop's insistence, from the start, that they not go to the authorities. That if they found the boy, they were not to try to retrieve him from his father. Of the search for Jonah before his death. Of the investigations after the murder. And of their concerns that something about the bishop and his actions wasn't quite right.

First of all, now that Jonah was dead, why was the bishop proceeding so cautiously? Then, since the boy was still missing, why hadn't the bishop gone to the sheriff and told everything he knew?

Now that the truck had been found, there was evidently more trouble than Branden had earlier realized. Why would Jonah and Jeremiah sink the truck in the swamp? And if they didn't, who did? Millie Dravenstott had been holding clothes for Jonah Miller in Fredericksburg, in case his father rejected him. Now why would Jonah save back a suit of English clothes and not an exceedingly more valuable truck? And more importantly, if Jonah and Jeremiah were simply heading home and Jonah had turned up dead, then why would Bishop Eli Miller hunker down at home without so much as a word? Unless the bishop, as Caroline had surmised, was still protecting the boy.

At the bishop's house, they parked out on the lane and walked openly up the driveway. There were hammering sounds coming from the rear. No one answered their knock at the front door.

In the back, they found Isaac Miller putting up frame on the poured concrete foundation on the knoll behind the barn. He wore a straw hat identical to Jonah's and a denim carpenter's apron over trousers. His light blue shirtsleeves were rolled up neatly, precisely to the elbows. Isaac Miller said little. He would only remark that his father was in the fields, pointing into the rolling valley behind the barns.

They took a path around a vegetable garden where two teenagers were hoeing weeds. The children looked up shyly, without speaking, and quickly returned to their work. There was a bricked well in the backyard, with a hand pump and a tin cup hung on the spigot. A long run of clothesline, with clothes fluttering black, with a sprinkling of subtle Amish hues.

Branden and Niell ducked under a tall grape arbor of weathered boards and stood to gaze at the fields of Bishop Eli Miller. The wide valley was planted in Amish crops. Corn, barley, oats. The dark soil at their feet was trampled by the hooves of horses. The short rows of grain in numerous small fields fanned in several directions, blown first this way and then another by a warm, irregular breeze. Purple martins skirmished through the air from a triple-decked martin house on a tall pole. A dinner bell rode high atop another pole.

On the far side of the valley, a line of timber showed white patches where the trunks of sycamores marked a stream. The sky was unusually blue for northern Ohio, but showed heavy gray clouds to the south. Branden, like many Buckeyes, was essentially forest bred. Accustomed to hills, trees, and vistas foreshortened by clouds. To him, sky blue was just another shade of grey, and any sunny day could hold the promise of rain. He stood at the edge of Eli Miller's fields and studied the sky. He lifted his hat and used a handkerchief to wipe out the hat band, confident that the approaching storm would drop the temperature ten degrees in as many minutes. Thinking that the next few moments would hold the fate of Jeremiah Miller.

In the farthest field, near the wooded stream, they found Bishop Miller sitting quietly on the buckboard of a hay wagon, reins limp in his hands, head bowed. Cut hay lay scattered in the field in arching rows that roughly followed the curves of the wandering stream.

At the sound of their approach, Bishop Miller looked up. He was obviously startled by the new Amish trim of the professor's beard. After gazing at the Amish-Branden for several minutes, apparently working on a decision, Miller climbed down wearily from the bench and grasped one of the tall wooden-spoked wagon wheels, which bore knobbed steel rims.

Branden's stance before the bishop was rigid and silent, feet planted somewhat apart, hands clasped behind his back, waiting for the bishop to begin. Niell stood to the side, a pace back.

After a silent interval, the bishop spoke falteringly. "I've been praying, Herrn Professor, for guidance."

Branden waited.

"I see that you've understood about Jonah's clothes. About his beard. What it means, that is."

"He was coming home on your terms, Bishop," Branden said. Then he held his peace, eyes steady and confident, partly accusing, mostly just waiting.

"It's not easy to know what to do. We are a simple people. Thoughts come slowly, decisions even more so."

The bishop seemed bewildered, not secretive as Branden had expected. Branden eased his stance somewhat.

"We've all been praying, first for Jonah and now for Jeremiah."

He reached up under his straw hat and pulled out a tattered paper. He held the folded page with trembling hands, his thumbs up, as he had obviously done through many hours of prayer. His head bowed slightly, out of habit.

Then the bishop offered the folded page to Branden, and looked beseechingly into Branden's eyes.

Branden unfolded the page and read an erratic scrawl:

$75,000 or the kid will never come home.
Jonah knows nothing.
Tell no one.
Dont go to the police.
Wait for instructions.
Dont try to find us, or they both die.
One month, so be ready!

Branden, flabbergasted, handed the page silently to Niell, who read it and then ran his fingertips through his hair with an indignant groan.

Branden asked, "How long have you known?"

"This note came at the same time we got Jonah's note, when Jeremiah was taken."

"You knew this when you first came to see me?"

"We knew Jonah had the boy, and we knew someone had delivered that note."

"That's why you didn't want us to let on that we were searching for Jeremiah?"

The bishop nodded yes.

"And why you haven't come for help, now that Jonah is dead?"

The bishop nodded again.

"And you knew the day Jonah was murdered that he had been coming home? He'd repented. You wrote his obituary?"

The bishop nodded yes again, his mind numbed by the cruel circumstances. Branden noticed especially that Miller had not argued with his assertion that Jonah had repented.

Niell stepped forward angrily and asked, "Do you know where the boy is? Who has him?"

"No," the bishop said, looking helpless.

"Have you looked for the boy?" Niell asked and then to Branden, "What's his name? Jeremiah?"

"Jeremiah," Branden acknowledged and waited for the bishop to answer.

"We have not," the bishop said, anguish in his eyes. "We thought it best to let the professor do the looking, while we kept up our usuals and prepared the money. In case."

Niell paced in a circle, manifestly indignant.

Branden peered into the eyes of the bishop and saw uncertainty and heartbreak. He realized instinctively that, with the death of Jonah Miller, there would be more to the ransom scheme than was first intended.

Softly he asked, "Have you heard again from these people?"

The bishop produced another worn and tattered page.

Warned you about Jonah.
$100,000 now!
Five Days.
Be ready.

Branden handed the second page to Niell, who read it while pacing and then stopped and eyed Branden, astounded.

"How long have you had this second ransom note?" Branden asked.

"Four days," the bishop said.

"So that's why you wanted me to keep searching for three more days. After that it wouldn't matter anymore."

The bishop nodded, "Yes."

"We saw your son Isaac back at the house," Branden said, deliberately calm. "I presume he's building a *Daadihaus*?"

The bishop nodded yes, speechlessly.

"Then you plan to retire?"

"Yes," the bishop said and then explained, "Isaac is to have the big house. The little *Daadihaus* is for the Mrs. and me."

Branden took the two pages from Niell, refolded them, and held them, hesitating a moment before saying, "I gather you've not yet decided whether or not you'll pay the ransom."

23

BRANDEN and Niell parked at the Millersburg Courthouse amid a noisy procession of autos, trucks, and buggies. At the curb marked for horses only, some of the rigs were plain in the extreme, and flat black. Others were more elaborate, and sported mirrors, reflectors, and other fixtures. Some of the Amish had unhitched their horses and pushed their buggies to the side. Those on shorter errands had left their horses hitched at the rail along the eastern sidewalk on the courthouse grounds. Tourists slowed traffic on the square or congregated on the sidewalk, taking pictures, pointing crassly, and talking loudly.

The morning had been breezy and warm, but now the advance clouds of thunderstorms had started to gather as Branden and Niell made their way around the brown and tan sandstone courthouse, Branden seething at the tourists. He glanced up to gauge the coming storm, dark clouds setting off the green copper roof of the old, boxy building.

As they came around the courthouse and passed the war monument, the clouds opened and heavy drops began pelting down. Niell and Branden sprinted across the small lawn in the downpour and ducked into the north door of the jail, the rain pinging loudly on the hand-hammered tin moldings over the jail's windows and doors. Shaking rain off his cap, Niell commented, "The sheriff's not gonna go for this at all."

An hour later, Branden glanced ruefully at Niell, having come to regard the young deputy as an accomplished master of understatement.

"I still can't believe it," Robertson was saying, calmer now, but still clearly incensed.

Ellie Troyer had not mustered the wherewithal to press her ear to the wall boards. Until now, she hadn't needed to.

"I couldn't risk it, Bruce," Branden said, defending himself. "We only had suspicions about the boy. Nothing to go on, and, for all we knew, it was Isaac, or someone close to the family, who had Jeremiah. If I had pushed too hard on that, we might have precipitated something unintended."

Robertson scowled bitterly, not liking any angle on the matter. He paced behind his desk, eventually retrieved his overturned swivel chair from the corner, and sat down heavily.

"You couldn't have trusted me to handle it?"

Branden gave his friend a look that answered, gently, no. Then he said, "Until now, I thought it best to proceed as the bishop had wanted. He had brought me in on those terms, and I figured he would know the problem better than anyone."

"Well he didn't!" Robertson shouted. He reached for a cigarette, lit it, inhaled deeply, and crushed it out. "What's Caroline doing out at the Millers'?"

"We called her from a gas station. She's going to talk with Mrs. Miller. Their youngest daughter apparently saw a policeman in a car on the lane the day Jeremiah was taken. Maybe Caroline can get her to remember some more details."

Robertson listened and tried to relax. Eventually he took another Winston out of its red and white pack and leaned back in his chair, smoking without comment. From time to time he pulled his gaze down off the ceiling and shot Branden a look.

Then he got up and went out to the front counter, spoke with Ellie for several minutes, came back to his chair with something like a smile on his face, lit another smoke, and sat down. At his desk, he sorted, again, through the items retrieved from Jonah's truck and from reports brought in that day by the deputies. Branden and Niell waited, Niell in the straight wooden chair in front of the sheriff's desk, Branden in the soft leather one to the side.

Robertson thumbed out his cigarette, blew smoke and said, "I've questioned your little waitress friend this morning, Mike."

Branden nodded. "I told you about her at dinner last night."

"Did you know that she had seen Jonah recently?"

Branden shrugged.

"And just when were you going to tell me that?"

Branden didn't answer.

"Well, she ran into Jonah up in Cleveland this spring, and told him he had a son. Said it shook him up plenty. Also said she'd told Jeff Hostettler about the whole thing."

Branden rolled his eyes and sat back with a groan. After an uncomfortable interval, he rose, moved to the window, and stared out. Traffic had slackened on the courthouse square as the afternoon had progressed. Eventually, Branden reclaimed his seat and sprawled in it.

Ellie Troyer carried in a fresh pot of coffee, poured for the sheriff, and offered to Branden and Niell, who both declined. She lingered, standing beside Niell's chair, somewhat back, eyeing the sheriff.

"What am I gonna do here, Ellie?" Robertson said. "The professor thinks I should wait for his wife to come in."

"Perhaps," Ellie said.

Robertson thought for a moment while tapping a book of paper matches on his desk and then asked, "Who've we got on patrol this evening, Ellie?"

"Schrauzer, Wilsher, Jones, and Nelson," Ellie said.

"And who'd you recommend to send out to the Millers'?"

After a pause, Ellie said, "I think Wilsher."

"Right," the sheriff agreed. "But tell him to handle things slowly with the Millers. He'll understand. He's to stay there with them. I don't want his unit parked on the lane, so have

Schrauzer or Jones run him out. Tell him I'll be out after we've finished here. Might be late tonight. Got it?"

Ellie said, "Got it," and waited.

Robertson glanced at his deputy with an air of decisiveness. He pushed back from his desk, opened its center drawer, withdrew a note pad, wrote several lines, tore off the top page with a flourish, folded the page, handed the note to Ellie and said, "You and Niell work on that."

Ellie opened the note, read, motioned for Niell to follow, and left with him.

Branden stood up awkwardly after the long spell in the low chair and paced in front of the sheriff's desk, hands in his pockets, easing the stiffness out of his legs.

Robertson rocked back in his swivel chair and studied the high, ornate, hammered-tin ceiling tiles, where a fan made slow revolutions. Then he pulled up to his desk and sorted through the accumulating evidence. To Branden he said, "I've had deputies checking roofing crews in the area since I talked to Missy about the smudges on Jonah's boots. But everything we've got from the truck points to Lake Erie, instead."

Branden tried the straight wooden chair, found it uncomfortable, and returned to the low leather one. He dropped into it and slouched with his feet stretched out, his back low to the seat cushion, struggling to relax, thinking it typical of Robertson to have tracked down every lead he had. So he had spoken to Ester Yoder. Probably also to Isaac. Maybe he had actually interrogated them as suspects.

Outside the sheriff's window, the thunderstorm had dropped the temperature by twenty degrees. Leaves, broken twigs, and branches lay randomly about the lawn and the sidewalks. Only a single buggy remained, and the usual complement of tourists had departed in their air-conditioned bus.

Eventually Caroline arrived with Deputy Schrauzer and laid the ransom notes, in a brown envelope, on the sheriff's desk. Robertson read them without comment.

Branden held to his leather chair and Caroline took the straight one. Schrauzer stood. They all waited on the sheriff, who sat thoughtfully at his desk. Time passed.

Robertson sorted through details in his mind, shoved the Jon Mills evidence around on his desk with a pencil, and eventually spoke with a tone of restless irritation. "Jon Mills has got himself a speeding violation out of Port Clinton, up on Lake Erie," he said, indicating the general scatter of documents on his desk. "That fits with other items from Jonah's truck. Still doesn't give us much to go on, finding the boy, that is."

Robertson picked up the ransom notes again, reread them and said, "We still can't be sure that these were written by anybody up at Port Clinton." He sounded negative. He wondered, momentarily, how Ellie was coming along with his instructions.

"None of the Millers can have done this," Caroline asserted.

"Maybe so, but neither is any of them gonna be the least little bit of help," Robertson retorted. He stood, stepped to one of the windows in his office and looked out onto the courthouse square.

"They don't know what to do," Caroline said. "You can't blame them, Bruce."

"Their grandson's been kidnapped and they can't think what to do?"

"They've been praying."

"Great, that's a marvelous comfort to know," Robertson said with intense sarcasm.

"Knock it off, Bruce," Branden said, openly irritated. "What would you expect them to have done?"

"They could at least have come to me, or have gotten some cash together," Robertson declared, glaring out the window at nothing in particular. Then he twisted at the waist to glare at Branden. "You think they wouldn't have paid anyways. That sound at all normal to you?" It was spoken scornfully.

"That sounds Amish to me," Branden said. "That's what makes me think the people who kidnapped Jeremiah can't be

Amish. Who'd expect Old Order Amish to have that kind of money?"

"Then they could damn well sell some land!" Robertson exploded.

"You know better than that, Bruce," Branden argued. "You wouldn't have advised them to pay, at any rate."

Caroline said, "Selling land is something they wouldn't readily do. You know that, Bruce. Their salvation's mixed into it. To give up land would be to put them all at risk, not just Jeremiah. That's why Michael's right. The kidnappers cannot have known the Amish."

Robertson scoffed, "How about someone like Isaac Miller, who stands to benefit from Jonah's death, and won't return Jeremiah until he has the farm?"

Branden challenged him instantly. "Name one case, here or anywhere else, Bruce, that such a thing has happened among the Amish."

Robertson made a disagreeable expression that grudgingly acknowledged Branden's point. Then the sheriff thought again of Ellie and Ricky Niell. They should be almost ready, he mused. After a few restless moments in front of the window, Robertson asked Caroline, in a gentler tone, "What did you learn out there, anyways?"

"Their youngest daughter, Ruth, might have seen something the morning Jeremiah was taken," Caroline said. "A policeman. Stopping by the mailbox."

"That's it?" Robertson asked.

"The girl's only six," Caroline said. "The family knows to take things slowly, if she is going to be able to remember anything more."

Branden sat more upright in his leather chair and took up an earlier point. "It's not that they wouldn't sell land, Bruce. Rather, they've been slow to come to the conclusion that they might actually have to do it. Slow to pray it through. Cautious.

Thinking slowly. Not knowing what to do, or whom to trust. For all they know, one of us might have the boy. English are English, so to speak."

Caroline said, "I agree. There's not a soul out there who doesn't want to see Jeremiah brought home. From what the women have said, they've checked with the families in the district. Totaled their funds."

"And?" Robertson asked, while noting that Branden had taken the ransom notes and was studying them, slouched again in his leather chair.

"And there isn't a family who would withhold a cent. The Millers have got the funds. All they have to do is ask, and dozens of buggies would appear in their yard that very day, cash in hand."

"A hundred thousand?" the sheriff asked.

"More if they needed it. Everybody's waiting for the bishop to decide."

"He wouldn't spend a hundred thousand to save his grandson?" Robertson asked.

"He feels he's responsible for deciding if the safety of one is to be balanced against the well-being of all," Caroline said.

Robertson grimaced as if he thought the decision obvious. He watched curiously as Branden read the ransom notes.

"We've still got Jeff Hostettler," Deputy Schrauzer offered.

"I've always liked him for this one," Robertson said. "How's this sound for our precious Amish saints? The way Hostettler tells it, Brenda Hostettler tried talking to Eli Miller before she killed herself. She begged him to send after Jonah. Figured it was her only way of getting him back. Brenda Hostettler begged Eli Miller to ask his son home. And Miller wouldn't so much as lift a finger."

Caroline answered, "They lead separated lives for a reason. You can't have part of the Amish and not the whole."

"This is one part of the Amish I can do without."

"It's their faith, Bruce."

"No, Caroline, I'm sorry. It's a boy's life," Robertson said, quarrelsome. "Mike, I want you to tell me why I shouldn't charge you for not reporting the missing kid the first thing you knew about him."

Branden rose, paced along the windows and defended himself. "As far back as we go, Bruce, you're not going to charge me with anything."

"How about interfering with a sheriff's investigation?" Robertson griped.

"You didn't have an investigation involving the boy."

"That's my point, Professor. I should have had one."

"When I first got involved in this matter, there was only a family dispute, maybe not even that, over Jermiah's spending time with his father. Bishop Miller would have denied there was a problem, if I had taken the matter to you. We know that now, because of the ransom notes. His entire approach was to try to find the boy without drawing attention to the search."

"Doesn't matter," Robertson said. "You knew there was a problem once Jonah turned up dead. You should have brought the case to me then, at the very least."

"The bishop wouldn't let me."

"Oh, that's supposed to impress me?" Robertson shot back.

"At that point, at most, it was a case of a missing child. And the bishop told me he'd deny the matter if I talked to you. Now we know why. The ransom deadline hadn't expired. I didn't know that then, but I made a judgment call. Either I could bring you in, and lose the Millers' cooperation, or I could try to do some good in the three days Miller had given me. And what if it had been someone close to the Millers who had the boy? Then what, Bruce? At the most, you can charge me with bad judgment."

"You concealed a kidnapping."

"That's not true!" Branden snapped. "I brought you the case the first thing after I knew about the kidnapping. Ask Niell."

Robertson shouted, "Mike, I swear I'm gonna . . . ," and stopped.

Branden turned from the windows and squared up to the sheriff, heated.

"OK," Robertson said. "OK," the intensity rinsing out of him quickly.

Branden relaxed and stood by the windows. Then he crossed the room and lifted a water-soaked matchbook from the evidence scattered across the sheriff's desk. "You said most of this stuff from the truck comes from Port Clinton?"

"The truck's registered in Texas, but everything in it comes from Port Clinton and places around the bass islands," Robertson said.

Branden saw the traces of a satisfied smile on Robertson's face. "What are those keys?" Branden asked, indicating a set on the sheriff's desk, chained to a small red and white plastic float that resembled a marine buoy.

"He had a boat on Lake Erie," Robertson said, "and a trailer hitch on the truck to match."

"Then someone's going to have to go up there," Branden said. "How about you and me?"

"Not me," Robertson said with a chortle. "I've got to be here, working with the FBI." A broad smile appeared on his face. It was a smile that said, "I've been ahead of you all along, Professor."

"You called in the FBI?" Branden said, sounding incredulous. "We're too close, now, to have to stop and bring the FBI up to speed."

"I've got no choice, Mike. Kidnapping's a federal offense. That's what Ellie's been working on."

Branden remembered the note Robertson had handed Ellie and said, "The FBI will not go about this the right way, Bruce. Not with the Amish."

"Not down here, they won't," Robertson chuckled. "As soon as they move into this case, we'll have to do things their way, here. I figure that'll be later tonight. At the moment, I've got Wilsher camped out at the Millers, and I've still to hear what the Miller girl might have seen. I'm not very hopeful, but most of our leads come from the items we recovered from that truck, and they all indicate Jonah Miller was living and working near Port Clinton. We've got restaurant matchbooks. Rent receipts. Boat repairs. Marine fuel receipts. Everything points to that."

"And?"

"And, Professor," Robertson said, "by the time the FBI gets anything out of the Millers, and then manages to drag the rest of it out of me, you and Deputy Niell, there," nodding smugly at the door behind them, "will have had about a half-day head start, up on the lake."

They turned to the door and saw the deputy, equipped thoroughly for the work the sheriff had scribbled down earlier for Ellie. In his left hand he carried a bulking black canvas duffel. On his feet were high-lacing black leather boots. He was dressed otherwise in his gray and black Holmes County Deputy Sheriff's uniform with gold trim and insignias. In his right hand he carried a Colt Gold Cup .45 ACP pistol mounted in a black leather shoulder harness with extra magazines. His sheriff deputy's service revolver was strapped to his belt, as were a double set of speed loaders, handcuffs, flashlight, and a canister of mace.

"I'm beginning to like that Ellie Troyer," Robertson commented dryly. "Girl knows how to follow orders."

24

Thursday, June 25
11:30 P.M.

AGENT Stan Walters, FBI, was trying his best to control his temper, but he felt a growing impatience with Sheriff Robertson. He had spent two inactive hours in the sheriff's office, and although the Amish lore and the sheriff's concern that matters be handled correctly made sense to Stan, he also realized that a good portion of those two hours had been "down time." Time when the sheriff had not been focused on task. In truth, Stan Walters thought, they could have been out here much sooner. OK, so they weren't locals, but really, two hours to bring them up to speed on the kidnapping and to give him advice about how to handle Amish folk? Either the sheriff and Ellie Troyer had been stalling, or they simply hadn't gotten with the program. All right, a man had been killed. A cowboy, from what they had said, dressed Amish. And OK, he thought, that clearly connected up with the kidnapping. But really, sheriff, he thought, you could have given me that much on the ride out.

Walters was thin, five-ten, dark-haired, and dressed in a plain gray suit, white shirt, and a simple red tie. His hair was cut medium short, combed neatly, and evidently always stayed that way. His badge was out on the breast pocket of his suit, and he held a cell phone in his left hand. He switched it off and pushed past Robertson in the dark, having decided enough was enough.

He mounted the wooden steps onto the Millers' front porch

in near-total darkness. Agent Jim Galloway followed. Walters fumbled for a doorbell for a confusing moment and then settled for a few soft raps on the screen door. "Are you sure they're going to be home?" Galloway asked from the steps.

Robertson, standing wordlessly down on the lawn in front of the large porch, might have laughed if he hadn't spent the last two hours with the FBI, trying to explain to them how best to handle the Amish.

These two had arrived at nine. Ricky Niell and Mike Branden had left earlier, by seven. By nine thirty, whatever else might happen that night, Robertson had promised himself resolutely that he would not take Walters and Galloway out to the Millers' until close to midnight. Maybe later. Perhaps not even until tomorrow.

From the front lawn, Robertson spoke softly up to the porch, "Walters, this is not the way." He shook his head in the dark.

Walters turned to knock again on the door. As he raised his knuckles, a match was struck behind the screen, and he stepped back, startled, as it flared. The silk mantle caught on a Coleman lantern, and he stepped closer to the screen and saw Isaac Miller in denim trousers, his suspenders hanging down.

"Stan Walters, FBI," he announced and showed his badge. He pulled the screen door open from the outside and started to move inside, but Isaac held his position at the threshold with the lantern at shoulder height, the light glaring directly into Walters's eyes. Galloway moved a step closer. Walters stopped, surprised and confused, and the screen door closed gently against his back.

"I said, FBI," he said again. He was here from Columbus because he had a reputation for handling delicate matters with soft hands, but Walters found himself put out that the people here were not responding to his authority in the way he had come to expect. Still, he recognized the irritation that was mounting in him, and he choked it back. Stay cool, he thought.

Isaac held a blank expression and did not move.

Robertson moved forward on the lawn below and came into the edge of the light thrown by the lantern. He caught Isaac's gaze and shook his head. Walters saw Isaac glance past him to Robertson and turned in the doorway to say, "Tell him, please, Sheriff. We are here to help."

Robertson said, "These agents are from Columbus, Isaac. They're from the Federal Bureau of Investigation."

When Agent Walters turned again to face Isaac, a woman in a long plain dress and white apron had appeared behind him. To the woman he said, "Ma'am, can we please get started."

Robertson motioned silently for Isaac, and waited for him on the lawn in front of the porch. Isaac glanced briefly back at his mother, set the lantern down inside the house, hooked up his suspenders with a swing of each shoulder, and came out to the sheriff, who drew him aside in the dark, whispered in German dialect, and sent him off. Then Robertson came lazily up the steps.

Walters studied the woman in front of him. White chambray prayer cap, tied under her chin. Pleated high-necked dress of surf turquoise. White apron. A small girl came forward, in a long nightshirt, and stood slightly behind her mother, barefoot.

"Your granddaughter?" Walters asked, trying to sound pleasant.

"My daughter, Mr. Walters."

Walters said, "Again, Ma'am, I'm with the FBI. This is agent Galloway." He held out his hand.

Mrs. Miller shook it gently, politely, somewhat bashfully.

Still on the threshold, with the screen door pressed against his back, Walters asked, "Are you Mrs. Miller?"

"Yes," she said. "Bishop Miller is my husband."

As she said this, Walters heard the hooves of a horse pound furiously on the drive and then fade on the lane. He turned to look back, saw nothing in the dark, and then held the door open for Galloway. Robertson stepped forward onto the porch and watched intently through the screen, curious to see how Gertie would handle the FBI.

"As I understand it, Mrs. Miller, it is your grandson, then, who is being ransomed."

Gertie Miller agreed with the slightest nod of her head. She looked out to Sheriff Robertson with both puzzlement and concern. She drew her daughter closer to her and waited.

Walters eased himself a bit further into the doorway, and Mrs. Miller stepped back. He said, "Can we talk inside, Mrs. Miller?" and motioned for Galloway to follow.

"The bishop's not here presently," Gertie said and waited. The young girl at her side watched Walters curiously from behind her mother's dress.

Walters said again, "Where can we talk?" and looked around in the dim light of the Coleman lantern on the floor. He, Galloway, Gertie Miller, and her daughter all stood just inside the door in the front hall, with Isaac's propane lantern glowing at their feet. Galloway felt for a light switch beside the door and then let his hand fall to his side, embarrassed.

Gertie Miller looked blankly at Agent Walters. She acknowledged the sheriff with a bashful look, picked up the Coleman lantern, ushered her daughter outside, came slowly down the steps, and turned to stand peacefully with her little girl under the branches of the large oak. Walters and Galloway followed her down the steps.

"As I have said," she said politely, "the bishop is not home just this minute. Perhaps we can do our talking out here."

"Mrs. Miller. The FBI is here to help in rescuing your grandson," Galloway said. "Jeremiah, as the sheriff has told us. How long has he been missing?"

"A few weeks, already," Gertie said, and "I'm sure you'll be wanting to speak with the bishop."

Walters knelt to try with the girl, but the child eased out of his reach.

Gertie Miller calmly laid her hand on her daughter's shoulder and spoke a few words in German dialect. She stood erect beside the lantern and said, "The bishop will be along, directly, Mr. Walters. I'd rather we didn't wake the other children."

Robertson, standing to the side with his hat in his hands, listened with great interest.

A match sputtered and caught behind him. A lantern was lit, and a man dressed in Amish style came forward toward Robertson, greeted him with a gentle hand on his shoulder, and stood beside the sheriff.

"Andy," Robertson said in a greeting tone.

"Sheriff."

Galloway came over and asked, "Bishop Miller?"

Andy Yoder shook his head "no."

Another lantern flared to life under the oak. A buggy came up the drive, the harness jangling and the horse snorting in front of a whip.

To the driver Galloway said, "Are you Eli Miller?"

"Yes," softly.

"Bishop Miller?"

"That would be Eli P. Miller."

Galloway shook his head and almost laughed. He gave Walters a wry look that said, "How are we going to sort this out, Stan?"

More men arrived. More lanterns glowed. Eight in all, and now agents Walters and Galloway stood in the center of a ring of Amish lights under a heavy oak tree, after midnight, on the lawn in front of the Miller home. The light fell on Walters and was amplified by the heavy green canopy of the oak overhead and by the glistening lawn.

A horse, galloping on the lane beyond the picket fence,

slowed and turned into the drive. Walters watched as Isaac slid off and whispered to Robertson in German.

Then Robertson allowed himself the faintest of smiles and said, "Agent Walters, I'd be more than happy to introduce you to Bishop Miller."

The bishop emerged from beyond the ring of lanterns and stood beside his wife.

"OK. Mr. Miller. Bishop," Walters said, "We are here to help find your grandson."

Robertson showed no reaction. Inside, privately, he celebrated the small victory of his last few hours. Niell and Branden would surely be at Port Clinton by now. Isaac had gathered the district, and Gertie Miller, unprepared, had nevertheless handled the FBI as he had hoped she would. Distrusting the law. Yielding to her husband, who now stood before the two agents in his everyday denim suit.

Walters said, "Your wife preferred to wait for you to arrive."

"She recognizes my authority," the bishop answered and smiled at his wife.

"Please, Mr. Miller. We need to ask you both a few questions."

"I am her husband."

"I understand that. "

"And bishop."

"Which means?"

"Which means, I answer to a higher authority."

Walters said, "I appreciate that, Mr. Miller, but we need to get started. In truth, we need your help, if we are to help you. You do want to find your grandson?"

"Of course," Miller said.

Galloway tried, "We want to bring your grandson home to you, Mr. Miller."

Miller thought about that for a moment and said, "We are powerless to save, if the Lord will not."

Walters studied the bishop's eyes. They remained steady, peaceful.

Miller spoke briefly in soft, authoritative German and the lanterns were shut off around the circle, leaving only the one at the feet of Gertie Miller. The bishop reached down to it and turned it off as well and said, "I trust you'll allow us a moment to ourselves," and left Robertson, Galloway, and Walters under the oak with their retinas glowing white from memory of the light.

Robertson quietly stood his post on the lawn, satisfied.

Walters asked, "What do you think they are doing?"

Robertson said, "Praying, Agent Walters," and added, "I reckon we'll have to do things their way for a spell."

Then Robertson turned and ambled over the low hill beside the big house, leaving Walters and Galloway under the oaks, listening alone in the dark to the opening strains of a German martyr hymn rising from the bank barn where Jeremiah Miller had first met his father.

25

BRANDEN cast off from the marina on Catawba Island Peninsula, dressed in jeans, sneakers, and a green and white Millersburg College sweatshirt. He started the engine of the Bayliner and pointed it out into the waters of Lake Erie. He waved to Ricky Niell, heading up the marina steps to return to Port Clinton, where they had spent the night after their hurried drive north.

They had first called the neighboring Marblehead police station, but their only response, both last night and this morning, had been a recorded message. At breakfast, Branden had called the marina where Jonah Miller's Bayliner was docked for repairs. He had gotten directions. Route 163 East to 269, and then north onto the Catawba Island Peninsula.

Then he had called Tarshish Construction. Yes, they employed Jon Mills. Certainly, he could talk with Ray Tarshish, the owner of the construction company, but he'd have to get himself out to the condo project on the islands.

At the marina on the Catawba Peninsula, Niell, in uniform, had presented the boat's registration, with the keys on Jonah Miller's buoy keychain, explaining that the late Jon Mills was a murder victim in a case they were investigating for the Holmes County Sheriff's Department. Niell had paid the repair bills with cash that Robertson had instructed Ellie Troyer to give him the evening before, and the marina had released Jonah's boat.

Branden eased the boat away from the docks, out through the narrow channel between the break walls, and into the larger waters among the islands, sharing the channel with the last of the fishing guides who puttered out of West Harbor in single file and then jammed into high once clear of the break walls, racing with their customers to sweet holes near the islands where the walleye were known to be running. The ferries had begun their rounds, stopping near Perry's Monument at Put-in-Bay and at Kelleys Island to the east.

Once clear of the channel, Branden made for Middle Bass Island. Far to the west he could make out the inverted cone evaporator at the Davis-Besse nuclear power plant and its white plumes of steam against blue sky. To the southeast, the entrance to Sandusky Harbor was obscured by the Marblehead Peninsula. The famous roller coasters at Cedar Point stood out above the trees, the view in the eastern distance fading into a hazy blur in the morning sun.

As he motored to the island, Branden was keenly aware that he traveled the same waters as the great Commodore Oliver Hazard Perry, who had defeated the British fleet northwest of Put-in-Bay, in September of 1813. The professor in him came to the fore, and he found himself reciting Perry's famous dispatch announcing the end of the War of 1812 in the North: "We have met the enemy and they are ours."

Branden tied up at the construction site on Middle Bass Island's eastern shore and scrambled onto a floating pier. As he steadied himself on the slow-rolling platform, gentle waves broke on the shore. He caught the smell of sea grass and rotting driftwood as the water rose and fell, teasing a jumbled pile of floating debris along the shore. He stepped off the pier onto a black stone and gray boulder beach where a trail began at the base of cliffs, leading up about thirty feet to a construction site hugging the edge of the bluff. There was a sign indicating that Tarshish Construction was putting up luxury condos. The trail branched, the left fork offering a direct and steep ascent, while the right led along the shore several paces to a scaffolding with an elevator cage and crane.

He took the steeper trail to the left, which skirted the face of the cliff at an angle. After forging his way to the top, he paused to catch his breath while looking out across the water, now serenely blue-green. On the horizon, he saw one of the massive ore boats riding high in the water, empty, bow pointed west. Branden turned to face the condos under construction in a narrow glade between the edge of the cliffs and the island's vineyards to the rear.

The site was filled with the sounds and smells of construction. There were shrill, ripping screams from a dozen power saws and the clatter of rapping hammers. A fire barrel gave off slow curls of smoke.

At the far end, the last unit had been framed out, windowed, and roofed only recently. In units closer, electricians and plumbers were busy with their various tasks. Closer still, drywallers worked in units nine and ten. Roofers were laying shingles on units fifteen and sixteen.

The units to his left looked nearer to completion and showed the gray and white vinyl siding and scarlet roofing that the other units eventually would wear. Under all the units, the white concrete block foundations, painted with black waterproofing compound, had long since been laid. They were still exposed, surrounded by jumbled piles of dirt, rock, cast-off lumber scraps, metal sheeting, concrete block fragments, torn roofing shingles, empty cans of roofing cement, and bottles, pop cans, and paper lunch bags. Wooden planks had been laid in several directions over the muddy debris.

Branden started at the first unit, found it empty, and moved to unit two. There he found a carpenter working alone on molding trim. He was Eric Sutton, an older, slender, weathered man who had known Jon Mills, and took the news of his death hard.

Branden stood near the large window in the front room of the unit, gazing out awkwardly past pink manufacturer's stickers on dirty glass. Sutton stood in the back room, in an efficiency-style kitchen separated from the living room by an unfinished counter where bar stools would be used. Sutton had his hands planted on the countertop, elbows locked, shaking his head at the news. Branden wished he had handled it better. That he'd somehow managed to bring the news to Sutton more gently.

"You say his name wasn't Jon?" Sutton asked, studying the countertop.

"He changed his name to Jon Mills, evidently down in Texas, but he was born Jonah Miller, in Millersburg," Branden explained. He turned from the window and studied Sutton, who was dressed in a flannel shirt with the sleeves torn off, jeans, and work boots. Sutton had a heavy leather tool belt strapped to his waist.

"How did he die?" Sutton asked, straightening up and facing Branden.

"Shot," Branden said. "Down in Holmes County."

"That's where his son came from," Sutton remarked absently.

Branden took an involuntary step forward. "You know Jeremiah?"

"Jon called him Jerry. Or Little Jer. Saw him once or twice, when he first came up here, and then saw a bit more of him lately," Sutton replied. "Jon'd bring him to work sometimes."

"Can you tell me about him?"

"What was he doing back in Millersburg?" Sutton asked, shaken.

"We think he was going home with his son," Branden said, and then tried again with, "What can you tell me about Jeremiah?"

Sutton acquired a distant look in his eyes and then said, "I never knew he had a son until a month ago."

He slipped his hammer out of its loop on the tool belt, pried a bent nail out of a length of red oak trim, tossed the nail to the floor, and threw the trim into the front room. Then Sutton shook his head, disbelieving. "We both signed on with Ray in Texas. Trim carpenters in a boom town. Got any idea how good construction work is in a boom town?"

Branden didn't.

"Plenty good, let me tell ya. But, when the oil went bust, Tarshish went bankrupt, and moved here to the lakes to start over. Lately, it hasn't been boom-town great, but at least it's been steady."

"I'm hoping to find Tarshish here today."

"He'll be along," Sutton replied, and returned to his work in the kitchen. Branden stood in the front room and watched Sutton, thinking.

In the kitchen, along a vertical seam between a cabinet and a wall, Sutton drew out his tape rule, noted the length, snapped the rule into its case, slid the metal case onto its hook on his tool belt, and came around the counter into the front room. From a stack of red oak trim, he selected a piece of suitable length. At the table saw, he made quick marks with a carpenter's pencil, blew sawdust off the top of the saw, threw the switch, made two precise cuts, and immediately shut power to the blade.

As the blade whined to a stop, Sutton lifted his hammer out of its belt loop, and, back in the kitchen, carefully pried the defective trim from its place. He tossed the flawed trim onto the floor, and inserted the new piece.

Two gentle taps with his hammer started the first nail, and

two more started the second. His eyes fluttered and closed part-way against the dust he had made. He squinted in the direct sun, guided the new piece into position, drove the nails home, reached for a counter punch from his belt pouch, sank the nails, and stepped back. His arms dropped listlessly to his side, and he turned to study Branden. The table saw had run to a stop, leaving the room quiet except for the shuffle of Sutton's boots on the plywood flooring. The slight haze of rising saw-dust glinted in the rays of the morning sun as it broke through the front window at an angle. Branden caught the aroma of freshly cut oak.

"I can't tell you all that much about the boy," Sutton resumed. "One day Jon said that he was going to 'fetch his son.' Wouldn't be back for a few days." Sutton shrugged. "First I'd heard of a son."

Branden suppressed an urge to question. Eventually Sutton continued.

"But I can tell you plenty about Mills. Miller. Whatever." He shook his head.

Branden waited.

"Jon Mills was a true-born master carpenter. Must have grown up with it. He loved wood, and he was good at it. That's why Tarshish brought him up from Texas."

Sutton fought back a tightening in his throat, cleared it with an awkward cough, and continued. "And Tarshish brought me along because Mills insisted.

"Jon was good at only two things. Carpentry like I said, and drinking. Flat wore me out. Between his drinking and his friends, Jon just flat wore me out."

"His friends?"

"Jon might have been good with wood, but he didn't know the first thing about people. Trusted everyone. Had no sense who was good people and who wasn't. He ran with the worst there was. Almost like a compulsion. It was a wonder he got any work done at all. Seemed to burn it at both ends. Drink nights and work days, and he never missed a beat. Like he was showboatin'. You know, show up drunk or hung over, and still tie a knot in your spine.

"Then, sometime after his son came up—that was over a month now—Jon's work started to suffer. Sometimes he'd show up, but he was distracted. Like he was making a decision. Last week or so, it was awful. I never saw Jon do a piece of bad work before, drunk or sober, but look at this junk. I'm cleaning up after him here. Ray had to put him on roofing."

Sutton made an expression of mild disgust and went to work in a second corner of the kitchen, on another length of red oak trim that didn't suit him. With the measurements committed to memory, he went to the uncut wood pile, selected another piece, cut it to length at the saw, and then double-checked the angles. Back in the kitchen, he worked the flawed trim loose from its position and tossed the reject into the front room to join the first one. With a knife from the back loop of his carpenter's belt, he shaved off the slightest bit of wood, and, four nails later, the second repair was finished.

As he stepped around the kitchen counter, they heard the sputter of an engine down at the pier. "That'll be Tarshish," he said. "I recognize his engine."

Branden looked through the window briefly, then turned back to Sutton and said, "Why do you think his work deteriorated? Was it having his son here?"

Sutton thought and then said, hesitantly, "I don't think that was it. At least, not entirely. Not at first."

"But?"

"Might have been something else, I don't know. The kid was awful troublesome at first. Someone had to watch him all the time. Jon was real worried the boy wasn't going to take to him. Wasn't going to adjust to having a dad, you know. Then he eventually warmed up to Jon, and they started acting more like a family. At least as much like a family as Jon Mills could ever've managed. They did the kinds of things you'd want to see a father and son do together. Fishing out on the lake. Amusement parks. Sometimes he'd bring the kid to work. Now that I think about it, lately Jon hasn't been drinking. Hadn't been drinking." Sutton shook his head as he remembered that his friend was really gone. "I figure they got two good weeks together."

"Where did the boy stay?" Branden asked, fighting an urge to push.

"Someone watched him. I'm not sure," Sutton said, turning back to his work. "Look, I'll think about it, OK? Maybe I'll come up with something. But if it's all the same to you, I need to get some work done here."

26

RAY Tarshish, short and rotund, bounced over the rough two-by-four planks, up toward unit two, carrying several tight rolls of building plans under his arm, springing the boards with each of his awkward steps. The planks set up a swaying motion in rhythm with his gait, causing him to wobble out of balance. He teetered awkwardly on his stocky legs, saved himself at the last only by grabbing for the door frame with his free hand, and pulled himself into the unit.

After a curious nod acknowledging Branden's presence, Tarshish took out a large red handkerchief and wiped perspiration from his round face, dabbed at the top of his bald head, and paced a slow circle in the front room of the condo to catch his breath.

Eric Sutton interrupted his work to introduce Tarshish to Branden. He briefly explained about Jon Mills, leaving Branden to supply the details. Tarshish cried out at the news, dropped his blueprints in a corner, and stepped to the window, shaken.

His breathing had regulated somewhat, but a hard pulse beat in his temples. His shirt had come undone beneath his belly, so he unfastened his belt, smoothed out the shirttail, tucked in as much as he could manage, and sucked in heavily to fasten his pants and then his belt, saying, "I knew he had changed his first name, but his last name wasn't Mills?"

"Miller," Branden said. "Jonah Miller, but he evidently changed it to Jon Mills in Texas."

"We knew him as Jon."

"You first met him in Texas?" Branden asked.

"Yes, I believe it was Texas," Ray said distantly. After a moment with his thoughts, Tarshish said, "Funny how you forget."

He paused.

"When we first met, Jon said he had changed his name because it suited Texans better. Must have meant Jon versus Jonah. Same reason I started using Ray. For the Texans. Much better than Raymonde, don't you think?"

Tarshish held a position at the front window and stood with his hands in his pockets, looking vacantly down to the silver-green water meeting an advancing bank of heavy gray clouds. Nearer shore, the water had taken on a dirtier khaki hue. Whitecaps dotted the lake. His mind struggled with the news of Jon Mill's death.

Distracted, Tarshish said, "Tarshish is a Spanish name, and Ray is short for Raymonde, and Texans like it simple. My people fled Iran after the Shah.

"Can you imagine that," Ray said and turned from the window. "We were Spanish Christians, living in Iran, and fled to Texas. Jon used to say we were both running from an Ayatollah. I think it would have helped if I had known his name was Jonah. Like in the Bible."

At the window again, standing with Branden, Tarshish watched the clouds gather over the lake, and remembered.

Branden waited.

Tarshish sorted through his memories sadly, taking his time, and finally spoke.

"Texans," Ray said, shaking his head, using a tone that pronounced them all scoundrels. "But Jon loved it down there." Then, "I'm the one who brought him back to Ohio," spoken as a self-indictment.

"Jon was a fancy dresser. Fancy western clothes. The fancier the better." He turned to Branden and asked, "Any idea why?"

Branden said, "Jon was raised Amish," and remembered the teacher, Miss Beachey, and her story of a rebellious Amish lad, rolling a tight cuff in his denim jeans.

Tarshish looked puzzled.

Branden explained. "For religious reasons, the Amish strive to be plain, both in dress and in lifestyle. They are farmers, mostly in Ohio and Pennsylvania."

"They drive those buggies?" Tarshish asked.

Branden nodded.

"Did you know he had a son?" Tarshish asked.

"Yes," Branden said. "He'd only recently learned that."

Tarshish gathered up his building plans and motioned for Branden to walk with him outside. They stood for some time at the edge of the cliffs, looking over the water as the wind built and the temperature dropped. Ray talked about Jon Mills, his recent announcement that he had a son, and the change that Mills had undergone, for the better, once he had brought the boy up to the lake. The good influence the boy had been on him at first. Before the startling decline in Jon's work.

He turned to face Branden and said, "Jon changed once his son had been here for a while. It was a marvelous thing to see. He stopped drinking so much. Started cleaning up his language. Then one night he showed up at my house over in Port Clinton. Wanted to know if I knew any preachers."

"Did you?"

"I sent him to see Father Timothy at St. Mary's."

"Do you know if he went?"

"I think he did, but he also disappeared soon after that. Now you tell me he's dead."

Branden questioned Tarshish further about Jon and Jeremiah. He learned that they had lived in a trailer along the water west of Lakeside, that Jeremiah had stayed there with an older lady when Jon was at work, that Jeremiah had seemed hostile at first and then more content, eventually even happy, or so it had seemed to Tarshish, to stay with Jon for the summer.

But, the last Ray Tarshish remembered of Jon Mills, he had changed. He had asked about a preacher, turned inward, and left town shortly after.

As they stood together on the cliffs, Branden's mind carried the image of a man who had walked into a general store in Fredericksburg and bought a new suit of plain Amish clothes. A man changed for the better by an Amish boy of ten, camped beside a truck in the swamps of the Killbuck Marsh.

27

THE Marblehead Police Station occupied a corner room in a boxy building made of white quarry stone. A square patch of grass in front served as a tidy spot, close to the road, for a flag pole and a small black-and-white sign. A faded page taped to the door suggested that the station was infrequently staffed. The parking spot for a single cruiser was vacant. On the door, there was a number for the mayor's secretary in the event the police were ever needed.

Ricky Niell took one of his business cards from the neatly creased breast pocket on his uniform shirt, wrote a note asking that he be contacted at the Water's Edge Motel in Port Clinton, indicated it was an urgent matter involving a missing child, and dropped it through the "Pay Fines" slot in the door. On another of his cards he copied down the phone number of the mayor's secretary. He tried the doorknob one more time, cupped his hands around his eyes, and bent forward to take a last disapproving look through the glass. Then he climbed high into his black 4x4. There were remote-operated spotlights mounted on a silver roll bar, and a full bar of flashers on the cab. The aftermarket lifters put the running boards a good three feet off the pavement.

He rolled out in low gear onto the highway, cruised slowly westward, and turned into the parking lot at the Marblehead

Coast Guard Station, adjacent to a ferry landing. He backed the truck into one of the spots marked for visitors, shut down the engine, and watched the ferry from Kelleys Island make its docking. As the ferry gates came down, motorcycles roared to life and several dozen bikers in leather jackets sped away, two at a time, past the Coast Guard Station, shouting back and forth over the noise of their engines. Inside the modern brick Coast Guard structure, Niell reported to the command center and asked for the Officer of the Day.

An officer standing behind the counter said, "I'm Chief Petty Officer Johnson," looking at him inquiringly while keeping part of his attention on the bikers. Two Seamen lounged in chairs behind the counter. A large window behind them gave a view of the docks below, where two Coast Guard boats strained on their lines in tall, surging waves. Kelleys Island stood out on the horizon beyond. Niell presented his credentials and explained his search for the missing Jeremiah Miller, beginning with the murder of Jeremiah's father, and ending with the ransom scheme that still hadn't worked itself to a conclusion.

The radio claimed CPO Johnson's attention. He eyed one of the young men seated behind him and tilted his head toward Niell. In response, an affable young man stepped out from behind the counter and introduced himself to Niell as Seaman Munson.

As they shook hands, Seaman Munson drew him a few paces away from the radio and said, "You said you're on a kidnapping case?" with obvious interest. He had friendly eyes and a confident manner.

Niell replied simply, "Yes," and fixed his gaze on the boats docked below the window.

Munson ran his eyes along Niell's line of sight, turned back and asked, "You want a tour?"

Niell glanced at CPO Johnson, still busy at the radio, shrugged and said, "Sure, maybe a quick one." They descended a set of gray steps to the basement and walked out onto the lower level toward the dock. The last of the bikers cleared the landing. On board the first boat, Munson started in the wheel room, pointing out electronic equipment, radios, navigation electronics, sirens, and the like, all with obvious pride.

"This is a forty-one," Munson announced. He showed Niell belowdecks and then onto the stern, where he opened an engine compartment amidships and said, with one eyebrow cocked and a grand smile, "Twin Cummings, 903s."

He closed the engine-room hatch and remarked, "The forty-one will eat up eight-footers all day long," indicating waves on the lake by rolling a curving palm in the air.

"You call it a cruiser?" Niell asked.

"UTB. It's a Utility Boat. A forty-one," Munson explained. "The number indicates length. This is a forty-one-foot UTB. Number 443. UTB 41-443."

The boat was spotless, painted white and deck gray, with an orange and blue Coast Guard stripe slanting along its bow. The waves came relentlessly into the small harbor, and rocked the UTB again and again. Munson stood with pride on the stern and let his legs carry the swells. Niell steadied himself against a rail as Munson locked the engine hatch. "And if I should need to call the Coast Guard?" Niell asked, thinking again of Jeremiah.

Munson led him back into the wheelhouse and tapped the radio console. "Start out on VHF/FM Channel 16. That's 156.80, the International Hail and Distress Frequency. Then we'll probably switch you to 21."

Then Munson pointed out the boat in the second slip. "That's a Raider 22. Hostage rescue, that kind of thing. Our antiterrorist units train up here on the lake. You can cut that boat in half and it'll still float. Still run its guns on half a deck."

Back at the command center, Munson returned Niell to CPO Johnson. Johnson agreed to monitor LEERN on the scanner next to his desk for any news from the Marblehead or Port Clinton police and reassured Niell that they'd get a line on all of the law enforcement radio traffic, one way or another.

Neill thanked CPO Johnson and Seaman Munson. He was about to head for the door, but on impulse returned to the counter and asked, "What can you tell me about the Marblehead Police?"

Seaman Munson smiled openly. CPO Johnson chuckled and punched out a number on his telephone, got a recording, and put it on a loudspeaker. "That's about all you're gonna get out of Marblehead," he commented over the recording of the voice of the mayor's secretary.

"Sheriff Robertson was going to phone ahead this morning," Niell said. "To try to talk to the various departments in the area. I was expecting to find someone at the station, if Robertson got the word out, that is."

Johnson smiled, stopped to take a call, hung up, came around the counter and said, "There's only one policeman at the Marblehead station. One cruiser and one parking spot. You've been there?"

"Just now."

"Then you've seen the whole operation. Not a big department."

"Who's the one officer, and how does he handle three shifts?" Niell asked.

"He doesn't try," Munson said and chuckled. "They just keep a sign on the door when he's not in."

"I've seen it."

"Whoever needs police is supposed to know that number," Munson said. "Otherwise, they get cooperation from the force at Port Clinton. It's a good relationship and Paul does a good job considering he's the only one."

"Paul would be the policeman at Marblehead?" Niell asked.

"Yes. Paul Lively," Johnson said. "He's got a cottage at Lakeside and a boat at a small marina on East Harbor. Sometimes he guides. Fishing."

Niell got out his notebook and copied down addresses for the cottage and the boat dock.

"If Paul's not at home," Munson added, "then he's either gone fishing, in which case you'll have to wait until dark, or he's having breakfast at Big Boppers."

Niell gave him a look.

"It's a small family restaurant, back down 163 about two miles on the right. A favorite with the locals."

CPO Johnson took another call.

Niell flipped in his notebook to the page with the address for Jon Mills and got directions from the seaman. On the way out to his truck, he watched the ferry make another landing in noticeably rougher seas. A steady line of tourist traffic had accumulated on Highway 163. Most of it lazily followed the highway to Marblehead at the end of the peninsula, turned around, and joined the line of traffic in the reverse direction.

Niell pulled out onto the highway amid the traffic, found the Big Bopper, and checked the gravel parking lot, out front and in the back, for the Marblehead police cruiser, with negative results.

Then he worked his way slowly along North Shore Boulevard, heading back toward Lakeside, checking the small street signs for the road where Munson had said Jonah Miller's trailer should be parked.

It was a single, gravel lane, little more than two tire tracks and a middle line of weeds, running toward the water on East Harbor. He waited out in front for a car to clear the lane and then turned in.

At the end of the lane, behind a group of dilapidated summer cottages in an old orchard, he found a single-wide trailer parked at the very edge of the bay, abutting a disorderly pile of broken concrete pavement slabs that had been dumped to make a seawall. Small wooden steps gave access over the concrete slabs to the water, where there was a private dock labeled with a weather-beaten sign stating that the dock was reserved for the exclusive use of the cottage residents. The placard carried the usual warnings about trespassers, prosecution, and the full extent of the law.

Niell climbed back over the seawall and stepped around to the trailer, which he found to be locked. He thought about forcing the door and then decided against it. Instead, he searched outside.

The trailer was old, aluminum sided, and had small awnings hung over smaller windows. A short TV antenna was strapped haphazardly to one end. The aluminum siding, dented and stained heavily with tree sap and bark dust, was done in a light green-and-white style that had been popular in the fifties. The tongue of the trailer rested on a leaning pile of concrete blocks, and the rubber tires were blocked off the ground by rusted iron pyramid braces that carried the weight of the axles. The corners of the trailer were also braced with concrete blocks that long ago had settled into the sand. A few ill-tended apple trees in back had dropped more than one season of dirty branches, fruit, and blossoms on an unkempt yard. Two fishing poles stood against the back of the trailer, lines tangled. He checked each of the windows. None of them permitted him a view inside.

He bent over and studied the storage space under the trailer. A rusty barbecue grill and a scattering of broken boat parts had been stuffed there long ago. Nothing recently. Back at his truck, he reached in for a camera on the front seat, snapped several pictures of the trailer, climbed over the broken slabs of the seawall, and stood on the boat dock to take several more pictures of the area. The bay opened to the west where clouds had started to gather in profusion. Boat traffic coming in off the lake congested the channel around the small rocky island guarding the entrance to the bay.

Back at the truck, Niell dropped the camera onto the front seat, stepped around intending to make another inspection of the trailer, and was greeted by a middle-aged woman in overalls, who offered her hand and said, "Officer, I'm Melanie Brikker. My husband and I run this place. Landlords."

Niell shook her hand and said, "Deputy Ricky Niell."

"I'm not really supposed to let anyone other than tenants on the docks," Melanie said, "but it's OK."

"Sorry," Niell said. "I'm interested in the man who lives in the trailer."

"Right," Melanie said, and gave a little laugh. "That's Jon Mills. He's a good friend of ours. Look, Deputy. If you want a better look at those docks, it's OK, really."

Niell indicated that he would and they stepped over the seawall and walked out to the end of the docks. Niell studied the line of boats at the docks.

"Jon's boat isn't there, if you're looking for it," Melanie volunteered. "He took it over to the marina at West Harbor for repairs."

Niell suppressed the reflex to respond and asked instead, "How long ago was that?"

"Dunno. Must have been more than a week ago. I wondered what happened," Melanie added. "We haven't seen his boat, and he's been gone a spell, too. He's paid up on his rent, though."

Niell decided to try for information he already knew. "Do you have any idea where he went?"

"He used to drink a lot," Melanie said. "With my husband most of the time. But lately, we haven't seen him, and from what Bobby tells me, he wasn't too keen on drinking the last few weeks, anyways."

"Bobby?"

"My husband," Melanie said. "Jonah was his drinking buddy. But like I said, we haven't seen him for a spell. Maybe he went somewhere to dry out."

"It's possible," Niell remarked.

"Nothing would suit me finer," Mel said. "Those two drink too much as it is."

Niell reached into his uniform shirt pocket, took out one of his cards, and gave it to her. "If you get any word, please call."

Melanie Brikker studied the card and said, "Holmes County?"

"It's a ways south of here," Niell explained.

"Whatever you need, Deputy. Just take your time looking around. If he shows up, I'll call."

"Thanks, Mrs. Brikker."

"Melanie," she corrected.

"Melanie," Niell said. "Again, thanks."

At the Big Bopper, Ricky scanned the lot again for the Marblehead cruiser. He checked in at the Coast Guard Station where Seaman Munson, alone at the counter for the moment, said that the Marblehead Police had not made an appearance. Out again on Highway 163, he stopped at the Cheesehaven Barn, advertising meat, wine, donuts, bread, and candy. He stood in line with teenagers in swim suits and baggy sweatshirts, bought an assortment of crackers, cheese, and fruit juice, and then drove back east through the small town of Marblehead, with its inns, art galleries, restaurants, marinas, curio shops, and real estate agents. Still no police cruiser at the station.

Near the end of the peninsula, he noticed a neat brown and white sign for the Marblehead Lighthouse. On impulse, he followed the sign, turning just beyond the St. Mary Byzantine Catholic Church that advertised Bingo on Monday nights. He drove along a narrow road to the water, where a caretaker's two-story white frame house stood beside the lighthouse. The caretaker's house was old, with a plaque marking it as historic.

Its siding boards drooped in the middle of their long horizontal runs. The roof was mostly of gray shingles, but showed the original red in damaged patches.

The lighthouse was a white stucco circular tower painted red on top. Its parapet was surrounded by an iron railing, also red. The historical marker declared that the lighthouse had been erected in 1822, and that it occupied the easternmost point on the peninsula. Today it guarded gray slate rocks slippery with green moss, and large gray boulders cut from nearby quarries. Trees grew among the boulders. Beyond the trees, wind and waves came ashore on an expanse of flat stone.

Niell took out his snack and sat at a picnic table under the trees, watching an assortment of boats taking shelter from the seas in a small cove beside the Byzantine Church. Beyond the point where the lighthouse stood, he surveyed a high chop on open waters.

Where to next? As ordered, phone Robertson and try to sound competent. As before, he'd have nothing to report.

Well, almost nothing. He had found the trailer. At least he had that much. "Leave nothing out," he imagined the sheriff's insistent voice on the phone.

Then he'd meet up with Branden back at the marina, find Officer Lively, and work through official channels to open the trailer. Would Robertson say he should have forced the door? Probably. Another good reason not to make that call just yet, Niell thought.

But there was something else, he realized slowly. Something he had missed. Something that nagged at him subtlely. Robertson would insist on knowing exactly what that was. And Niell knew, now, that he wouldn't be able to tell him. Wouldn't be able to explain what it was that bothered him.

He stopped eating and stared unhappily at the water. It was something that had not seemed right at the time. Perhaps something at the police station that wasn't open, or the bikers at the

Coast Guard Station, or the restaurant, or the trailer, or the private dock beyond the concrete sea wall.

Drive past the trailer once more, Niell thought. Look for the Marblehead cruiser. Run the scanner on your radio and listen to law enforcement in the area. Maybe check in with the Coast Guard again.

And then what? He screwed the lid back on a half-finished bottle of orange juice. Big mistake to call in now, he told himself. Let Robertson wait. Call when you're ready.

At least find the Marblehead policeman. Try his cottage at Lakeside. Or his boat on East Harbor. Call the mayor's secretary, as the sign on the one-room police station had instructed. Last, check with the Port Clinton police, in case Marblehead's single cop didn't turn up. And then what?

That's the trouble, Niell told himself, tossing the remains of his lunch into the bed of his truck. You still can't pin what's got you rattled. He sat in his truck, looking toward the water, making a list in his mind of Robertson's inevitable questions.

A priest from the Byzantine Church stepped out in full vestments and walked down to the shore to watch the boats in the cove, a steady breeze tearing at his robe. For the first time, Ricky noticed the four ornate Byzantine crosses on top of the church. The crosses consisted of an upright post and three crosspieces. The top crossbar short, the second longer, and the third set low and at an angle. The four crosses sailed the darkening skies amid several onion-domed Byzantine turrets. About as far as you can get from Amish country, he mused.

An image of Jonah Miller in the ditch crossed his mind. Then the image of Branden in Amish clothes, confronting the bishop in the far hayfields near the stream.

He thought of Jeremiah, and remembered Robertson warning that they'd have, at most, a half-day lead-off on the FBI. A torrent of pessimism washed through him. Jeremiah wouldn't be found. At least not here. Probably not alive.

Then what bothered him so? Something he bumped against. Saw vaguely then, but discounted. Consequently lost it. He imagined Robertson haranguing him about the details, and groaned. What was it?

"Think, Niell!" he muttered. His fingers tightened on the wheel, and his elbows locked in tension. He started the engine, revved it, and rolled the truck out toward Highway 163, convinced there was something he had overlooked. Something he needed to understand. They were not wasting their time here. He knew that now.

OUT on 163, Ricky Niell listened to his scanner, reviewing the places he had been that morning—the motel, the marina, the Marblehead Police, the Coast Guard Station with its parade of bikers next door at the ferry landing, the Big Bopper parking lot, the cottages in the orchard, the trailer, the seawall leading to the private boat dock, the Cheesehaven Barn, the lane just beyond the Byzantine Church, the red-and-white lighthouse with its gray and black rocky shore with a picnic table under the trees, and a Byzantine priest standing in a driving, onshore wind at the rocky edge of a protected cove.

Niell thought of calling Robertson and immediately decided against it, convinced more than before that he had missed something. Out on a straight length of 163, he laid on the horn and swung out into the passing lane, alarmed that somewhere today he had made a terrible mistake.

28

Friday, June 26
10:30 A.M.

THE storm arose quickly over the shallow waters of Lake Erie, and boaters familiar with the lake's inconstant nature sought cover through the channel into West Harbor, Branden among them. On the end of the first dock at the marina, Niell waved Branden over and jumped aboard without waiting for Branden to tie up. He gave a brief explanation of his concerns, and took the wheel from Branden.

A cold northerly had settled into a confident pattern, skimming across from Canada. Whitecaps snapped on all sides.

"I just want a look at that dock from the water," Niell shouted over the rising wind and the engine. Beyond the break wall, the boat slammed into three-foot waves and threw up heavy spray.

Branden gripped the rail, tried to keep his footing, and settled for a seat on the edge of the boat cushions. Niell pushed the Bayliner eastward toward the vicinity of Lakeside, where the private dock stood on the other side of the seawall from Jonah Miller's trailer.

Branden squinted forward, trying to judge the distance, alarmed by the suddenness of the storm. He shouted over at Niell, "You called Robertson?"

"Not yet," Niell shouted, wrestling fiercely with the wheel. He turned his cap around so the bill wouldn't catch the wind.

Near the entrance to East Harbor, Niell brought the Bayliner close in to shore and skirted the point. He came around into the entrance past the small island, dropped into the calmer harbor, and turned immediately to port, into the easternmost cove. Twenty feet out, he reversed throttle, shut down, and stood off from the dock.

Three boats were tied there, bobbing in the water, and two more docked while they watched. An elderly couple clambered out of one boat, a family with children out of the other, all taking note of the storm.

"Looks pretty normal here to me," Branden said and eyed open waters nervously.

"I'd hoped something would jar a memory," Niell said, disappointed.

"It's a rental trailer?" Branden asked.

Niell braced himself behind the wheel, studying the dock, and then turned his cap around forward and nervously rocked it into position tightly on his head. "Right. A junker trailer. At the end of a run of several cottages in an old orchard."

"And Jonah rented the trailer?" Branden asked. "You double-checked that?"

Niell nodded yes. "Rented it from the Brikkers," Niell said, "Melanie and her husband Bobby." Then Niell frowned heavily, took a quick glance at the boat traffic in the harbor, and started the engines. To Branden he said, "She never mentioned Jeremiah."

"That's not what you'd expect, Ricky," Branden said, immediately concerned.

"I know," Niell said and pushed in behind the wheel.

In the waters outside East Harbor, whitecaps danced on a four-foot chop. Cold spray lashed fiercely over the windshield. Niell pushed the boat harder into the coming storm, bracing himself with one forearm against the wheel and with the other against the cabin wall. Water poured into the boat and drained out aft whenever a swell lifted the bow and then the stern. Niell pounded the Bayliner across the swells, heading back to the channel into West Harbor. He concentrated his thoughts on Melanie Brikker in front of Jonah's trailer. His boots proved incapable of holding the deck.

His cap caught the wind and sailed away. He grabbed for it by reflex, but was forced immediately, by the next hammering wave, to brace himself again with both hands. He clung to the wheel and rode the throttle, forcing his way through the storm, driving his mind to comprehend. At length he maneuvered the boat into the long, dangerous channel between the break walls at West Harbor.

Once inside the channel, Niell eased back on the throttle, and the boat settled low and rode its own wake forward into quieter waters. In a driving rain, only the Sohio sign at the docks was visible to guide him to the marina.

Branden let go his grip on the rails and shouted against the wind, "What else, Ricky? She didn't mention Jeremiah, but what else?"

Niell flashed a helpless expression.

"Describe her for me. What did she look like?" Branden asked in the rain.

Niell described her.

"Tell me what the two of you did."

Niell told him.

"What, precisely, did she say?"

Niell gave it back to him word for word, and Branden's face blanched, as he realized what it meant.

29

Friday, June 26
12 noon

NIELL shot down 269 on the Catawba Peninsula, under lights and siren, at fifty plus miles per hour.

As he drove, he reached to the seat for his pistol, magazines, and shoulder harness.

"Steer," he shouted on a straightway and gave Branden the wheel.

Niell ducked into the shoulder rig, pulled it into place, and grabbed the wheel.

Then he looked over at Branden and said, "Robertson says you handle guns."

"Right," Branden said.

Niell drew his revolver, a stainless steel Smith and Wesson model 66, handed it sideways to Branden, and accelerated.

At the intersection with 163, Niell ignored the stop sign, took the corner fishtailing, skidded sideways through the gravel on two wheels, and tore east into the downpour.

Branden pushed the cylinder release button on the .357 magnum, swung the cylinder open, ejected six live rounds into his lap, and closed the cylinder. He then tried the trigger against pressure on the hammer from his thumb, both single and double action, gave Niell an approving look, and reloaded.

Niell smiled halfheartedly, slipped two speed loaders off his belt, handed them to Branden, and said, "The sights are set low. Six o'clock on a 9 bull at 25 yards."

Branden slipped the speed loaders onto the right side of his belt, rebuckled, gripped the .357 authoritatively in his right palm, and glared into the pounding storm.

The windshield wipers snapped left and right, throwing off water. In the hard afternoon storm, there was little more than the light of dusk.

Niell keyed his mike, punched up the Intercity Channel, and broadcast using the Buckeye Deputy Sheriff's Codes.

"This is Deputy Sheriff Ricky Niell. Code 44, eastbound on 163, kidnapping at the Orchard Grove Cottages."

Then a similar message using the 10-codes. "This is Deputy Sheriff Ricky Niell. Eastbound on 163, Code 20 on a 207. Code 3 and 10-54 at the Orchard Grove Cottages. Kidnapped child, Jeremiah Miller, age ten."

He came up to a slow-moving camper, swung around abruptly, punched up the Law Enforcement Emergency Radio Network, and broadcast again in the 10-codes.

At North Shore Boulevard, Niell overshot, slammed to a stop, backed, bounced the 4x4 left over the curb stones, and accelerated with a skid onto the blacktop.

"Watch for the Orchard Grove Cottages," he said and threw the switch, cutting the siren.

Almost immediately, he came upon the two-track lane to Jonah Miller's trailer, swung hard left, and slid the truck sideways into the orchard towards the trailer.

Then he broadcast his position on both the Intercity channel and LEERN.

Without precautions for silence, he jerked to a stop beside the trailer. The nose end of the truck bounced abruptly against the jumbled concrete seawall.

Niell bolted out, leaving the door ajar, and drew his .45 automatic. Branden followed with Niell's .357.

Niell pulled a large crowbar out of the truck bed, ran up to the trailer, popped the trailer's door open with a vicious thrust, tossed the crowbar into the sand, and scaled the two steps, pistol in his right hand leading his eyes into the trailer.

Branden covered outside, revolver drawn.

In seconds, Niell stepped out making a disgusted grunt and said, "There's a policeman dead in there."

Branden poked his head in and saw enough to know not to enter.

Niell stepped to the driver's side of the truck, stood in the downpour, and reached for the mike. Distant sirens came to his ears.

"Code 32 at the Orchard Grove Cottages."

Almost instantly, two cruisers with lights and sirens shot into the lane at the front of the cottage properties and headed for Niell's truck, which was still running flashers in the rain.

Branden stepped around the trailer and peered into the stormy darkness back toward the cottages.

Niell threw power to the spotlights on his truck and started searching the grounds with twin shafts of light.

"There's a body in the trailer," Niell shouted as the first cruiser skidded in behind his unit, blocking his rear.

Two Port Clinton policemen scrambled into the trailer, came out directly, and returned to their unit.

One radioed in, and the other came over to Niell.

"That's Paul Lively in there," the officer said, shaken.

"I think he's been in there a while," Niell said and briefly explained about the missing Jeremiah and the Brikkers who ran the place.

Another Port Clinton unit arrived, officers got out, and Niell hurriedly gathered them in the rain at the back of his truck, explaining again about the kidnapping of Jeremiah Miller.

"That's Mel Brikker," one of the officers said. "Runs the cottages with her husband when he's not in jail."

Branden shouted "Ricky!" from the edge of the trailer and ran toward Niell, pointing back down the lane.

"They just took off. I saw the boy!"

Niell motioned for the two cruisers to back out of his way and realized that there wouldn't be time. He jumped in behind the wheel and roared the 4x4 up onto the jagged pile of concrete slabs, backed down a bit, lunged forward onto the pile again, tilted the truck at an extreme angle, backed a second time, and then bounced forward and pulled hard right, the two left wheels riding high on the seawall.

Once clear of the concrete slabs, he motioned wildly through his open window for Branden to jump in, and then raced without caution around the trailer and through the orchard, knocking off low branches, between the cottages, and fishtailed back out onto North Shore Boulevard.

The police cruisers backed down the lane, swerving erratically, lights and sirens piercing the rain.

Branden shouted, "The other way, Ricky!" and Niell whipped the 4x4 around on the slick pavement, headed for 163, and then followed the fleeing car toward Marblehead.

On 163, they overtook a slow-moving Gremlin hatchback, raced by, and then saw a blue sedan some distance ahead, careening wildly under the Marblehead streetlights. On impulse, Niell punched up channel 21 and raised the Coast Guard.

Near the point at Marblehead, Niell again broadcast his position on LEERN, pounded the wheel when he realized where the car was headed, and followed it on in, past the Byzantine Church, down the short road to the lighthouse and the waters off the Marblehead point.

Niell skidded to a stop in the gravel, ran his spotlights over the area, caught a glimpse of the sedan at the water's edge, and focused the beam on two figures, a woman and a man, struggling to load a squirming bundle into a boat tied among the trees beneath the lighthouse.

Niell drew his pistol, ran along the shafts of light toward the boat, and shouted, "Freeze!"

The boat engine sputtered, caught, fired, and growled into life.

The man spun the wheel, and turned the boat toward open water.

Rain blew hard in Ricky's eyes. He closed the distance to the boat as it pulled away.

Niell dodged trees, hit the flat rocks at a run, leapt for the boat, splashed into the water with his left hand locked on the starboard gunwale, spilled water into the boat, and heard the engine cough, sputter, and die.

By reflex he brought his right hand up with the pistol, and last remembered the bulking form of the woman, who lunged to the gunwale with a wooden paddle, and smashed it viciously onto Ricky's head.

Niell groaned, rolled onto his back, sank, popped up on his stomach, and bobbed in the shallow water, unconscious.

Branden waded into the water, grabbed Niell by the front of his collar, held him half-floating face-up at his side, and trained the barrel of Ricky Niell's cocked .357 magnum on the man, who worked furiously to restart the engine, not more than five feet away.

Niell's unconscious body lurched with the waves against Branden's thigh. The rain pounded into Branden's face. Lightning struck on the opposite side of the cove, lighting the scene in white flashes. Gasoline fumes from the boat's motor filled the air.

Branden shouted, "At this range, I'll never miss!" and stared coldly at the man.

Mel Brikker scoffed, jerked Jeremiah to his feet, and held him in front of her, bound, gagged, and groggy.

"Back off!" she shouted. "We're taking the kid!" She reached into the bottom of the boat and brought up a sawed-off shotgun, pointing it toward Branden.

Branden snapped his arm toward her, fired once, and immediately cocked the hammer again.

The round struck Mel Brikker at the base of her neck. She dropped the shotgun, grabbed at her throat, and fell over backwards, blood spurting between her fingers.

Jeremiah fell sideways into the bottom of the boat.

A Coast Guard UTB appeared from behind the shoreline to the west, its screaming sirens set on wail.

Bobby Brikker managed to restart the engine and pulled away abruptly, leaving Branden struggling in the waves to bring his sights, one-handed, onto Brikker's back. Niell floated heavily in the water at his side.

Port Clinton officers arrived on shore, splashed into the water, and took charge of the unconscious Niell.

Branden regained the bank and tore along its edge, past the lighthouse, pushing recklessly through the tangle of branches and rocks to the point, trailing Brikker's boat as it left the cove.

He took up a position in waist-deep waters off the point, planted his feet, and drew down, double-fisted, on Brikker, his finger tightening against the smooth combat trigger.

Around the point, in a driving rain, lights and sirens caught his attention and he eased off on the trigger, still charged with adrenaline, frantically wanting the shot. Driven to take it, as he waded deeper into the water.

Seaman Munson careened the Coast Guard UTB in front of Branden into a tight circle around Brikker's boat, and switched his sirens to an intimidating yelp. Then he threw the switch to loud hail and spoke with command. "This is the U.S. Coast Guard. Stand to, and prepare to be boarded."

As Munson came alongside Brikker's small boat, two men from the hostage rescue team boarded with drawn nine millimeter Berettas, while others on the bow and stern of UTB 41-443 covered with M16s.

The wake of the UTB came ashore and knocked Branden

over backwards amid the boulders of Marblehead Point. When he had managed to struggle to his feet, he could see Jeremiah standing in the boat, with one seaman from the UTB working to untie him, while another wrestled Bobby Brikker into handcuffs.

30

A DISGRUNTLED nurse stormed up to Ricky Niell's room at Magruder Hospital, held the door ajar with her foot, and said, "Out. Both of you. Mr. Niell needs to rest."

Robertson, equally disgruntled, followed Munson out into the hall and traded scowls with the nurse. Once the nurse had disappeared around a corner, Robertson stuck his head back into the room and said, "You never called."

Niell managed a weak smile, shrugged, and said nothing.

"When you wake up, you need to call Ellie," Robertson added.

Niell blanked and rubbed the back of his head, and Robertson explained. "She's been asking about you all night, and I'm tired of explaining to her that you're not dead. OK? Call her!"

Niell nodded voicelessly, and Robertson let the door close softly.

Then he pushed the door open again abruptly and asked, "They say you had the professor out on the lake under a small crafts warning. You got anything to say about that?"

Niell rolled his eyes painfully, and Robertson backed out of the room grumbling.

"He'll be all right," Robertson said out in the hall. "Just a concussion."

Seaman Munson asked, "You know how he figured it out?"

"Not yet," Robertson said, still irritated with the nurses. "They haven't let me stay long enough to ask him."

"Down in Holmes County," Munson said, "I bet Niell's sort of a hot dog. Does things his own way."

Robertson smiled broadly and eyed the nurse's station for a chance to slip back in.

"He's like me," Munson smiled. "He likes the action. Worries that if he starts carrying too much brass on his collar, he'll end up on a desk job."

Robertson said, "Sounds like Ricky." He took out a pack of cigarettes, nodded at the no smoking sign on the wall, and said, "Let's go outside."

Under the canopy at the emergency room entrance, Robertson lit up, shook the match out, and walked with Munson toward the parking lot. The sun was up strong, burning off the morning haze, steam rising from the blacktop.

"You found Niell's pistol underwater?" Robertson asked, trying to tie up all of the loose ends, cover all of the details.

"Right."

"And you say Branden fired once?" Robertson asked and drew on his cigarette with his eyes narrowed.

"One shot at the woman and then prepared to take a second, at the man," Munson said. "Right as we came alongside."

"The woman died instantly?" Robertson asked. He knew she had, but wanted Munson's account of it.

"Dead in the boat by the time we boarded," Munson said. "If Branden had got off another shot, the man'd be gonners, too."

"You saw her point a shotgun at him?"

"Right, but we were still a ways out, at that point."

"So, there'll be no charges."

"Shouldn't be."

"And the boy?"

"Found him tied up in the bottom of the boat," Munson

said. "The woman bled all over him. The kid had been tied and drugged."

"He's going to be fine," Robertson said and looked back toward the hospital from the parking lot. "They're going to observe him for a few hours more, and then I'll take him home."

Munson shaded his eyes to look up toward Niell's room. "If you find out what put him onto the Brikkers, let me know, will you?" Then he shook Robertson's hand, slid into the seat of a small convertible, and backed out of the parking place.

Before he drove away, Munson looked up from his two-seater and said, "Sheriff, we're supposed to handle kidnappings, anything federal, through channels. Toledo, Cleveland, and then Washington. You got any idea why Niell didn't do that?"

"*Loose as ashes in the wind.*"

Munson looked puzzled.

"That's a line from an Ian Tyson cowboy song, Seaman Munson," Robertson explained. He grinned and added, "It's the same reason Niell paid you boys a visit on his own initiative, yesterday."

"Which is?"

"Ricky Niell's not carrying too much brass on his collars," Robertson said.

Then, Robertson finished his cigarette, crushed it out with the toe of his shoe and asked, "You got time to show me where the trailer is?"

Munson led Robertson to North Shore Boulevard, slowed in front of the Orchard Grove Cottages, pointed down the lane, waved, and sped away. Down by the water, at the end of the lane to the trailer, Robertson parked beside Niell's truck and a Port Clinton police cruiser and found Branden, with an officer, in the trailer.

"How's Ricky?" Branden asked immediately. He had parked himself in a well-worn recliner, and had several books stacked in his lap, with a few more open on the floor at his feet. Empty spaces in a bookshelf beside him roughly matched the volumes Branden had gathered to himself.

"Niell's gonna be fine," Robertson said and then, "Is this where they found the cop?"

"Back there," Branden said, indicating a small bedroom set off with a folding partition.

The Port Clinton cop came forward from the bedroom and said, "His name was Paul Lively. When we found him, he'd been dead maybe three days."

"You figure he caught on to the Brikkers?" Robertson asked. "With the kid, I mean."

"Must have," the policeman said and walked out, stepping over the collection of books at Branden's feet.

Robertson took a seat at a small metal table in the corner that served as a kitchen and looked around at the inside of the trailer. There was a closet door ajar, with outlandish western clothes on hangers and piled loosely in a basket on the floor. Dirty dishes lay in the sink and on the kitchen table. There was an over-full ashtray and a rusty fishing knife. Several snapshots were scattered on the table where he sat.

Robertson gathered up the pictures and asked, "Have you seen these?"

Branden nodded, absorbed with one book, and Robertson eased back on his chair and flipped through the photos, shots of Jonah and Jeremiah, fishing with an older man and woman.

"Are these the Brikkers?" Robertson asked and tapped one of the snapshots with his finger.

"Melanie and Bobby Brikker," Branden said distastefully, looking up for a moment from his reading.

In one photograph, Robertson saw Jeremiah next to a gruff-looking Melanie Brikker, who held him tightly by the shoulders on the stern of a Baha Cruiser. Jonah stood next to Jeremiah, smiling unconcerned into the camera. Robertson shook his head, disgusted by the way the Brikkers had betrayed their friend, and scattered the snapshots back onto the table. "They must have played up to Jonah while they ran the blackmail scheme secretly."

"Trouble was, when Jonah started talking about going home with Jeremiah, the Brikkers' secret ransom scheme caved in around their ears," Branden said.

Robertson stood, studied the inside of the small trailer for a moment, and decided he had seen enough. "I'm going back to check on Niell and the boy," Robertson said. "Want to join me?"

"Not just yet, Bruce," Branden said, distracted. "I'd like to pack up a few things here. Caroline knows a teacher who'd probably like to see some of these books."

Robertson eased himself down the two steps of the trailer and turned back to Branden. "They say you got off one clean shot, Mike." He watched Branden's face for a reaction.

Branden pulled his eyes from the book and looked back at Robertson calmly.

"You gonna be OK with that?" Robertson asked.

"Yes," Branden answered directly.

"You know you saved young Miller's life," Robertson said, intending encouragement.

"What are you worried about, Sheriff?"

"It's not so easy, sometimes, Mike. Living with a shooting is not at all easy."

Branden closed the book in his lap, looked at his friend, thought for a moment, and said, "When she brought out the shotgun, my arm snapped left immediately. But it plays back through my mind in slow motion. Everything is still up here, in my eyes, as if it has just happened, only slow. Bobby Brikker cursing at the engine that wouldn't start. The smell of gasoline all around me. The rain and the wind. The way everything felt cold, wet. The boat rocking in the waves. That wretched woman. Her scorn, contempt. Niell floating against my thigh. Sirens and lights behind me, coming down the lane to the lighthouse. She stooped down and brought up the shotgun and started to point it. I can still feel Ricky washing in the waves against my leg, cold. Still feel the concussion of the shot against my palm. A brief gust of gunpowder in my face. The adrenaline when I chased the boat along the shore. A nearly unstoppable surge, driving me for a second shot. I study that sort of thing all the time—in the memoirs of Civil War soldiers. The rush of combat, a high of unbelievable intensity.

"I've always wondered about that. The question of valor. You know, strength of will. And I remembered the boy tied in ropes, the cop in the trailer with a knife in his belly. And Jonah Miller lying in his ditch."

He paused.

"And?" Robertson asked.

"And I don't think I'm going to have any trouble getting over killing Melanie Brikker."

Robertson remembered Munson's account of it and said, "From what people tell me, you'd have capped off Bobby Brikker, too."

Branden looked steadily back at the sheriff, thought about an answer, and shrugged.

31

Thursday, July 2
8:00 A.M.

IT WAS the day of Jonah Miller's memorial service. His plain burial had taken place several days earlier in a family cemetery on a rise overlooking the Doughty Valley.

Caroline Branden climbed the worn sandstone steps to Leeper School carrying a brown paper grocery bag and a key. She wore a long, pleated dress of a plain dark plum color. It had a high collar and long sleeves. Her long auburn hair was tied in a bun at the back of her head, out of deference to the Amish.

She had found an Amish neighbor to the school, explained her intentions, and had borrowed the key to the school with a promise to return it after the services. Branden waited beside the car.

Summer had come convincingly, at last, to the Amish farms on the hills and in the valleys of Holmes County. In an assortment of small fields beyond the school, Branden saw hay wagons drawn by horses, corn waist-high in a corner field, a man on a bicycle, and a matched pair of Amish brothers setting fence posts. Branden was dressed modestly, as he knew the bishop would prefer, in the new suit of Amish clothes he had bought with Caroline in Fredericksburg. His short brown beard was trimmed neatly, the skin shaved smooth, top and bottom, around his mouth, anticipating the Amish service to come.

Inside, Caroline took three tattered books out of a paper sack and arranged them on Miss Beachey's old desk. Into the pages of one of the books she inserted a single-page note, written in a heavy, unpracticed hand.

Then she took a second note out of an envelope and reread it.

Dear Miss Beachey:

Thank you for taking my call yesterday. By now I'm sure you'll have heard the details of the death of Jonah Miller and of the rescue of his son.

It is our hope that you can derive some comfort from the fact that Jonah took "Fenimore" for his middle name. You obviously made a great impression on a fifth-grade scholar.

In Jonah's home, among a collection of numerous books, my husband found these three—a collection of American poems, plus Moby Dick and The Last of the Mohicans— which I am sure Jonah would want you to have. As you'll note, they were often read.

In between the pages of The Last of the Mohicans, we also found this note. We are not certain when it was written, but Jonah obviously meant it for you. It is evidently several years old.

Sincerely yours,
Caroline Branden

Then she put her letter into its envelope, laid it on the teacher's desk, and opened *The Last of the Mohicans* to the page with Jonah's note. It was an old, yellowed page, started long ago and never sent.

Dear Miss Beachey:

I am not hopeful that you will remember who I am, but I remember you.

All my life I have wanted to thank you for the books.

Lately, I have been thinking

32

AT THE Miller house, Branden parked some distance back, behind an assortment of buggies on the lane, where two Amish boys tended horses beside the wooden fence.

Cal Troyer met them at the sliding doors to the bank barn, on the lower level. Inside, Caroline took a seat on benches with the women, and Cal led Branden to a bench on the side for the men.

The services proceeded for two and a half hours, the preacher and the deacons presiding in front with the bishop, the benches for the women facing those for the men.

There were numerous hymns in German, sung a cappella with a strange, hurried cadence and without harmony.

The first sermon was in German. Cal translated for Branden at times. At one moment, Cal caught a glimpse through the sliding barn doors of Bruce Robertson, listening from outside to the service.

Before the second sermon, the bishop stood and addressed the congregation first in German briefly, and then at length in English, explaining that Brother Roy Miller would preach shortly but, though it was not their custom for him to do so, he allowed as how the death of his son and the ordeal of his grandson gave him, as bishop, a little leeway in this regard.

He explained how he had come reluctantly to the conclusion

219

that Pastor Troyer and Professor Branden should be approached to help them locate Jeremiah. He spoke of the dismay he had felt when the ransom note had first arrived. He spoke of the hours on his knees in prayer, and thanked the deacons for their service to him in that regard.

He thanked the people, whom he considered with justifiable satisfaction, had stood by him and his family, faithfully.

He thanked Pastor Caleb Troyer, who again had proven his friendship and goodwill among the *Gemie*, remarking that if there were to be any persons other than farmers in heaven, let it be the likes of Pastor Caleb Troyer.

He turned in Branden's direction and told the congregation of the general nature of Jeremiah's rescue, without mention of the shooting.

And he opened The Book, read from it in High German, and continued for forty minutes, explaining what he had learned through his recent ordeals.

First he read from the book of Jonah. In Chapter Two, he read as far as verse eight, paused, and read it again in English, giving it word-by-word emphasis: "They that cling to worthless idols, forfeit the grace that could have been theirs"—tying it to the story of his late son Jonah, explaining how their Jonah, just as the Jonah of old, had run not from them, but from God.

The bishop emphasized that he considered it an exceedingly great mercy that he had been shown, on the day of their Jonah's death, that, like Jonah of the Bible, his son had come to his senses. That he had turned, at last, back into the will of the Almighty.

Then the bishop turned to face little Jeremiah, who was seated on the front bench among the older men. He opened an English Bible to Psalm 139, read it, and then spoke directly to Jeremiah.

"Jeremiah, you are seated with the men today in a place that should have been your father's."

His voice faltered. Tears filled his eyes. Branden fought a

tightening in his throat and found his cheeks wet with tears. He looked over to Caroline, who watched the bishop, also with tears.

"And I say to you today, Jeremiah, that your father was truly a prodigal. A wanderer, when he need not have been. And although it was not your lot to have known your father long, he died on the land of his people, trying to bring you home. In truth, bringing himself home, too.

"I also say to you that Psalm 139 is now yours, as it was your father's. You carry his blood in your veins, and you'll need Psalm 139 when your time of the *Rumschpringe* arrives."

The bishop then turned to address the entire congregation.

"The Lord has shown me two voices speaking in Psalm 139.

"First there is the voice of Jonah. It is a voice that proclaims that one cannot outrun the reach of God. This is the promise that has sustained me since the *Meidung*. That our Jonah could not run so far away as to escape God's call on his life. The Jonah of scriptures could not do this and neither could our Jonah. This first voice, a promise from God, has sustained my prayers in all the years that Jonah has been gone.

"And in all these days that Jeremiah has been gone, the second voice of Psalm 139 . . . ."

The bishop stopped, struggled with his emotions, brought a handkerchief to his eyes, and wept. Jeremiah rose from his seat on the bench, came forward and embraced his grandfather. The bishop knelt down, whispered in Jeremiah's ear, kissed his hair, and waited for him to reclaim his place among the men.

"The second voice of Psalm 139 promises that we cannot be found so far along into harm's way, or be taken so far into our enemy's grasp, as to outdistance the abilities of God to provide for our safety."

He concluded his remarks by reading again from Psalm 139, verses seven through ten, in English for the benefit of the Brandens:

⁷Where can I go from your Spirit?
Where can I flee from your presence?

⁸If I go up to the heavens, You are there.
If I make my bed in the depths, You are there.

⁹If I rise on the wings of the dawn,
If I settle on the far side of the sea,

¹⁰Even there, Your hand will guide me,
Your right hand will hold me fast.

After a second sermon and a little more singing, the bishop's wife and her daughters-in-law served a meal in shifts in the big house. The men sat together, eating heartily, talking little. The women ate next, also together, while the men gathered outside under the trees on the front lawn and talked. Some smoked. Others carried benches up from the barn and sat together, with the hooks of their vests undone.

Out by the fence at the lane, young Jeremiah stood in the middle of a ring of eager Amish boys and told the story again of how his father had taken him up to the great lake.

After a period of time, the bishop appeared with Mrs. Miller and Isaac, as women gathered on the front porch to watch. Several lads came forward, carrying a large wooden table and six hickory chairs. They placed the furniture on the lawn in front of the Brandens and stepped back to allow the bishop to speak.

"Mrs. Branden. My wife and I want to express our appreciation for your kindness and for the efforts of your husband."

He stepped to the long table and ran his fingers over the grain, remembering. It was made of curly maple, stained a light cream color, hand rubbed and hand waxed, the elaborate grain of the wood giving it an elegant pattern of rich curls. The six chairs with maple seats and bent hickory backs fit easily under the long table, three on a side with room to spare. A patina of dust covered both table and chairs.

"My wife has kept this table in the barn all these years against my better judgment. It is plainly too fancy for an Amish home. Our son Jonah made it many years ago, and we'd like you to have it now. The chairs too."

Caroline looked to Cal, who smiled his approval.

"Then, my son Isaac will deliver it tomorrow, if that is acceptable to you, Mrs. Branden."

Then Bishop Miller motioned for the people to gather beside him on the lawn. Cal stepped back and joined the crowd. Bishop Miller positioned Caroline and the professor at one end of the table, and then stood at the other end of the table and waited for the people to gather around and settle down. Jeremiah pressed forward and stood by his grandfather.

"Herrn Professor Branden. We are a plain and simple people. We think, some would say, too slowly. And our judgments are not always perfect. But, once we are sure of our course, we are a determined and steadfast folk.

"It is not our way to take oaths, and I will not do that now. But neither is it our way to say one thing and do another. We do not swear or pledge, but our word is our bond.

"I do say this much, though. You are known among us, Professor. The people here in this valley will stand by you in anything you may ever need."

Later, at their car, men and women gathered again to say their good-byes. When the small crowd had cleared, Cal came forward and leaned over at Caroline's window on the passenger's side.

"I'm still not certain what it was that you and Ricky Niell noticed about Mel Brikker," Cal said. "Robertson hasn't seemed to get anything about it out of Niell either."

Branden sat behind the wheel with a smirk and said, "Mel Brikker called him Jonah." Then he drove away smiling mischievously at Cal in his rearview mirror, letting the pastor figure out what it meant on his own.

33

Saturday, July 4
11:30 A.M.

ON THE Fourth of July, Ricky Niell strolled into the Brandens' backyard with a beaming Ellie Troyer on his arm. He nodded to Cal Troyer, and Cal brought them onto the large screened porch where Caroline greeted them. The four took seats in the wicker chairs near the screens and studied the collection below of two dozen or so neighborhood children, parents, college deans, professors, students, friends, and families who gathered each Fourth of July on the Brandens' lawn.

Sheriff Robertson stood with Arne Laughton, president of Millersburg College, beside Branden, out at the cliff edge of the yard, where Branden's Civil War cannon was trained over the eastern valleys. The president had been speaking earnestly of salaries, chairs, and commitment, saying, "We'll never be able to match an offer from a university, Mike. You know that as well as anyone."

Branden smiled in his wool uniform, Union blue. The cannon was charged and fused. He held a smoldering linstock in one hand, and it gave off a lazy, meandering line of smoke. "It's not the money." he said, toying idly with the linstock. It never was, he thought. Never would be. It hadn't been when he had finally given the unopened FedEx package to Caroline. He had told her that she could open it, if she wanted. She had let it lie unopened on their kitchen table for a week and then had given it back to him, saying, "As you said, Michael, it might become entirely too complicated to open it." He had smiled gratefully.

"It's not the money," he said again, absently.

"Then what?" Laughton pushed. "You already occupy the most prestigious chair at the college."

"I'm going to explain this to you only once more, Arne. Then you're going to give us what we want." He looked up to Caroline and then back to Laughton. "I've got a wife who gets up every day at five A.M. and stands on the porch to greet the dawn. Watches the sunrise and reads the 139th Psalm. She and Cal Troyer have been working on a way to turn her unusual sensitivity to children's struggles for good, and that's what we intend to do."

"Whatever you want. We intend to keep you," Laughton said expansively.

Sheriff Robertson's eyes glinted delightfully, and he folded his big arms, more than a little amused by the way Branden was handling the college president.

Intently, Branden said, "I want the tuition benefit for ten children."

Laughton's expression clutched. He almost blurted out, "But you've got no children!" but caught himself, astonished.

Branden noted this and said, directly, "Right, Arne. We have no children."

Laughton's eyes registered dismay, unaccustomed as he was to level forthrightness.

Branden continued, "We want the tuition benefit for ten children, five to be designated by me, the others by Caroline. Anyone we choose, any time, now or in the future. They're going to go to Amish kids who are trying to make the change into English life. A memorial, if you will, to Jonah Miller."

Laughton's jaw hung slack. Robertson grinned from ear to ear. Branden's face showed strength of will.

"The price of my staying on at Millersburg College is the education of ten children."

Laughton realized he had been called. "Tuition for ten students?"

"Full tuition, now or in the future. Five for those I'll designate. Five for Caroline."

"Mike, you're out of your mind."

Branden shrugged as if he could not have cared less.

"Free tuition at Millersburg College for ten students?"

"Free tuition at any college in the nation," Branden insisted, "for four years each, five years if any of them should need it."

"The Board'll never accept that, Mike."

"That's our price."

Laughton blurted, "The tuition benefit's exclusively for the children of faculty," instantly regretting it.

"By the end of summer, you'll have my resignation."

"Don't be rash."

"The way I figure it, Arne, a FedEx envelope on my desk makes it considerably less than rash. Makes it, in fact, eminently reasonable," Branden said and smiled up to Caroline on the porch. She waved an encouragement, knowing full well what the subject of her husband's conversation with the college president would be.

"Ten free rides?" Laughton groaned.

"Anywhere in the country. At any college or university. Tuition for ten students, designated at any time, by either Caroline or me."

"You've got to be joking."

Branden's eyes went cold, flat with determination. "We have no children of our own, Arne. We're never going to have any. So, that's the way it is. A chair at a university, or the one here. It makes little difference to me. Flatly, it'll be Millersburg College with ten tuition benefits in our control, or we'll be gone by Fall Semester."

With resignation, Laughton said, "I'll have to square it with the Board."

"I'll need an answer by August 1," Branden said with an almost offhand nonchalance.

Robertson smiled broadly at Branden's triumph.

Laughton smiled weakly, then frowned openly, shook his head, and walked slowly back up the slope of the yard, away from the cliffs, bewildered.

Robertson snickered, shook his head, and asked, "You'd leave?"

"Caroline could never do it," Branden said.

"Then that was a bluff?"

"No. That was a fair price for my staying."

"Why for Amish kids?" Robertson asked.

"You know how tough the transition is into the English world. There are too many Jonah Millers out there, as it is. Even for the ones who finish high school or finish up an equivalency degree, there's still a tremendous adjustment. Cal Troyer's got whole families like that in his church. Well, Caroline and I are going to help. At least help those who truly are moving out of the Amish life. The first one goes to that waitress, Ester Yoder, if she'll finish her high school."

"You'll just end up encouraging folk to leave their families," Robertson said.

"We'll be careful to avoid that," Branden said. "We're not trying to lure anyone away. Besides, take Jeremiah Miller. As much as he has his father's blood in him, and as much of the world as he's seen, the day might come when he'll want out too, and why not help him then?"

"I'd expect that his father's lesson would keep him on the farm."

"Either way, we're going be ready," Branden said.

Robertson eyed him respectfully for a moment, and then changed the subject. "Have you had a chance to talk with Jeremiah Miller?"

"Not really," Branden said.

Robertson said, "We got a lot from him after he was released from the hospital. Some when I drove him back home from Port Clinton, the rest later. Turns out that Jonah Miller never knew until the very end that the Brikkers had been ransoming his son to the bishop. They had a falling out up on the lake when Jonah started talking about going back to Amish ways. But before that, he had never known about the ransom."

Branden shook his head.

"And you were right about Jonah," Robertson said. "He was coming home Amish when he was killed on the lane. Coming home to his father."

"Then he left the pickup," Branden said, "intending, if his father would not take him back, to return to the truck, retrieve his clothes from the store in Fredericksburg, and drive away forever."

"Right," the sheriff said. "But home was the one place they couldn't let Jonah go. So they waited in their car for father and son to come down the lane that morning and then confronted Jonah about the ransom scheme."

"Jeremiah saw it all?" Branden asked.

"Everything. His father refused to join them. The money wouldn't have meant anything to him. Anyway, Jeremiah says Melanie Brikker lost her cool, boiled over, shouted bad things about Jonah's newfound religion, and grabbed Jeremiah and pinned him against the car. Then he saw his father shot point blank, struggling with Bobby Brikker for the gun."

"That's a lot for a kid of ten to handle."

Robertson nodded agreement.

"Did Jeremiah say anything about the truck?" Branden asked.

"The Brikkers forced Jeremiah to show them where Jonah's truck was parked in the marsh, and then they sank it in the swamp. They only needed to hide it for a day or two, when they'd collect the ransom."

"What about Paul Lively?" Branden asked. "Just an innocent bystander who eventually figured something out, or part of the ransom scheme from the start?"

"Jeremiah doesn't know," Robertson said, "but he did say that, on the day he was taken, Officer Lively drove the car for Jonah."

"Lively delivered the first ransom note with Jonah's note to his father," Branden said. "I figure he was in on it at the start, but got himself killed after Jonah was murdered."

"We don't know if Lively knew what was in the first envelope," Robertson noted.

"Maybe we never will."

"We'll get it out of Bobby Brikker," Robertson said confidently. "But that still leaves one other thing not yet tied together," Robertson added. "Ricky Niell has not been altogether forthcoming about the matter of how you two caught on to the Brikkers." His expression coaxed an answer.

"Melanie Brikker gave herself away," Branden said, obviously amused.

Robertson waited impatiently.

Branden glanced at his watch, and looked up to Caroline with a satisfied smile. He watched President Laughton step onto the back porch and saw Caroline hand Laughton an envelope. He watched with satisfaction as Laughton opened it, knowing what it said: "First Tuition Designee—Ester Yoder, should she, someday, be inclined to accept."

Then Branden turned again to Robertson and said "Melanie Brikker called him *Jonah* when she was talking with Niell."

After a moment looking at his watch as the seconds brought on noon, Branden explained by saying, "Melanie Brikker had no business knowing his name was anything other than Jon. Jon Mills from Texas. But she called him by his Amish name. That was the key."

And then, as the sheriff thought it through, Branden laid the smoking linstock against the short fuse of his cannon.